'Vengeance is what I want.

'I want Falstone's sister, I want his land and I want his life.'

The wound was making Alex light-headed, for the image of Madeleine's naked pale limbs entwined about his own kept surfacing. And resurfacing.

Angrily he slammed his clay goblet down. He remembered the living flame of her hair as she had been bustled from the room and the cool feel of her skin when she had touched his hand.

I can help you.

Alex shook his head in disquiet. She was a hostage, that was all. A valuable means of vengeance and retribution when expediency demanded he find a way to exact conditions from the rampant greed of her brother.

A convenient pawn.

Sophia James lives in a big old house in Chelsea Bay, on Auckland's North Shore, with her husband, who is an artist, three kids, two cats, a turtle and a new guide dog puppy. Life is busy because, as well as teaching adults English at the local Migrant School, she helps her husband take art tours to Italy and France each September. Sophia has a degree in English and History from Auckland University, and believes her love of writing was formed reading Georgette Heyer with her twin sister on the porch of her grandmother's house, overlooking the sandhills of Raglan.

A previous novel by the same author:

FALLEN ANGEL

ASHBLANE'S
LADY

Sophia James

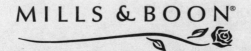

First published in Great Britain 2006
Harlequin Mills & Boon Limited,
Eton House, 18-24 Paradise Road, Richmond, Surrey TW9 1SR

© Sophia James 2006

Standard ISBN 0 263 84665 2
Promotional ISBN 0 263 85143 5

Set in Times Roman 11 on 14½ pt.
04-0806-68329

Printed and bound in Spain
by Litografia Rosés S.A., Barcelona

Bonny Laird of Ullyot

Oh, bold border ranger
Dark vengeance and danger
Stalk thee relentless
'Tween Jedburgh and Sark

On come the reivers
And wily South thievers
Hail, soldiers of Ashblane
Fight on till the end

Chapter One

Heathwater Castle, northwest England.
30 September, 1358

> 'There is a grounde called the Debatable Grounde, lying between the Realme of England and Scotland...'

'Ian!'

The anguished keening cry of a name travelled on the wind over Heathwater as Laird Alexander Ullyot tore off his jacket and rocked back and forth across the dead body of his clansman.

Lady Madeleine Randwick, watching from the woods, could barely believe such emotion to come from him, for the Chief of the clan of Ullyot, born and bred in the Scottish Highlands and the bastard son of a royal father who had never claimed him, was far better known for his cruelty and callousness.

And she could well understand why. With the rain pouring down in earnest, his face looked hewn from cold hard marble. Not pretty. Not comely. No young man's face this, full of dreams and promises, but a worn and tried visage underscored by danger and seasoned by tragedy. The scar that ran across his right cheek and into the hairline of his dark blond hair could be seen even from this distance, lending him a hardened beauty that took Madeleine's breath away. No healer worth her salt had worked on him, she thought, folding her cloak across the brightness of her hair as his double-handed claymore caught the sun.

Lord, if he saw her!

Crouching lower, she viewed the oozing wounds on his arm and back dispassionately. A deep gash might well poison his blood. With intent, she weighed up her options. If he died, her brother might relax his guard around Heathwater, giving her the chance she needed to escape.

Escape from Noel and Liam and Heathwater. How long had she dreamed of that? She was about to turn away when she noticed his shoulders shaking.

He was crying.

The hated Laird of Ullyot, scourge of the borderlands and instigator of a hundred bloody battles, was crying as he brought the fingers of the one he mourned to his lips in a tender last embrace.

Madeleine stayed still, the image of muscle and war-toughened invincibility strangely disconcerting against such grief. She noticed him stiffen as soon as he perceived a sound from further down the valley, the dirt on his hands marking his face as he swiped his eyes and stood, glance chilling and sword drawn.

So this was her enemy close up. This man, whose land ran north of her own along the border of Scotland and joined with the tracts of her brother's domain west of the River Esk.

She sensed his awareness of being watched as he scanned the undergrowth on the hillock behind her, but the arrival of a group of Ullyot men drew his attention away. She could hear his deep voice relaying orders as the bodies of fallen friends were separated from foe and placed on a dray pulled by two horses. She wondered where his own horse was, her curiosity appeased a moment later as he tilted his head and whistled to a steed of the deepest black. With a growing fear, Madeleine burrowed back into the root space and tried to recall all she had ever heard of the clan Ullyot.

Ashblane.

His keep hewn of stone, tall and windowless, the little light allowed in banished by dirtied cattle skin. Terence, her brother's servant, had told her this once just after her mother had died. A cautionary tale, she had guessed, to balance her own lot against that of others, for no one could live more bleakly than Alexander, the powerful and arrogant Chief of Ullyot.

The bodies had been stacked now and angry drifts of conversation reached her fleetingly before the rising wind snatched them away and pulled at the plaid Ullyot had draped across the faces of his fallen. The dirty tartan was stained in red. His arm, she supposed. Or his nose. Or the slash she could see deep across his back as he turned, the marks of battle mingling with the rusty blush of blood.

His men crowded around him as if for comfort. Fleetingly she wondered who would give him comfort, the wayward thought catching her as being so absurd that she had to stifle a laugh. A man like Ullyot would need no comfort, no cosiness nor succour to lighten his way. The Laird had chosen his pathway, after all, and rumour had it that it did not include the support of anyone or anything. Loneliness was his code, and hatred his inspiration.

Glancing up at the sky, she tried to judge the time of day as the party disappeared through the wooded hills leading to the river. She dared not start for Heathwater Castle till the sun was lower, the ridges protecting her only marginally from the scouts and sentries she knew would be posted until the Ullyot party was well out of sight. Resisting the urge to creep forward to tend to any of her brother's men, she stayed still until she could be certain that they truly had gone. Already she could imagine the knells and peels of the chapel bells at Noel's castle, and she dreaded going back. Dreaded seeing the mothers of sons lying fallen, the colour of the Ullyot plaid not shading their faces as the cold and rolling mists settled in from the Scottish Lowlands.

* * *

An hour or so later Madeleine deemed it safe to move, and she had almost reached the line of trees where she had instructed her sister—dressed, as always, as her page and who was safer here than at Heathwater—to wait, when a movement caught her attention. One of the Ullyot soldiers appeared out of nowhere and was shouting as he tracked into the glade, sword drawn. A prickling fear enveloped her. Something was wrong. Even from this far she could see that it was wrong.

'Jemmie,' she screamed and raised her hand, surprised to find it whipped behind her back in a punishing grip.

'Keep still, lassie.' The voice at her ear was deep and imbued with the tones of a Highland Scot, and her whole world narrowed as she turned.

It was him, Alexander Ullyot, and she had not heard even the whisper of a footstep.

Eyes of the palest silver ran across her from head to foot, narrowing as the nails on her right hand raked down the ragged flesh on his arm.

'Cease,' he cursed and pulled her against him, pulled her into sinew and muscle and war-sculptured bone. Pulled her into warmth and sweat and the tantalising scent of pure male. And for a second everything slowed.

Safety. Strength. Potency. When had she ever touched a man who felt like this? Who looked like this? Her breath fanned out against the wide bare skin at his throat and lust swamped her.

A warrior.

A fighter.

A leader who knew his worth in a land that gave no second chances to those who didn't. She wanted to place her cheek against his chest and beg for refuge. She wanted to hold him as a shield against a world she could no longer fathom…did not want to fathom.

'Who the hell are you?'

No angel's voice. The anger grounded her, as did the blood from his shoulder, dark against her arm and powdered into blackness. He would likely kill her if she gave her name. Red dizziness blossomed and the beat of her heart angled into panic.

'Who are you?' he repeated, his hand clamped hard across her shoulders. Maddy's breath caught and thickened and when she tried to turn to see what was happening to Jemmie, the roiling tunnel of blackness stripped her of balance and she tumbled into nothingness.

Chapter Two

Madeleine came to in a filthy cell littered with marsh reeds. Jemmie lay beside her, unconscious, the fastenings on her thin wrists mirroring her own; already the rats were grouping. The cote-hardie she had worn was gone and her kirtle had been overlaid with the Ullyot plaid, the squares of blue, red and black dull in this light and barely respectable given the linen on her shift was ripped in a number of places and the ties at her bodice cut. Shock made her tremble; even in the coldness of this day she was sweating. Why were they here? And where was here? Not Ashblane, she mused, for a banner draped across the wall showed the crest of the Armstrongs.

Her movement brought a face to the cell door. A gap-toothed man with long dirty hair peered in through the bars, though he covered his eyes with his hand as soon as he perceived her watching him.

'She's awake.' The slippery vowels of Gaelic. She'd

never learnt the language past the rudiments and could not catch the gist of the reply from further out.

The sackcloth surprised her as two men strode inside. As they wrapped it firmly around her head, she wondered why they should want to carry her this way and began fighting as soon as her wrists were released. She was rewarded with a harsh smack across her cheek and tears stung her eyes. These men would kill her. Fear throbbed deep as she listened to the passage they took. Up some stairs, she guessed, and into a room warmer than the others. The slight smell of charcoal assailed her nostrils, and also the more astringent aroma of sweat, as the men placed her on her feet.

'Remove the covering.' The voice was chilling and she straightened, her eyes blinking in the harsh and sudden lightness.

Laird Alexander Ullyot stood before her, flanked by two men almost as tall as he. He had not bathed since she had seen him last, though now he wore a coarse woollen over-jacket. The hard planes of his face in the glow of a banked fire were ominous, as were the leather bindings that anchored his left arm. She knew without being told that they hurt him, for he kept himself strangely still even as he held the attention of all those around him.

'The Armstrong laird names you as Madeleine Randwick? Sister to Baron Noel Falstone of Heathwater? Is this the truth?'

Nodding, her glance fell to his heavy bladed falchion

before regaining his face. The surprise she had noticed
fleetingly a moment ago had escalated into anger as he
strode forward, tipping her chin up and rubbing at the
bruise on her cheekbone.

'Who hit her?'

'She struggled, Laird, and I had to—'

The man who had taken her from the cell got no further.
A backhanded jab from Alexander Ullyot knocked him flat.

'Replace him, Marcus.'

One of the men beside him nodded and Maddy felt
heartened by the exchange, though Ullyot's next words
were not at all comforting.

'You are a prisoner here, Lady Randwick. A hostage to
make your brother see sense.'

'He will not—'

'Silence.' The quiet order was more disconcerting than
an outright shout. She noticed simultaneously the corded
veins in his neck and the chips of dark silver in his eyes.
She also saw the intricate crest that topped the gold ring
on his little finger. The lion of Scotland! Danger spiralled
into dizzying fear and she stumbled and would have fallen
had he not come forward to steady her. His hand was cold
and the hard shape of a dagger strapped in the fold of his
sleeve unnerved her further. He felt the need to carry
hidden weaponry even in the company of his own men and
allies? What laws did he live by?

The answer came easily.

None.

Paling as the implications of her deduction hit her, she dug her nails into her arms to distract panic with pain, ceasing only when she caught him looking at the red crescents left on her skin.

Distaste crept into slate-cold eyes. 'Why were ye there? In the dying fields?'

She blanched. Could he think her part of the battle? 'I am a healer,' she said, defiantly.

'A healer, is it? Rumour says differently,' Ullyot said with distaste. 'Quinlan, take her back to the dungeon.'

'No.'

'No?' A light of warmth had finally entered his eyes, though the effect in a face etched with none was unsettling. 'You would question me?' He stood so close now she could see the blond tips on his lashes. Long eyelashes and sooty at the base.

'There are rats.' The laughter of those around her made her jump and she fought to hide fear. The ill-tied plaid she was dressed in dropped below the line of the torn kirtle and she noticed keen eyes upon her breasts. Just another humiliation—she sighed and edged the warmer wool up with shaking arms.

'Take her back.'

'Please. If it's money you are after I can pay you. Handsomely.' Every man she had ever known had his price, although this one's frown was not promising.

'It's flesh and blood I'm wanting from your brother, Lady Randwick. Gold canna' bring back those men that I have lost.'

'So you mean to kill us?'

Before she could say more he placed one hand around the column of her throat and squeezed gently. 'Unlike your brother, I do not kill women and children.'

She felt the breath leave her body in a sharp punch of relief, though a new worry threatened. She had seen what Noel did to the captives at Heathwater and rape could be as brutal as murder.

A living death.

And such harm could come from any number of these men present. Indeed, when she looked around the room she saw many eyes brush across her body as the Ullyot soldiers contemplated their share of the easy spoils of battle.

Summoning courage, she stood her ground as Alexander Ullyot's eyes darkened, fathomless for ever, eyes drenched in the colder undertones of sorrow. Grief juxtaposed with fury. Grief for the man he had cradled and wept over. Madeleine was lost in what she saw.

'I can help you.' Her words came from nowhere and she felt him start as she laid her fingers across the heated skin of his hand. Grief was as much of an ailment as the ague or an aching stomach, and the healer in her sought a remedy.

'I do not need your help.' He snatched away his arm, angrier now than when she had first been brought into the room. 'Take her away.'

The irritable bark of instruction was quickly obeyed as two men stepped forward, though as she looked back she saw that he still watched her. Framed against the light, the

Ullyot laird looked like a man from legend: huge, ruthless and unyielding. But something else played in the very depths of his pale eyes. Something she had seen before many times on the faces of many men.

Interest. Lust. Desire.

She smiled as he was lost from sight and bent her thoughts to wondering as to how she could best use this to her own advantage.

'What do ye think of her, Alex?'

Quinlan's voice penetrated Alexander's thoughts as he upended his glass. 'Madeleine Randwick looks rather more like a dirty angel than the conniving heartless witch it is said that she is.'

'She's taller than I thought she would be.'

'And a thousand times more beautiful, aye?'

Anger levelled him. 'A pretty face can be as deceiving as a plain one, Quinlan.'

'She was scared of the rats.'

'Then get rid of them.'

'The rats?'

'Tomorrow we leave for Ashblane and we've not the time to waste transporting a sick woman. Put her in another room and post a guard at the door.'

He made himself stop. His left shoulder throbbed, the paste the physician had applied to the wound searing into the flesh. As he tried to lift his arm the breath caught in his throat, his heart pounding with the effort it had taken.

Ian. Dead.

Everything was changed. Diminished.

'Damn Noel Falstone to hell,' he whispered fiercely and walked to the window, trying to search out the dark shape of the Cheviots to the east and tensing as Adam Armstrong came to stand beside him.

'I am sorry. I ken how close you and Ian were and—'

Alex held up his hand. Anger was far easier to deal with than sympathy and much more satisfying. 'I should have ridden into Heathwater with the men I had left and flushed the bastard out. Ian would have done that for me were I to have been lying on the cold slab of your chapel with the salt upon my belly.'

'And you'd have died doing it.' Adam, as always, sought the calm logic of reason. 'Nay, far better to wait and continue the fight on another day when the element of surprise is on your side and you are not so battle-wearied. Besides, you are wounded. At least let me see to your arm.'

'No. Hale has already done so.' Moving back, Alex brought his left arm into his body. He wanted no one close. No one to see what he could feel. The wound was not small and he was far from home. Tomorrow when they reached Ashblane there would be time enough. For the moment, here in the keep of the Armstrongs, he wanted control. Or at least the illusion of it, he amended, as a wave of dizziness sent him down to the chair beside the table.

'Ian should'na have come with so few men.'

'Why did he, then?' Interest was plain in Adam's voice and, pouring himself another draught of ale, Alex was pleased for the distraction. It gave him a moment to swallow and settle the nausea. When he felt steadier he began to speak, though the beat of his heart was constant in his ears, the normal tones of his speech masked by rushing blood.

'Noel Falstone had burnt down cottages and taken womenfolk from a village west of Ashblane, and Ian left in fury before I had a chance to join him. If he had waited, we could have hit the bastard together.'

'Waited?'

'I have been away in Edinburgh with the King.'

'And when the King knows of the Falstone treachery? Will he act?'

'Our liege lord has lost heart after his long captivity under the English and prefers diplomacy these days to battle.' Alex was careful with his words.

'You may well be right; besides, David will'na slay a man as wily as the Baron Falstone no matter what the provocation. He is too useful to him with his lands on the border and the Marches completely in disarray.'

'Which is exactly why I will have to do it myself.' Alex pulled himself up. This time the room did not sway. 'Falstone is a braggart and a risk taker. Bur he is also a man of habit. He spends each January in Egremont and travels by way of Carlisle with only a small guard of men. He thinks himself safe.'

'You could not breach the sanctity of England so far south. Not like that.'

'Could I not?' His eyes hardened.

'As it is now, you stand in favour with the King. Imperil the treaty and you will lose Ashblane under the banner of treason. No one could save you.'

'No one will see me.'

'You would not wear the plaid? Lord, let me warn you of the pitfalls in this pathway. David may be your kin, but he is first and foremost King and he allows you Ashblane as a royal fortress. Should there be any instability here, any hint of falseness…?' He spread out his hands across the table in a quietly eloquent gesture. 'I am your friend, Alex, and from my experience men with a single purpose often bury their logic to define what they were not sure of in the first place. Take your clan safe back to Ashblane where Falstone cannot harm you, neither in siege nor battle. And while you are at that, toss the Randwick woman back to her brother with a note of clemency. Falstone may even thank you for it and David certainly will with the ink on the parchment of the Berwick Treaty hardly dry.'

Anger exploded as Alexander drew himself up from the chair and threw the last dregs of his ale into the fire.

'It is not thanks I am seeking,' he growled and watched as the pure alcohol caught with alacrity and the flames licked upward. 'Nay, Adam. Vengeance is what I want. I want Falstone's sister, I want his land and I want his life.'

'And the de Cargne sorcery? How will you still that in

Madeleine Randwick when it is said she can make a man
believe anything?'

This time Alex did laugh. 'You've a strange way to interpret the Holy Scripture. Thou shall not worship false
idols, and are not sorcery and witchery the falsest of them
all? If it is the magic you fear, then do so no longer, for the
Bible would'na countenance the existence of such inexpli-
cable unreason.'

Adam Armstrong brought his hand down hard. 'You
have stayed in the world of warfare for too long, Alexander, and strayed from the gentler teachings of God, so do
not lecture me on the interpretation of scripture. The border
lore is full of the tales of the de Cargne women whether
you deem to listen or not. Josephine Anthony. Eleanor de
Cargne. And now Madeleine Randwick. She uses her
beauty to tie men to promises they canna remember
making when they wake in her bed come the dawn. Strong
men. Brave men. Brought down by the wiles of a witch.'

Alex took a deep breath and groped for normality. One
more day and he would be at Ashblane. Twenty-four hours
and the malady of what burned in his bones could be
healed. Aye, the wound was making him light-headed, for
the image of Madeleine Randwick's naked pale limbs
entwined about his own kept surfacing. And resurfacing.

Angrily he slammed his clay goblet down. He remembered the living flame of her hair as she had been bustled
from the room and the cool feel of her skin when she had
touched his hand.

I can help you.

He shook his head in disquiet. She was a hostage, that was all. A valuable means of vengeance and retribution when expediency demanded he find a way to exact conditions from the rampant greed of her brother.

A convenient pawn. A woman whose very name was synonymous with treason and immorality.

The Black Widow of Heathwater.

With an angry swipe at the ale beside him he upended the bottle and felt the pain in his arm numb. She would be gone before the week's end. He swore it. And Ashblane would stay safe.

She had hardly got back to her cell when the man named Quinlan came down the stairs.

'Unshackle her,' he called to the guard and waited as this was done.

Maddy tensed—she had seen the anger in the Laird of Ullyot's eyes. Had he rethought his plan and sent his minion to kill her? Panic made her struggle and pull back.

'Where are you taking me?' Deciding indignation was the best way to push her advantage further, she stood.

'To a room without rats.' His reply was measured, and the humour in his words struck her as odd. She struggled to make sense of it all.

'Why?'

'Our Laird wants you fit to travel north in the morning.'

The significance of this reply hit her with a blinding

euphoria. They were not to die tonight? Perhaps, after all, there was a chance.

'Please. Could you free my page, Jemmie, too? He is only young and the cold is bitter here.'

A wary puzzlement filtered into the eyes of the soldier opposite as his glance skimmed the floor.

'The offer is for you alone, Lady Randwick.'

'Then I am sorry, but I cannot accept it.' Already the faintness of blue marked the pale face of her sister as the chill crept in through granite flagstones. She held out her arms for the manacles and turned her head away. She felt the chains re-locked as tangibly as she felt the indecision of the man opposite, though she did not look at him as he left, the heavy iron door clanging shut with a dreadful finality.

Sitting down, she put her head between her legs and willed calm as the small fingers of panic wrenched aside composure. She was trapped in the dungeon of an Armstrong keep by a Laird known well for his lack of mercy, and, if that was not bad enough, Jemmie was in a disguise that would tip the balance further were she to be unmasked. Everything was worsened yet again by the fearful nature of the Laird of Ullyot himself.

She made herself stop.

Unlike your brother, I do not kill women and children. Were those not the exact words he had used?

The thought cooled panic and kindled hope. If the rumours about the Ullyot's appearance had been so misleading, then perhaps his character was also unjustly slandered?

'Please, God, let it be so,' she prayed; as the tightness around her chest loosened, she crept across to Jemmie, frightened by her stillness. If her sister died, how could she keep living? A sob of terror escaped her before she could stop it, before she could again assemble the core of strength that she very seldom lost a hold of. She had been in worse predicaments before and had survived. With the grace of God and a little luck, perhaps they would both survive this one, too.

Quinlan returned to the Great Hall less than ten minutes after he had left it.

'She says she will'na leave her young servant.'

'She what?' Alexander turned to his second-in-command, wincing as the movement tore into the wound on his shoulder.

'She says she will'na go without the boy. Jemmie, she calls him. He has'na regained consciousness yet and she's worrit by the cold.'

'Then leave her there. Place a blanket across them both and leave them there.' But Quinlan wasn't quite yet finished.

'She smells nice, Alex, and her manners are more than fine....'

Sharp laughter filled the room. 'She's Noel Falstone's sister, Quin. She takes place in his raids.'

Quinlan shook his head. 'And yet when the plaid fell from her shoulders in the cell I saw a scar on one breast fashioned into the sign of the cross. Remember Jock Ullyot's words, Alex. He told us that the woman from Heathwater

Castle who had helped him bore the sign of a cross. And her hair. He spoke of a fiery angel who healed people…'

'He was dying. Delirious and dying. And if it be a fiery angel we are searching for, I doubt Madeleine Randwick would qualify.'

'The rumours could be wrong—'

Alex cut him off. 'They're not. Leave it at that, aye?'

'I would, save Geordie is on guard duty tonight.'

Swearing, Alexander reached for his dagger on the chair, tucking it into the belt at his waist with difficulty. 'And his son is laid out on a slab in the chapel. Ye dinna think it wise to change the watch, then?'

Quinlan shrugged in resignation. 'He's as close to the edge as I've seen him. To insult him further…'

He didn't finish as Alex Ullyot led the way out of the Great Hall, his shadow lying uneasily against stone as they made their passage to the dungeons below.

The cell was quiet save for the night-time wind that howled around the corners of the draughty passageways. Madeleine Randwick had hooked herself around the scrawny body of the boy she had been brought in with. An uncomfortable position, Alexander reflected, given the space between them. He noticed how her hands were taut white with the effort of stretching so far left.

'Get up.' He strode in as soon as the locks were freed and pulled her to her feet, ripping the plaid off her in one quick movement and turning her around to the light to find the scar of which Quinlan had spoken. A dainty cross of gold surprised him and he fingered it briefly before turning his mind back to the scar. 'Who marked you so?'

Maddy was stiff with shock. 'Liam Williamson, the Earl of Harrington.'

'You are his?'

'Yes.' Her heart beat fast in her chest and her mouth was dry. She saw the knife in his hand before she felt it and looking down, saw that her breast ran with the blood of a shallow cut. The red of her blood stained his hands as he drew away.

'Under the spoils of battle I relinquish his claim. Untie her, Quinlan, and bring her to the chamber off the solar.'

'You mean to—?'

'Now.' He said the word through his teeth and the soldiers in the cell all hurried to obey him. She felt their rough hands take liberties and knew that the Laird had seen it, too. This time he offered no retribution.

A large bed dominated the room they repaired to and it was on this the soldiers placed her. She noticed them fan out across the room as if they meant to stay through the deed, though the one named Quinlan was clearly agitated.

'She is a Lady, Alex.'

'She is Harrington's whore.'

'No, I'm not—' A hand clamped across her mouth.

'Speak again and I *will* kill you.' He released her only as she nodded. The blood at her breast made her faint, made her shake, made her sick to her stomach and she retched across the floor the contents of a frugal meal from the morning.

Now she would die. Looking up, she blotted the spittle with the borrowed arisaid and waited for retribution. Kill her or ravish her. It was all the same—if this Laird did not do the deed, then Liam Williamson surely would before too much time had passed.

She was sick of caring, sick of worrying, sick of the effort it took to live into another day and the absolute absence of any viable alternative. 'End it here,' she thought and stood, challenging him, before the rush of unbalance took her and she crumpled on to the floor of the raised dais.

Alex swore as the redness of her hair spilled across his boots, the white sheen of her body dappled now with blood and bruises. She was young and thin and strangely vulnerable, this Madeleine Randwick. Bending, he touched the fiery tumble of her silken curls. In unconsciousness her fear had been wiped away and moulded into something else entirely, the gentle line of her throat running up to a face that was unexpected.

He turned, his stomach no longer in this public ravishment. 'Settle her into a bedchamber upstairs and bring the young page to her,' he ordered, his eyes flicking to the wound he had inflicted on her breast. He suddenly wanted to cover it, but knew that to do so would invite comment. Stripping a flare from the wall, he made for the door, dismissing the sentries with a sharp order and glad that he could trust Quinlan's honour to make certain that the Lady of Heathwater stayed safe.

* * *

Madeleine woke in a bed, the feather-tick covers pulled up over her, and Jemmie beside her in a makeshift cot on the floor. Reaching her hand across the space, she was relieved when the blankets stirred. Jemmie was alive and unhurt. That was all that mattered. Outside it was dark; she could see a quarter moon through the clouds between the ill-fitting shutters.

'Are you hurt badly, Maddy?'

'Only a little.' Sitting up, she pulled at her plaid to reveal the cut Ullyot had marked her with. It still oozed slightly, though a skin had formed across the edges of the wound. Spitting into the palm of her hand, she rubbed the mark briskly and swallowed back tears.

'It feels better already, and, if Ullyot has not killed us by now, I doubt that he means to.'

'But the mark. He will take you—'

She cut off the worry. 'He will take me as a mistress, mark or no mark, Jemmie. It's the least of our problems.' Rising from the bed, she went to the window, pulling back the shutter and opening it carefully. Three storeys from the ground and no foothole to allow leverage. The Laird was taking no chances. She knew the door would have a guard standing watch.

'We have a knife and a gold crown.' She pulled both objects from a hidden pocket sewn deep inside her petticoats, putting her herbal powders that were also hidden there aside. 'It may be enough.'

'To escape?'

'Nay, to send a message.'

'To whom?'

'To Goult. If we could get away from here and ride west towards Annan—'

Jemmie interrupted her. 'No, nothing is safe.' As the words stopped, Madeleine noticed the thin band of sweat across her sister's brow. Could she be sickening from the cold night on the floor already, or was this a sign of being as frightened by the Laird of Ullyot as she herself was?

Her heart raced in fear. The Laird of Ullyot was not at all as other men—she had seen the auras that surrounded him the moment he had turned towards her. Silver and black. Eleanor had always warned her of such a mix; years ago she had come across her mother in the stables with her gowns around her thighs and entwined in the arms of a stranger who had breathed silver.

Silver and black. And something else, too. Something unspoken and forbidden. Something primal and reckless.

Shaking her head, she pocketed the dagger and the coin and began to think how she could turn this adversity to her own advantage.

'We will watch for our chance to escape; when it does come, we will make for France.' Covering her hands with the folds of her skirt, she was glad Jemmie could not see the whitened knuckles of her clenched fist. Glad she could not know the other thoughts that rushed around inside her head and had her rigid with panic.

'And we will be together, Maddy?'

The voice was shaky and years of her own fears allowed Madeleine to easily see fright in others.

'We will always be together, Jemmie, I promise. But now you must sleep, for it will be a long march on the morrow.'

She watched as the blankets shifted and then stilled before turning her eyes to the light beneath the door and sitting up. If they came, she would be ready, and the knife in her hand was honed sharp.

The Laird of Ullyot came to her room just as the pinkness of dawn blushed the eastern sky, his surprise at finding her awake masked quickly.

'I would speak with you, Lady Randwick, and without your page. My men will take him.'

Jemmie stood uncertainly, movements clumsy with sleep, and Maddy felt her stomach lurch in fright. 'Where will you take him?' She tried to temper her desperation.

'To the room next door. We will return him to you later.'

Her eyes went to the two guards. How dependable did they look? She was thankful to notice one was an old man with kindness stamped in his eyes.

'I will be safe, Jemmie. Go with the men.'

'But I think—'

Maddy shook her head as Jemmie began to speak, but the gesture did not seem to sway any intent as a bony chin went up and thinly covered shoulders straightened. 'Will you give me your word, Laird Ullyot, that you will not hurt her?'

A young, uncertain demand given without weapon or strength. Holding her breath, Madeleine waited for reaction.

'Get out.'

Not a knife through the ribs then, or a fist against the thin bones of Jemmie's face. Reciting a prayer of thankfulness in her mind, she watched as her sister was taken from the chamber. As the door shut behind the group, Ullyot began to speak.

'You have one who would vouch for your character, it seems, Lady Randwick, though many would say you are a whore and a liar known throughout two kingdoms for your loose ways and dark magic.'

She made herself smile. 'I have been incarcerated at Heathwater for the past ten years, my Lord.'

'Hardly incarcerated, my Lady, for your exploits at the Castle are chronicled well by those who have enjoyed your favours.'

Unexpectedly, she felt herself blush bright red. Angry at doing so, she stood and walked to the window.

Why was he here? And alone?

'How many retainers does your brother keep at Heathwater?'

Her relief was visible. He was here to find out about Noel's fighting capabilities?

'A thousand,' she lied, knowing the number to be almost twice that.

'A thousand without the retainers of Harrington?'

She knew the question was not lightly asked and looked

away. 'My brother has not the numbers your domain yields, sir, though there is a certain safety implicit in depending on others.'

'How so?' His eyes were instantly alert, the mark on his cheek below puckered badly in the harsh dawn light.

'The Ashblane soldiers are weighty in number. Too weighty, I have heard it whispered. Royalty likes to have strong men on the edges of their land as a first defence against invasion, but, when they become too powerful, any king is apt to worry.'

He laughed, the sound threaded with such ill-hidden arrogance it could only denote a man truly at ease with his own capabilities. 'If you want to help your brother, I would advise you not to lie.'

'Because my betrayal would yield him a quick death as opposed to a slow one?' She thought of Goult trapped in the middle of a battle, but he ignored her question and posed one of his own.

'Your page, Jemmie. How important is he to you?'

For a second Madeleine thought she might faint. Indeed, she grasped at the sill beneath the window and closed her eyes, every single thing she had ever heard about the Laird of Ullyot suddenly true. He had neither soul nor heart nor honour. And he was clever. She could barely believe the turn this conversation had taken. Had he guessed?

Desperately she faced him. 'If lives are to be traded, Laird Ullyot, I would prefer to barter my own.'

'Would you indeed, Lady Randwick? And I wonder why that might be the case?'

She dared not speak again. What was it he wanted of her? Everybody wanted something.

'Now, how many? What are the numbers?'

'Three thousand.' She did not look up as she recited the retainers and their strengths, careful not to leave out the Western allies. She was truthful with the demands of number. With her sister's life at stake and a Laird renowned for his lack of leniency, Goult would just have to take his chances.

'Thank you.' The words were as bleak as his eyes as she watched him. Slate grey. The colour of a lake before rain. Pale. Unreadable. Distant. For a moment she felt disorientated and exposed.

'The safety of my clan is paramount to me, Lady Randwick, and I will do anything to protect it. Anything. Remember that and ye may yet live to be reunited with your beloved Heathwater.'

She nodded because he expected it and watched him leave. *Heathwater…beloved?*

If she could burn the castle down herself she would, and if Noel was caught in the flames with Liam Williamson then all the better for it. The ghosts of ten years of hatred floated dangerously near and she closed her eyes against the screams of her murdered husband as the tightness in her chest caught her. Groping for the chair, she sat down. Not here. Not now. Not again. First she must get Jemmie to safety. And after that…

She would pray that the black Baron of Ullyot would scourge Heathwater from the earth on which it stood, leaving nothing for her ever to remember it by. And no one.

Alexander strode to the chapel. The candles burning in the vestry lit his passage as he crossed to where Ian lay. Lifting the plaid blanket away, he ran a finger in the sign of the cross over a cold forehead and pinched the salt in a dish on Ian's stomach to the four corners of the room. 'A charaid. May the Devil be far from your soul and your journey into Heaven sweet.' With care he rearranged the rondel dagger tucked into the sleeve of his dead friend's jacket, pleased to see that someone had thought to clean the blade and sharpen it. 'I swear ye will be avenged,' he whispered into the dawn. 'I swear it on the soul of the Virgin Mary and the blood of our Lord.'

Our Lord?

How long was it since he had prayed? Crécy? Alexandria? Cairo? He looked up at the vaulted ceilings and across to the portraits in gold of the Holy Family that hung against the far wall. Adam Armstrong was a devout man and his chapel reflected this. A small likeness of the Virgin Mary caught his fancy, for she had hair the same colour as Madeleine Randwick's. Shaking his head, he cursed abducting her, cursed the porcelain sheen of her skin and her fire-red hair. He should leave her with Armstrong to send back to her brother. Hostages could only harm Ashblane and he was always careful as far as his castle was concerned. And yet he knew he would not do it.

'Why can I not just leave her here?' His whispered question seemed like a shout. Lord, to be even considering taking her? Protecting her?

'I think she has cursed me, Ian. I think she has used her magic and cursed me.' The blood in his arm beat loudly and he felt hot. Sick. Cursed.

Breathing out, he pulled up the sleeve of his jacket to get a better look at the wound at the elbow. Angry lines of dark red scoured the skin and tracked upwards, the pain surprising him. Even in Cairo, with his face slit open from cheekbone to temple, he had felt better.

He knelt and genuflected, holding his right arm against his side so that no movement jolted it. And when he had finished his prayers of deliverance he made his way out to the waiting soldiers, hoping like hell that his dizziness was a temporary condition and that he would not slide from his horse before he again saw the battlements of the Ashblane keep.

Chapter Three

They had been travelling north-east through the damp of a rising drizzle for three hours, the hooves of hundreds of horses making such a sound that any enemies thinking to engage a force of men this size had long since vanished. Madeleine rode in the middle of the column with Jemmie at her side, and as the red and gold banners of the Ullyot clan swirled about them and the cold numbed the skin on her face, she wondered how much longer they would ride.

Finally the wide valleys of the Esk lay before them, tree berries bold and the branches covered with flaming leaves, and beyond, the deeper green of a forest. Jemmie seemed stronger after a night's rest and Madeleine's own wound stung less now, the throbbing of the night giving way to a softer ache. Ahead of her Quinlan reined in his horse suddenly and bid them to halt and she felt Alexander Ullyot's presence before she saw him, bathed in a coat of dust. She could tell that his arm hurt him by the angle at which he held it. His wounds required more than the poultice his physician had laid upon him and the healer in her surveyed his symptoms carefully.

Already he sweated.

The beat of his heart had quickened as well. She could see it in the pulse at his throat.

'We will build camp here for the night. The Liddesdale Forest is dangerous to stop in and we will'na make the other side by nightfall.' He shielded his face as he scanned the sky and Madeleine had the impression of him reading both time and weather. As he looked down their eyes met, flinted silver less sharp now as the first waves of deep infection assailed his body.

Little time left, she thought and dropped her glance. He would be beyond her help by the morning.

'You are comfortable?'

His question made her start, as did the full frown on his brow.

'Pardon?'

'Do ye have all you need?' His glance went to her breast. 'I could send my physician.'

'No.' She bit at her bottom lip to stop saying more and looked away. Already he was leaving. She felt as much of a murderer as her brother.

Quinlan dismounted and stood ready to help her down and she laid her hand upon his sleeve. 'I would thank you for your help last night.' Her gaze flicked across to Jemmie.

It had been Quinlan who had brought Jemmie to her wrapped in a blanket.

The resentment that lay in his light blue eyes was momentarily replaced by perplexity. 'Your retainer was full of praise for you, my Lady. I've seldom heard a young boy chat so much.'

The statement brought laughter to her lips. 'Surrounded by such soldiers as these, any stranger could seem verbose.'

Quinlan frowned. 'Alexander instructed everyone to keep their distance for your own safety. He wants you protected.'

'Why?'

'You are his now. Since last night.' His eyes dropped to her breast. 'As a hostage. I thought you understood.'

'And if he dies?'

Alarm flickered in blue eyes as he sought her meaning. 'Ullyot is invincible. Who would fight him and win?'

'My God…' Maddy crossed herself and turned away, the twin emotions of dread and joy battling within as suddenly everything dropped into place.

Could Alexander Ullyot, the feared Laird of Ashblane, shield her from everyone? From Noel and Liam? Even from King Edward? If he took her as a mistress, and unwilling, could such an uneasy alliance allow her time to think and plan, to throw them off her scent and disappear? She closed her eyes, the force of her desires washing across the more familiar powerlessness. He had men and might and an authority of leadership that was unrivalled. And last night, after she'd been sick over his floor, he had not killed her.

Not all bad, then, she reasoned, and turned again to Quinlan, her mind made up.

'Without my help, your Laird will be dead by nightfall.'

She saw the hairs of Quinlan's arm rise and his face redden visibly.

'You curse him?' His voice was strangled as he drew his blade.

'Nay. I told your Laird, I have the power of healing.' All around men gathered, their own swords drawn in response to Quinlan's anger. She held his gaze. 'The wounds your Laird has will poison him. Another few hours and his blood will run with it and there will be nothing I can do.'

'Kill the Randwick witch,' a bold voice cried to her left, and further knives were unsheathed.

'No.' Quinlan bade the men retreat, and they did so, but uncertainly, the air crackling with an unguarded tension. Were she to say more, she doubted even he could save her, and thus she held her silence.

An impasse. Drawing her gaze upwards, she looked towards the sky. The sun beat down upon the land and she felt it reflected in her hair. Quietly she raised her hood. In times like these some men took merely such a sign as this to take their action further. She saw Quinlan frown suddenly and thought perhaps he was a mind reader. She had encountered such beings in the old chronicles at her grandmother's castle, and always their eyes were blue.

'I will take you to the Laird and you can check the wound yourself.' His voice was curt as he turned to his horse and called for hers. Beside her Jemmie made to rise, but she stopped the movement.

'No, it is safe.'

One small hand came around her wrist and she felt the applied pressure. 'You'll need your things.' Jemmie's voice was uncertain, her upturned face deeply edged in worry.

'What things?' Quinlan demanded an answer.

'My healing tools. They were left at the side of the battlefield when you took me.'

'Our physician has others.'

Her mind raced to the balms and poultices she would have liked to have had, but in the pockets of her petticoats were twists of complex herbal powders whose recipes she had learned from her grandmother. It might just be enough.

And if it wasn't? She refused to think of this problem yet. Everything was tenuous, but on the brink of disaster she sensed something different. If the Laird of Ullyot lived, she might yet have a life. For within the bosom of this clan she detected a glimmer of safety. Safety for her and for Jemmie. For a while. And if Alexander Ullyot lived, she would ask for her uncle's safe passage from Heathwater.

Jemmie and Goult. Her family. To keep them safe she would strike a bargain with the devil himself.

The Laird was much worse when they reached him, and Quinlan's fright mirrored her own.

Alexander Ullyot no longer knew them, the sweat on his brow so high now he had lapsed into delirium. An old man crouched at his side with a bowl full of leeches. Already she could see he had been bleeding him, the fat black bodies of the worms bloated with blood and glistening under the light of torches.

Quinlan hurried to his side, knocking away the other soldiers who knelt there. His hand felt for Ullyot's and he squeezed it firmly.

'Alex.'

A flicker of consciousness generated greater tugging, the black blood from his wrist leaving a trail of darkness in the dirt. Perhaps it was that, Maddy thought later, that made him push the elderly physician to one side and bring her into the light.

'What can *you* do for him?'

A general hum went around the crowd at his words and another one as she came to crouch down beside him, pinching salt from a container on the ground and sprinkling it across the leeches. They curled up and fell on to the mat beneath him. She resisted scrunching them beneath her shoes even as the clan physician gathered them up.

'I'll need water,' she said, her hands touching the heat of his brow. 'And strong whisky.' Both came within a second of her asking for it and she extracted her dirk and powders from her petticoat pocket.

Instantly she felt the prick of a well-honed sword in the sensitive folds of her neck.

'Leave her.' Quinlan's voice. Anxious. Harsh. She did not look back at her assailant as she picked up her knife again and opened the herbal pouches. The sleeve of his shirt she dealt with next, slicing the seam apart and looking over at Quinlan who was watching her carefully.

'He can mend it when he is better,' she said bluntly, registering a spark of both admiration and wariness.

Many men had called her a witch, but just as many had admired her skills of doctoring. Tonight Quinlan's respect buoyed up her courage, made her fearless, made the contact she had with bone and skin and blood more real. Closing her eyes, she held the palms of her hands against his skin, feeling the poison and tracing the pathways of darkness to healthier flesh. The shock of connection was like an almost-pain and she could sense a haunting, answering anger that shut off the moment she felt it. Deliberately? Beneath consciousness he could feel her? Her heartbeat accelerated markedly. That had never happened before. Ever.

With hesitation she pinpointed the dark blue lines of blood and drove the tip of her sharp blade inwards, tourniqueting all that lay beyond and squeezing out the badness.

If the collected men gasped and watched her with disquiet, she did not recognise their superstitions, so intent on hearing next the sound of his bones. When she held up her hand for silence, it came immediately.

'Here.' She grasped the elbow and slipped it up against

the run of muscle, the swollen joints popping as the dislocation righted.

Sweat pooled between her breasts because she could not
quite shake the unease of his awareness. Rolling him over,
she looked at the jagged gash beneath his shoulder blade,
red crossed by other scars from different battles and healed
knot-beaded white.

A warrior!

My warrior!

The voices of those who had hurt him crowded in
against her, the wraith cries of old battles full blown from
that time to this one and echo-loud as she placed two
fingers against the broken skin and pushed. When the heat
gathered, her arms began to shake. Another moment, she
told herself, another moment and the warmth would come.
If she had been alone, she would have used the healing-
fire inside her, but here the traditions of other people bound
her tightly, and she had Jemmie to think of.

Nay, the doctoring had to be as conventional as she
could show it. She smiled to herself when sharp heat made
her fingertips vibrate. They would never see. A small, important victory for the de Cargne magic, for with its
coming she knew that death had passed back into life.

Sitting back, she rested for a moment before swilling
herbs in the whisky and bringing it to the Laird's lips.
Quinlan's hand stopped her.

'What is in it?' The charge of poison lay as an
unspoken threat.

Without answering she lifted the rim to her own lips and took a sip. Heat threaded her throat and sent the world reeling, but the fingers withdrew.

'Go on.'

Readjusting her stance, she looked again at her patient. 'You must drink,' she whispered and pressed with her fingers on a certain point of his neck. Grey eyes flew open on cue and he swallowed the liquid in thirsty gulps before lapsing again into unconsciousness.

All about her men crossed themselves, the age-old reaction to something that was not understood. Few men at Heathwater looked her in the eyes. It would be the same here come morning, though Quinlan's measured glance surprised her.

'Your Laird will live.'

'Do ye ever doubt yourself, Lady Randwick?' he asked as she bent again to her patient. Ignoring the question, she touched Alexander Ullyot's brow.

'Already the fever lessens. It is a good sign. By the morning he will be much improved.' Threading his dark blond hair through her fingers, she felt the lump of a fall on his temple.

I live as close to the edge of life as you do.

For a second she felt a bonding and, shocked, pulled her hand away.

Quinlan mistook her reflex action.

'What is it? What is wrong?'

'Nothing,' she lied easily and turned to collect what

little was left of her powders, wiping the blade of her knife with a pad of alcohol and pulling at the material in her petticoat to cut a wide swathe from the hem.

Two long bandages of clean lawn soon lay across her hands and, removing the stopper from the flask, she soaked them in whisky before winding them about the wounds. Alexander Ullyot thrashed a little as she kneaded his elbow and she hurried at her task. In all her years of healing she had not seen a patient who had lain so still during the most painful manoeuvre of repositioning a dislocated shoulder.

When he stirred and his eyes fluttered open, she tried not to touch his skin lest he feel again that point of contact. Already he was coming into consciousness; she had no wish to be still kneeling at his side when he awoke.

'I'm finished.' Standing, she rubbed at the small of her back, the bending in the cold startling her with pain. Deliberately she did not catch the eye of a single onlooker.

Two hours later she was summoned back to the clearing where the Laird of Ullyot sat.

'Quinlan says ye to be a witch.' His voice was deep but tired. 'My men believe it, too,' he added. 'They say ye charmed the sickness from me.'

'Given the limited skills of your own physician, their superstitions do not surprise me.'

She frowned as he tipped back his head and laughed, though the humour did not touch his eyes—rather it shadowed them in an unspoken distance. 'And yet you were not afraid?'

He faced her directly now, his irises catching the red light of a setting sun. Not quite silver, more the burnished hue of the wings of the moth that lived in the glens. And angry. Feeling his censure, she returned crisply, 'Once I touched you I knew that you would not die. If I had thought you to be unsavable, I could have stood back and pleaded ignorance, leaving your physician to finish the bad job he had started.'

'But by then ye had cursed me out loud. Nobody would have forgotten that.'

She did not answer and he swore softly, shifting his position as if to better accommodate his shoulder.

'Quinlan says you closed your eyes and read my blood with your fingertips. He said you asked for silence so that you could hear the sound of my bones. Like a witch would listen. Hale, my physician, says the same.'

'Your men speak nonsense, Laird Ullyot.' She noticed his eyes up close were beaded with a dark blue. They disconcerted her with their directness and she struggled for normalcy. 'I need to see if your fever is lessened,' she explained as she placed her hand on his forehead.

'It has gone.' His voice was quiet and disengaged.

'Your wounds, then. Does the pain increase?'

'No.'

'I need to look.' Feeling him stiffen, she leaned forward to take his bandaged arm in her hands. The appendage was hotter than she would have liked, though the flesh beneath when she unravelled the cloth had the look of a wound knitting nicely. When she checked his back it was the same. Reaching for the last of her powders, she added only a few drops of water.

'This one will cool your flesh,' she explained as she rubbed in the salve, though he caught at her hand when she went to apply more.

'Enough, Lady Randwick. You have cured me.' Strong fingers closed around her own and a guarded irony laced his words. 'The tales of your accomplishments are not without foundation, I see.'

Tensing, Madeleine pulled away. Dangerous ground this, given the widespread knowledge of the de Cargne sorcery. Tempering her answer accordingly, she met his gaze. 'And now you wish to thank me?' She sought to remove as much emotion as she could from her voice.

He laughed loudly, the sound bringing his retainers close, swords at the ready. Waving them off, he turned again to look at her.

'Do men *often* thank you, Lady Randwick?'

The insult was implicit and she braced herself. So many men had looked at her the way he was doing now and for one fleeting moment she was sorry that it was him. Before she had a chance to answer, however, he got to his feet and she noticed him wince as the arm lowered with the pull of gravity. 'I could fasten a bandage,' she offered from the ground, the healer within overcoming her woman's chagrin.

'Nay, I have this.' Pulling straps of leather from his pocket he brought the arm into his side and wrapped the binding around his wrist before looping it over his neck and moving the two or three steps needed to bring him right beside her. Sensing his intent for further conversation, she stood and waited.

'I am indebted to you for your help,' he said at length, the utterance dragged from his mouth as though it pained him to say it. 'And if you've a request ye wish to voice as reparation, I will try my best to see that it is done.'

'Bring my uncle to your keep from Heathwater.'

Surprise ran freely across his face.

'Why?'

'Because Noel will hurt him.' She could barely get the words out.

'And that would matter to you?'

'Yes.'

He watched her closely. 'Do you know how it is you are called in the court of Scotland, Lady Randwick?'

She didn't answer.

'They call you the Black Widow.'

The Black Widow. Lucien. She felt her world tilt.

'Rumour holds it, you see, that love for the chatelaine of Heathwater is conducive to neither a man's heart nor health. Lucien Randwick was eighteen when you married him and not twenty-six when he died. And when the body of an English Baron was found five miles from your castle before Yuletide last year, an entry in his journal named you as his lover. The pattern has been noted, Lady Randwick, though I'm wondering where I fit into the scheme of things. You could just as easily have said nothing today and left me to die.'

'I could have.' She said the words quietly, schooling her emotions in the way she had perfected across the many years of living with her brother. Alexander Ullyot could believe what he liked of her. People always had. She was surprised, though, by the thin band of pain that wrapped itself around her throat, and the tears that threatened. Looking away, she dashed the evidence against her sleeve. She never cried. Not ever. She forced a smile.

Jesus, Alex thought as the truth hit him. She had not murdered Lucien at all. A lifetime of soldiering easily told him that. Relief and anger were strangely mixed. He wanted to hate her, he wanted to hate her as much as he hated her brother. But he couldn't. And that thought made him even more furious.

'It was Noel, wasn't it?'

'Pardon?'

'It was Noel who killed them,' he repeated, louder this time and with more authority. 'Lucien and the others. It makes more sense, damn it. He used you as his excuse?'

For a second every single fibre in her body longed to lie, but the hilt of her knife in Lucien's neck was too real, too recent, and too tangible. She recalled in minutiae the way his eyes had glazed in shock as he had fallen, the light stubble on his cheeks strangely out of place against the harsher face of death. She remembered knocking his pleading hands away from her ankles and standing there until she was absolutely certain that his lifeblood had flowed away. Lucien Randwick, the golden-haired, laughing son of the Earl of Dromorne. Dead and not yet twenty-six.

Visibly she blanched. 'Nay, I killed Lucien.'

'But not the others?'

'No.'

The hardness in her voice was palpable, but Alexander saw the flare of fear in her eyes before she hid it. And sorrow. Madeleine Randwick was good at hiding things, he thought suddenly. Her healing magic, for one—now, even hours after she had touched him, the skin at his back still tingled. No simple task for all she said of it.

Magic. And now, murder. Baldly confessed. The knuckles of her hands were white with tension and her whole body shook.

'Randwick was a friend of mine.' His voice was soft.

'Lucien?'

'No. Malcolm, his father. He killed himself last year.'

He saw her grip the skirt of her dress. 'Malcolm Randwick. Dead? I had not heard. He brought me a bunch of snowdrops once and a pendant fashioned in gold. And when Lucien would not see him—' She stopped and caught her words. 'He was a kind man, a gentleman.'

'Unlike his son?'

The question was so unexpected she could not trust

herself to speak. Instead she nodded, and the instant bolt of anger in icy, pale eyes stunned her.

Belief.

Belief in her. For the first time in two years the white-hot shame of murder waned and the reality of her brother's complicity crystallised. It was not her fault. Not all her fault. She could barely take it in.

Alex looked away, not trusting himself to speak. Had the Randwick bastard physically hurt her? His eyes scanned the cream-smooth skin at her throat and arms and his quietly voiced expletive held a wealth of meaning as the night drew in on them both, black and close, the secrets of state binding them into fragile harmony.

'You were betrothed to Randwick as a child?'

'Yes.'

'Under the auspices of King Edward?'

'Yes.'

The pain in her voice was brittle, and with exaggerated care Alex continued. 'Malcolm's wife was Edward's cousin. Did you know that? The king knew of his condition.'

Condition? Lord, suddenly everything clicked into place in Maddy's head. Lucien had always been mad. Her brother knew it. His father knew it. And Alexander Ullyot knew it.

'I see.' She remembered the substantial amount of money her brother had received for the exchange of her hand in marriage. Her welfare had been sacrificed for expediency and then sacrificed over and over ever since. If it had suited her brother to name her a murderer and incarcerate her and her dowry at Heathwater, then how much more so it must have suited the royal family of England. Aye, if the taint of madness was to be banished then she herself had to be discredited completely. How well her brother had done that with the procession of tipsy male visitors to her private chamber and the constant change-over of staff sent to see to her needs. Isolation had fuelled the rumours and solidified her as the mad and dangerous Lady Randwick. And up till this moment she had never been able to understand any of it.

The Black Widow. Sometimes she had heard the words in the drifts of drunken revelry at Heathwater.

'I think I should retire.' She did not want to speak further, for, were he to ask about the details, she knew that the unexpected softness in his eyes would falter noticeably. Pulling her cloak more firmly about her, she shivered, but he was not yet finished. His free left hand steadied her movement. The spark of contact triggered an almost-pain.

'If it helps, Lady Randwick, I could tell you that I have killed a hundred men in battle and a score of others without its sheltering banner. And yet still I breathe. And live.'

Dimples graced her cheeks for the first time in months as she assimilated his very masculine attempt at consolation.

'Thank you,' she answered simply and watched as he left, moving through the trees with a grace seldom seen in large men.

The Laird of Ullyot was a self-sufficient man and one who walked his world without the crippling doubt of con-science, his strength and confidence as legendary as his danger. Without him next to her Maddy felt an unfamiliar tug of loss, as a lack of sleep caught up on her. Swaying with light-headedness she leaned against the trunk of a tree whilst considering her options.

'I'm to take you back to your page, Lady Randwick.' A kind voice startled her and she turned. 'I'm Brian the Tall,' the man said. 'The Laird's cousin,' he added, seeing her frown. 'He said to give you this. For the medicine, he said.' The leather flask of whisky he put in her hands was roundly full and fashioned with plaited tongs and shells. 'Gillion made it.'

'Who is Gillion?'

'Alexander's son.'

The blood drained from her face. Alexander Ullyot was married? He had a wife at Ashblane? Lifting her chin, she tried not to let this Brian Ullyot see her quandary. If a wife was at his keep, everything was changed. She could not stay there at all. The sharp points of the seashell had drawn blood from her palm before she realised what she had been doing and let go. The man beside her looked away and Madeleine saw the movement of one hand crossing his chest.

It didn't surprise her, as he'd been there at the healing. Still, she would have liked him as a friend, the kindness in his voice drawing memories of times when her life had included laughter. And now she was to be thrown again into a no-man's land where any hope of sanctuary was futile. She felt the torn skin on her breast and could barely draw breath.

But what now?

She would never go back to Heathwater and she could not stay at Ashblane, either. Playing the whore for the promise of safety was one thing, but playing it in the presence of a wife and children was quite another.

Biting her lip, she tasted blood, cursing her woman's body and her lack of strength. She hoped her healing of the Laird had inspired some sense of gratitude, some slight advantage to effect a softening of guardianship and a moment to escape. With Jemmie, of course. She frowned; the task of finding safe passage for them both had become immeasurably harder, especially in the middle of a landscape she could not recognise and the possibility of two hundred well-honed soldiers on their heels.

And Alexander Ullyot.

Worried, she thought of their recent conversation. Would the tainted secret of her marriage now be his to use as Noel had? A weapon of compliance. An unforgivable sin. Murder, or self-defence? Witchcraft or healing? Would Ullyot banish her to the court of either Edward or David to face trial and sentence? Her breath quickened as she remembered the rumours that placed the Laird firmly in the camp of David's court. Bastard son of one of Robert the Bruce's brothers, was it not said? For the first time ever she wished she had listened more closely to the gossipy ramblings of Noel and his lover, Liam Williamson. Pray that tomorrow they would still be heading north-east. Pray that the healing would sanctify her life. Pray that Ullyot was as irreverent of the law as she had heard and that the comfort he had given her was sincere.

The questions turned around and around in her head as a single drop of blood from the sharpness of the shell rolled down her palm and dripped off the end of her ringless fingers, mingling with the mud on the ground.

Chapter Four

She saw the keep from a distance and it was every bit as ugly as Terence had said it to be. More so in reality, for the walls rose at least a hundred feet in the air on every side and there was no sign of any windows. Jemmie beside her looked as taken aback by the place as she was. They had not expected a palace by any means…but this? The architecture defied description. Certainly it conformed to no style she had ever seen. Rather, it echoed only the promise of being a structure that might well still be standing in another five hundred years.

Ashblane.

The spoils of battle for Ullyot clan loyalty to Robert the Bruce after Scotland's War of Independence from the hated English. No motte-and-bailey earth-and-wood keep this, but pure Scottish stone. And unassailable.

The noise of bagpipes rolled across the valley and a huge roar went up as the gates swung open, the occupants spilling out, searching for loved ones. No one as yet had come to the Laird of Ullyot and she wondered about it. Every person stood back from him rather, giving him room to coach his steed across the drawbridge and into the bailey proper.

She and Jemmie gained the bridge a few moments later and she saw the faces of those around her without really looking. If she had stared further, she knew she would read disdain and hatred. She was Noel Falstone's sister and he was their sworn enemy. Already she could hear the wails of those who had reached the cart with the bodies wrapped in plaid. She steadied her mount, jittery in the close crowd of people, and wondered where to go.

'You'll need to dismount. Follow me.'

Quinlan's voice shouted across the noise around them and she nodded as she carefully slipped from the horse, her body stiff from the hours of riding. Once down she turned to Jemmie, her fingers cupping a bony elbow as she helped her sister to the ground.

The hall inside was unremittingly plain. No tapestries hung to break the gloomy pall, no embroidered chairs or bowls of flowers. No banners that festooned the walls of other keeps, no decoration at all save the stuffed head of a deer pinned at an angle above the mantelpiece. Part of its antlers lay on the shelf beneath, in an odd juxtaposition of space. Alexander Ullyot stood there now, warming his hands against the flames and speaking to a man she had not seen before. He had removed the sling, though he held his arm in an awkward slant; when one of the dogs at his side inadvertently knocked him, he swore roundly.

Madeleine frowned and wondered if the rest of the keep was as frugal, her heart thumping as soon as she thought it. Would she be dragged to his bed tonight? Already the hour was late. Would he want to take her now? He looked like a man who never waited for anyone, least of all for a woman. Pure masculine power cloaked his every action. And what of his wife and son? Where were they?

'Food will be brought to you and water provided.' Ullyot had finished with his retainer and was speaking now directly to her.

'It is not the custom here to eat in the Great Hall?' Madeleine's question was breathlessly hopeful as she played for time.

'Not tonight,' he returned quietly. 'Tonight we will bury our dead.'

The pain in his words was tangible and she looked away.

'Ian.' The word slipped from her lips without thought as she remembered the name he had called out in the fields behind Heathwater.

'What did you say?' She flinched as he covered the distance between them.

'Your friend. I saw him fall.'

'Lord.' The chips of cold anger in his eyes burned bright. 'I had heard it said ye like to watch the slaughter. Like a game?' The words were barely whispered as disgust overwrote plain fury and he turned away.

'You listen well to the stories that are spread of the de Cargnes, Laird Ullyot, and it is wise that you do so.' Her voice was as hard as his had been and it caught his attention.

He turned back.

Madeleine forced herself to smile. For this moment he must believe all that was said of her family. The wound at her breast marked her as his and here as at Heathwater she needed to put a measure of protection in place. Men coveted women they could understand, soft women, weak women. Her armour lay in the foundations of superstition and magic. Even a man like Alexander Ullyot believed in superstitions.

She thought he might strike her—indeed, took a half step backwards before she stopped herself. At her side Jemmie had reddened dramatically and her eyes flicked with warning as she prayed her sister would not be foolish enough to try to defend her if Alexander Ullyot were to knock her down.

'Do you court death, Lady Randwick?' Ullyot's query was bland and she looked up, puzzled.

'Pardon?'

'This.' He had turned out the small dirk from her pocket before she could blink and it clinked uselessly on the dirt floor. 'For a witch your face is surprisingly unschooled. But take warning. Should you bear arms against me in the company of my soldiers, you may find a sword through your heart before you have the time to explain it otherwise.' His free hand ran across her breast in a surprisingly lewd caress. 'And that would be a waste of good woman flesh, witch or no, I think.'

Maddy pulled away, the imprint of his fingers burning into her skin, and was intimidated again by his very bigness. With one single smack of his hand she could be dead if she should anger him further than restraint would allow. Her mind sought the anecdotes of his temper and the stories were many. Still she could not resist saying something as she hitched up her plaid.

'I think your wife may object to such fondling should she be watching, Laird Ullyot.'

The chips in his eyes became colder. 'And you think as Laird here I would have no right of choice?'

The question was so baldly provocative that the blood flared in Madeleine's face as she comprehended his meaning.

'Any choice by force is hardly honourable, sir, as any wife of honour would know.' She drew herself up to her full height, which was not inconsiderable, and wished she were taller. 'You have just need to ask your own.'

For the very first time warmth marked his face.

'I am pleased to discover that mind reading is not one of your accomplishments, Lady Randwick,' he said cryptically, speaking rapidly to Quinlan in Gaelic before he bent to retrieve her blade and left. She saw a group of women near the kitchen watching him, though he did not acknowledge their presence. Absolute interest was scrawled across every feminine face.

Madeleine turned to check Jemmie was tucked in safely behind her and wondered what was to happen next. Where would they be bedded and would the food he had promised arrive? Her stomach was rumbling loudly, protesting the lack of sustenance during the last two days, when a boy of five or so scampered out from a passageway, a broom of some weight bearing down behind him.

'Away with ye, ye clattie imp.' A serving girl chased him and Maddy found herself between the assailant and the child and in the first second of looking at him she knew him to be Alexander Ullyot's child. He had the same eyes and hair. And the same sense of distance from everyone and everything around him. In a child the trait was heartbreaking.

'Have you lost your senses?' She turned on the woman and made an effort to snatch at the raised broom. 'What has the boy done?'

'Stolen buns from the evening's wake,' the woman wailed and Madeleine saw that, despite the etched lines across her brow, she was young. She turned to the child behind her for explanation, though none was forthcoming. He watched her with furtive eyes as he finished off the stolen goods.

Usually children denied their wrongdoings. The thought hit her forcibly. Other children she had seen dealt with in a disciplinary matter had been full of explanation as to why they had not possibly done what it was they stood accused of. This child did none of those things. He did not even run for shelter or brush the offending crumbs from his tunic.

'Why did you steal the cakes?' Madeleine made her voice as gentle as she could, bending so the child could see her face. She noticed he watched her lips and did not meet her eyes.

'Because he is light-heided and dim-witted as well as being bone-hard deaf.'

The boy's gaze caught the movement of the serving girl as she advanced upon him and with a swish of linen and wool he had run past them and up the stairs.

Turning to Quinlan, Madeleine saw he had distanced himself from the whole exchange. The child was known to him obviously, but he made no comment on the encounter at all as he walked towards the stairs and bade her and Jemmie to follow.

'I'm to see ye to your sleeping place.' He did not catch her eye. Was this a good sign or a bad one? Her fingers sought out the cross of gold at her throat and she rubbed it twice, stopping herself the instant she perceived herself doing such. Noel had chided her last week for the foolishness of such actions, castigating her again and again to rid herself of the cultivated habits of her childhood. At Heathwater everything was as measured as it must be here. No false moves, no reckless actions to place the weapon of knowledge in anyone's hands. Schooled temperance and aloofness were the maxims of the Falstone men and their women suffered if they should forget such governance.

Keep your distance and the strength to maintain decorum no matter what.

Madeleine lifted her chin, remembering the words of her mother, and the words became a mantra as she followed the party up the stairs and into a room built at the back of the keep overlooking a lake. Some windows at least, then. Maddy drew in her breath with gratitude.

'You will stay here, Lady Randwick, and the boy Jemmie next door until we find a job to set him to. Supper will be sent up on a tray as soon as it is ready.'

'Thank you.' She felt the tremor in her voice, though, as she bit back the question of the night's sleeping arrangements. Quinlan surprised her again with his uncanny ability to read what was on her mind.

'The mourning will keep the Laird busy for the next few days. You will'na be bothered tonight.' Momentarily his eyes met hers. Imprinted with perplexity, she perceived also a humanity etched into the blueness. An honourable man, then, Quinlan Ullyot, and one uncertain of the implications of her imprisonment. Could he be persuaded, then, to let her go? Assist in the escape of both herself and Jemmie? Dare she ask the question at all?

'I am a lady, sir,' she began, wishing for the first time in her entire life that she bore the gift some young women had of bringing tears to their eyes on demand. 'Your Laird has no right as a gentleman to keep me here against my will. If you could help me—'

She got no further.

'*Ladies* dinna wear the mark of lovers on their breast or watch the slaying of good men in battle from a close distance. It is wise you learn that the will of our Laird is obeyed unquestioningly before ye ask of another what you were about to ask of me. Betrayal is measured in the cost of a life and no one's life here is worth less than your own. One false step and ye shall be interred, Madeleine Randwick, with the bodies that this night will be laid in the coldness of Ashblane's dirt.'

Without pausing for an answer he bade Jemmie proceed outside with him, the turning of a key in the lock giving her notice again that she was a prisoner here.

The light of a thin sun struggling through the October clouds hit the wall behind her and made her turn to the window. Through the panes of polished horn the world was strangely distended and made unreal. In the far distance she saw some hills. The Cheviots, she guessed. And just beneath her the movement of a priest hurrying, the black folds of his garment glued by force of wind around his legs and whipping the tassel on his belt sideways. If she listened carefully, she could hear the first tunings of bagpipes keening in the rising wind off the Scottish Lowlands.

Tonight she felt lonely and frightened and confused. Her hands dug deeper into the pockets of her skirt, feeling the last dustings of age-worn leaves. Chamomile. Lemon balm. Marjoram. They grounded her. Made her real. Pulled her bones to the earth in a way few people had been willing to. Jemmie. Goult. Her mother and grandmother. Shutting her eyes, she imagined Eleanor and Josephine calling to her in the way the de Cargne women had summoned their ancestors for centuries. The true witchcraft lay here, she smiled wanly and laid her hand across her heart, listening as the footsteps of the soldiers receded.

When silence reigned she crossed the room and bent at the timbered wall that divided her room from Jemmie's. Knocking twice, she held her breath, releasing it only as two answering taps came back. Two for safety. Three for danger. The codes from Heathwater were so ingrained that she was suddenly and unreasonably angry. When would their lives ever really be safe? When would she be able to sleep at night without the edge of panic in her dreams? When could Jemmie set aside boy's clothes and claim her place in a world that would not harm her? Ashblane was as much as a jail as Heathwater had ever been with its powerful Lord and its isolation, and here, caught in the borderlands of mist and drizzle, all she had ever tried to accomplish slid into nothingness.

The Black Widow. She mouthed the words into the quiet around her, hating the sound of them. At twenty-four she had become as notorious as her mother had been, and as trapped.

Chapter Five

The next morning she was taken alone to the Great Hall where the hum of conversation was quickly silenced by her entry. Maddy caught Alexander Ullyot's glance as she walked by. Today he looked tired, the dark stubble of his beard unshaven and the clothes she had seen him in last night dishevelled and creased. He had not been to bed then, the wakes taking up all of the hours between then and now. The thought made the bile rise in her throat and she was thankful to note that the chair to which she was led at least afforded her a little privacy.

'You are to sit here, Lady Randwick, and I will fetch you the morning meal.'

The woman spoke nervously and crossed herself as she scuttled away to the kitchens. Looking around, Madeleine caught the scowl of a man who shaped his hand into the form of a knife and whipped it across his throat. Her glance dropped away in shock. Such harsh and raw hatred was jolting—even though at Heathwater it had been every bit as potent, it had never been quite as overt.

She made herself sit perfectly still, hands tightly fisted in her lap, teeth gritted. She had sat like this so many times at Heathwater as Noel and Liam Williamson had drunk themselves into oblivion. She had shielded her emotions from her husband, too, when the ghosts that ate at his sanity threatened to take it completely. Aye. She was a woman who had learned not to expect much. Here at least there was not a fist in her face or a barrage of angry expletives every time she deigned to leave her room.

Her room. The tower room in the western wing at Heathwater Castle, black drapes drawn across the sun for fear the ghoulies and silkies of a thousand years of fairytale should enter unseen. Lucien's gibberish and in the end her saviour. She liked the curtains closed and humanity shut out, the sounds of a world she could no longer fathom softened by the distance of darkness.

A movement at the top table caught her attention. Alexander Ullyot had summoned a young woman to speak with him, a girl with light hair and a blue gown and the complexion of someone who enjoyed a walk outdoors in the sunshine. A girl who was even now approaching her.

'Would ye mind if I joined you, Lady Randwick? My uncle has bid that I be polite.'

A barely concealed insult. An explanation of intent.

'I do not expect it,' Maddy returned. 'Tell your uncle that

I relinquish any duty regarding manners that you or he may feel bound to.'

She was surprised when the girl smiled and sat. 'My name is Katherine. I am the daughter of the Laird of Ullyot's first wife's oldest sister.'

'His first wife? How many wives have there been since?'

Katherine smiled again. 'Only that one. She died when Gillion, who you saw last night, was born.'

'Then he is not married?' Maddy did not question the silent spring of relief that rose in her breast.

'No. Alice Ullyot has been dead for these past five years. She died in the chamber you have been placed in, though there is no ghost or any such thing. Not that you would be afraid, I think, Lady Randwick, for I have watched you. It is you the others are afraid of. They cannot afford to believe in your magic, you see.'

'Magic?' Her voice was guarded.

'The way you heal. With your hands.'

'It is not magic. It is only good medicine.'

'And it makes you independent, doesn't it?'

Maddy frowned, troubled by the drift of this conversation.

'You've no husband,' Katherine qualified, 'and you need none. I, too, would like to become a woman without need of men.'

'And that is how you see me?'

'I overheard my uncle say it to Quinlan when first he brought you here. He also said you were a witch.'

'And you believe him?'

'Quinlan does and Dougal, and the men who watched your doctoring in the clearing before the Liddesdale Forest. I see them cross themselves after you have passed them by. For protection, I think, though my uncle frowns at them when they do so. I have heard, too, that at Heathwater you preferred your own company and were rarely seen in the fellowship of others and I wondered—is it sometimes not lonely to be you?'

The wave of desolation that rolled across Madeleine as a result of Katherine's question had her struggling for a semblance of calm.

Lonely.

When had she ever felt anything else?

'No.' Even to her ears the reply sounded brittle.

'I'm sorry. I must learn not to pry. Everyone is always telling me that. "Stop the questions, Katherine. Stop asking about things." It is a failing that I am reminded of often. Why, when I was a child, I lost count of the times that my mother chastised me for impertinence and that is, I fear, a fault that I have just repeated.'

The prattle went on and on and Maddy relaxed, even as she had the strange feeling that the girl was actually giving her time to recover her defences. For the first time in her life she was uncertain of motive. This girl should hate her and yet she offered something else entirely. Friendship. Kindness. The lighter edge of companionship and a place where Maddy had never before ventured.

With anyone.

They were interrupted by a fracas at one end of the room that had them both standing. A man was screaming in Gaelic. She noticed the soldiers at the doorway fan around the table where they sat. A signal from the Laird, she fancied, when she chanced to glance his way and saw how he watched her. His air of tiredness had vanished into prickling alertness, the food untouched upon his plate. He watched her like a general might watch a battle, eyes scouting around the edges of the room with vigilant intent. He stood suddenly and Madeleine's fingers tightened in a fearful grip. If these retainers meant to harm her, she would have no chance, though suddenly she sensed someone charging at her from behind. Turning to counteract the threat, she knocked Katherine out of danger, but the nearest soldier was faster, his body thrown between Maddy's and the flash of steel. Everything sped up as he collapsed, the blade pushed through his ribs and out again. She could see the reddened tip as her unknown protector fell and she lunged for the knife at his belt, thrusting it before her in protection.

Nothing made sense, not the shout from the end of the room, nor the keening wail that came from her lips, nor the group of retreating soldiers burdened with the scuffling body of her would-be assailant. Only the grey eyes of Alexander Ullyot pierced the haze of her paralysing shock as he came to stand beside her. Only the gulping sobs of Katherine as she was led away by an older woman.

'Give me the knife.'

A hundred Ullyot retainers stood near, each bristling with their own form of weaponry.

'Give me the knife,' he repeated. His voice shook as he held out his bare hand, and he seemed relieved when she placed it in his palm, secreting it in his tunic before motioning his men to a distance.

Madeleine knelt to the fallen soldier at her feet and taking a breath she cradled his head in her lap, the spittle from his mouth staining her bodice and blood wetting her skirts.

'Thank you.' Her words were soft and his eyes focused as he tried to smile. Soft brown eyes, and young. Everything inside her tightened. Already the paleness of dying tainted his skin, his focus looking inwards and glazing as the blood flow weakened.

He had saved her and given his life for her own. A soldier whose name she did not even know. She could feel the ache in her throat as she brought his body closer.

Still. Still. She summoned warmth and softness. She banished fear and pain with the de Cargne chant of harmony.

A hush fell across the Great Hall as soldiers strained to listen and watch. The steady drip of blood slowed further and then stopped. Madeleine Randwick's hands pressed hard against the entrance of the sword point, then wandered to the young soldier's face as his breathing eased into silence and life gave way to death.

The red of her hair mingled with blood and her linen kirtle sagged at the juncture of her breasts, leaving the swell of womanly flesh visible to all those who stood close. And Alexander noticed his men watching. After all, she was reputed to be a whore, and soldiers bound long in the regimen of battle could hardly be chastised for taking a good look. Though this morning, bathed in the light of a thin autumn sun and helping his man to die with dignity, Madeleine Randwick appeared nothing like what it was said she *could* be.

For the first time in his life Alexander felt a strange sense of affinity with a woman. Moving his hand for the Great Hall to be emptied he waited, the silence between them punctuated only by her breathing.

'I cannot stay here,' she began when she noticed the last of the onlookers gone. 'Even though that man failed to kill me, another one may be luckier.'

His glance perused her woman's body. 'There is no other choice, Madeleine,' he growled, surprised by his use of her name, for he had promised himself no real contact. Surely as the sister of the hated Noel Falstone she must have known her pathway might finally come to this? He softened his voice as he noticed her shaking. 'I promise you that the man who did this will be punished.'

'By whom?'

'By me.'

Breathing heavily, she garnered control as the familiar disdain cloaked his features. She was glad for it. The expression he had been wearing a moment before had been perilously close to pity. And compassion. And she wanted neither. Pure and utter loathing was easier to deal with. To discount. To fight back against.

She lifted the hand of the dead soldier to her lips before kissing the fingers and standing. 'What was his name?'

'Patrick of Jedburgh. He was sent to me for training three years ago.'

'You can train men to give their lives for a woman they despise?' An unbridled criticism threaded her question.

'Nay, my lady,' he returned implacably. 'I train men to perform their duty. Patrick's duty was to see you safe. He did his job.'

Not one whit of emotion showed in his eyes, no regret, no guilt and no apology. A soldier he had known for three years lay murdered at his feet and she felt more sorrow than he did. Again she saw the man legend had grown up around, and her heart chilled. She noticed a new gash on the inside of his wrist, the bandage soaked in redness. The Ullyot death-in-blood tie, she supposed. She had heard tell of it, the incision made in the wrist of the living to be pressed to the lips of the dead. Just another bestial tradition of a clan steeped in them, though today she felt the action was imbued with a certain honour. Pain had a way of reclaiming numbness. And at this moment she would have welcomed the relief.

'You will return to your chamber.' The same woman who had brought her down reappeared as if by some pre-arranged signal and Madeleine saw that the six soldiers escorting her were armed.

'And can I hope that these ones are as well trained as Patrick?' She could not help the taunt.

The anger in his eyes heartened her, as did the last glimpse she had of the Laird Ullyot before she rounded the steps. He had knelt to his downed retainer and lifted him up in his arms and she saw the gentle way he cradled the body to his chest as he made for the chapel.

He came back later that morning and stood just inside her door. Blood stained his shirt, and his hair was plaited at the sides to keep it back off his face. For once she saw he carried no weaponry.

'You will keep to your room for the next few days.'

'And my page? Is he also being held to his room?' She hoped to God that Jemmie would be. At least she would know where her sister was.

When he seemed disinclined to offer more she asked quietly, 'This is a punishment?'

'No. This is a way to keep you safe.'

'Because others will try to kill me?'

He ran his hands across his face. She noticed the dirt under his nails and a new scratch in the soft flesh at the base of his little finger. 'Ashblane is a fighting castle, Lady Randwick, but we draw a line at the slaughter of innocents.' His tone was wry.

'Like me?' she challenged, noting the humour that was there momentarily and then gone.

'No one will try to hurt you after today.'

'Because you instructed them not to?'

He ignored her question completely. 'Your assailant's dismembered body lies in the western fields to be taken by the wolves and his head is staked to the stone on Patrick's grave.'

She paled at his description, for at Heathwater such brutality was generally hidden. 'A grim reminder of duty, then?' Her pointed criticism was not taken in the spirit she had given it.

Indeed he seemed pleased by her words as he walked into the room and stood near the window looking out.

'But the children. They will see—'

'Enough.' Leaning forward, he flipped the tie from her hair and watched as it flowed down her back to settle almost to the line of her hips. 'I like your hair down.'

It was the first truly personal thing he had ever said to her and she was so surprised she could think of no re-joinder. This was the way most men initiated the love play that she had endured at Heathwater for years. But by the look of annoyance and anger on Alexander Ullyot's face, she could hardly think that was where his next thoughts lay.

'Is Noel your full brother?'

'No.' Again he had disconcerted her.

'Who is Goult?'

'My uncle. On my mother's side.'

'He lives with you at Heathwater?'

'Yes.'

'Because he wants to protect you by being close?'

'Yes.' He was the first person ever to determine the true motives of her uncle and she was duly impressed.

'Does he ever leave the castle?'

'He goes to his sister in Carlisle for his birthday.'

'Which is when?'

'The twenty-second of October.'

'Then I will send men to fetch him to Ashblane when he does.'

He could have said nothing to surprise or delight her more and for a moment she could barely breathe.

'You remembered,' she whispered as she finally found her voice. 'Thank you.'

He brushed off her gratitude and caught her hand, raising the palm in a curious upward movement as though he would read her lines of fate. She felt the pulse at her wrist speed up and hoped that he had not noticed. 'Unlike your brother, we pay our debts.' His voice was gravelly and deep.

Tentatively she smiled at him and he dropped her fingers as if he had been scalded.

'You will be brought lunch and dinner. You will stay in this room. If you require something else, you will call the servant outside. But be warned—if you leave this room unattended you will be locked in.'

'Because you would think of my safety?' Madeleine could not quite resist the taunt.

'Exactly.'

He walked past her and out the door, slamming it behind him.

Once outside he stopped. Lord, she was so beautiful he was becoming as duped as the numerous lovers he had heard spoken of. It was her firelight hair and her mysterious eyes and the soft low timbre of her voice, he decided.

And her strength.

He closed his eyes and leant his head back momentarily against cold stone. He was so used to needy women. This one threw him, with her stubborn streak of independence.

She was the Black Widow. Trussing up her victims in the web of lies and deceit before what—killing some? Leaving others to eternally bleat about her charms? She was a hostage, and a way to get under the skin of her brother; as a willing player in the murky game of borderland politics, he should have no compunction about using her for his own ends. Aye, he should use her here and now and put an end to the nonsense that was building in him; should slam inside her and feel the flesh of her sex around his own. Should ruin her as surely as he wanted to ruin her brother.

And instead…instead he was escorting her uncle into Ashblane and complimenting her.

I like your hair down.

Lord, when had he ever noticed the length of hair on a woman before, or the style?

A witch and a sorcerer. The de Cargne sorcery.

And she was practising it on him.

He slapped the wall beside him and resolved to stay well out of her way whilst he worked out what exactly to do about the Lady Madeleine Randwick.

Chapter Six

She woke, knowing nothing was as it should be.

She was being watched. She felt the eyes rather than saw them, heard the breathing of an unwelcome interloper without the true vibration of any sound. Whirling to the wall on her right, she scanned the structure, the glint of orbs pulled from a large shuttered hole a second after she had come across them, and reappearing when she stayed perfectly still. Bolder this time. She caught the outline of his face, the colour of his hair.

The child she had seen when she had first come to Ashblane. Alexander Ullyot's boy roaming the hollow walls in the dead of night. Rising from her bed, she donned a wrap left draped across a chest. Would he return? She stayed still to listen and heard instead the drunken murmuring of soldiers on the battlements below. She caught the cadence of the Laird himself and hurried to the window to open it. A black-cloaked woman leant comfortably against him, her long blond hair caught in the light of the moon and the shape of soft femininity easily seen in the lines of her clothes. Madeleine frowned. Nothing seemed as it ought. A woman who he was obviously close to and a child who walked the house in silence at an hour when children should be fast asleep and protected in their beds.

Her fingers edged the ridge of healing skin at her breast through the thin linen of her shift. Why had he marked her so when the hatred he felt was so tangible? The brand offered protection. Had not Quinlan said as much? If it was merely woman flesh he wanted, he hardly need ask. He could take her when and where he desired and any amount of struggle she put up would delay the inevitable only momentarily.

Footsteps and men's voices outside her door brought her thoughts back to more immediate concerns. The handle turned as she stood there, the slat taken from its holder and swinging her door free.

Three men she had not seen before came into her bed-chamber, the smell of liquor heavy on their breath. Would they rape her even with the mark of their Laird at her breast? And why would the soldiers she could see just outside the door stand back to allow this group entry? The pale face of the young man they carried in next explained things completely, for his leg was opened in a gash from his groin to his knee.

'We're here for help with Dougal, Lady Randwick,' one of the men claimed solemnly. 'Dougal's leg is ruptured and he has been unconscious for over an hour.'

'Who did it?' Oh, pray God, let it not be her own brother.

'A wild boar in the Hermitage Forest, early in the afternoon,' he clarified. 'Quinlan said you would help.' Rampant worry overran the very strangeness of their request and Madeleine gathered up her cloak, certain now they would not allow her time to change. Her nightgown was thin, yet not one man seemed to notice in the desperation of their request.

'I'll need hot water and the use of the herb garden.'

They all nodded in unison. 'The housekeeper will fetch what it is you have need of.'

The patient was gently laid on her bed, though the linen there was stripped and a heavier cloth laid down before they placed him on it. It was unusual for any man to notice such things, she thought again. Certainly at Heathwater the men gave no concern to the increased labour that a washerwoman might expect from such an action. A younger man came forward as the task of settling the injured man was done. He had the look of the other about him and Maddy presumed him to be a relative.

'I am Donald,' he said, and blushed the instant he caught her glance. 'Dougal is my twin brother.' The catch in his voice brought to mind the kin of other patients she had tended.

'The wound is new, Donald, and he is young.'

'And the blood…?'

She stopped him. 'His signs are good. His colour. His pulse.'

'They say your witchcraft brought Laird Ullyot back from the dead.'

'And yet still you brought your brother to me?' she challenged boldly as she noticed his hand cross his chest. But now was not the time to engender doubts. Besides, the dirt in Dougal's leg worried her, for caught in the smears of mud she had detected horse manure. At Heathwater she had lost two young and healthy men from similar wounds, their jaws locking in the slow grind of an agonising death; both had been contaminated by the droppings of their steeds.

A further death here would endanger her life. And Jemmie's. Still, many a time before Noel had threatened her with the hereafter should she fail to administer successfully to another of the Heathwater soldiers, and her grandmother's oath of healing had been most succinct.

A patient is never to be turned away on the grounds of your own fears, Madeleine.

My own fears. The light caught Donald's face as he looked at her. It was not her own anxiety that held her immobile, but that of the loved ones left behind. A twin brother. The stakes were high. Detailing a list of herbs she wished to be brought to the room, she began to steep the bandages they had already provided in the cauldron fitted on an iron hook above her newly built fire. The chore calmed her and lessened her anxiety. She could have been anywhere. In England, Scotland or France. At the courts of the kings or at her own rooms in Heathwater. Familiar known rituals and numbered tasks. The art of healing blurred both surroundings and faces as she settled to her craft.

* * *

Two hours later, just as the light of a new day began to flood into the room, she knew she could not clean the wound any better. No speck of mud remained, no tiny particle of dirt, yet still she was loath to stitch it.

'You'll close it now?' Donald's query.

'Nay. I will leave it open.'

Around her she heard the rumblings of anger. It would be an easier decision to bind the wound as they expected. If Dougal died anyway, the proprieties would at least have been observed and she could be held in no blame. This way the flesh lay open to the badness of air. A choice of two evils, then. But which one was right?

Alexander Ullyot's entrance pulled her eyes from the wound. She could smell rose oil on his clothes as he came closer, giving leave to her notion that his last few hours had been spent in the company of a woman. The blond woman probably, with her rounded bosom and soft femininity. So unlike her own distanced hardness and rigid independence.

'What the hell are you doing here?' He did not speak to her, but rather to the four men around the bed.

'It's Dougal, Laird. A wound from the hunting.'

'And you brought him here? Why?' His eyes ran across the nightgown beneath her cloak and Maddy blushed, hating herself for doing so.

'It is said she saved you, sir. And Hale loses more men than he redeems…' Donald's explanation petered out as Laird Ullyot stepped into the light.

'He's hurt badly?'

'Yes.' Maddy could barely meet his glance.

'You'll stitch him now, then?' His question was hard as he saw her hesitate.

'Nay, I do not want to.'

'You wish someone else to finish the job?' Frowning, he turned, ready to call in another.

'No.' He turned back. 'I mean I wish to leave the wound open to the air.'

'Why?'

'Because it has been tainted with the manure of horses, a dangerous thing, it seems, from my experience in tending deep wounds. I lost two men last year after cleansing and stitching.' With the reasons said aloud, she felt more composed and certain. She would not stitch it. Her decision was made.

'Very well.' Alexander ignored the talk behind him, his eyes glancing at the boy's leg. 'Do we bind it at all?'

We.

She expelled her breath. *We.* Whether he knew it or not, he had protected her again, the decision now not hers alone to catch on the rebound. Already the murmurs of dissent had disappeared, the knife-edged tension dissipating.

'I will bind his leg with linen, my lord,' she acquiesced, soaking it again in the scalding garlic water and standing away from the wound. 'And I'll need splints.'

Within a moment someone had fetched wood to do the job and Maddy completed her task quickly, her hand falling to her patient's forehead as she finished. She wanted to lay her fingers again on his leg and close her eyes just to check the danger, but in front of Alexander Ullyot she could not. Another hour would be enough. The boy himself was asleep now, the valerian keeping him still and quiet. She watched as Ullyot went to the door and bade the others gone before she turned and stretched. Every nerve ending in her body told her that the Laird still stood behind her.

'You think he might die?' His tone was anxious.

'I hope not,' she answered, looking directly at him. Today he seemed less formal, and she could smell ale on his breath, even from this distance. 'But I don't know if I should have…' She made herself stop.

'Sometimes the best decisions hold no logic.'

'If Dougal dies, it will be said that I should have bound the wound,' she offered flatly back into the growing silence.

'And if he lives you will be praised for the opposite.'

Madeleine drank in his certainty with relish.

Strength, certainty and decision. She suddenly knew at Heathwater what she had missed the most.

'Thank you.' She said the words slowly, the slight incline of his head all that told her he had heard them. In the harsh new light the raised scar across his right cheek threw a jagged shadow on the rest of his face.

She got the impression he wanted to ask her something else and watched him as he cocked his head slightly to one side, the sounds of voices reaching her a second later. The imminent arrival of others seemed to galvanise his tongue.

'You were the healer at Heathwater?'

'When Noel allowed it, which was not often.'

'Who taught you?'

'My mother.'

'Eleanor de Cargne?'

The small flare in his pupils worried her. 'She was not as others said she was.' Biting her tongue, she schooled her expression. She had not meant to say the words aloud, but was unable to take them back as his hand wrenched the door open. Quinlan entered, looking flushed.

'We have a problem, Laird.' His gaze encompassed her and Maddy knew their problem was her brother.

She should have known Noel would send others to do his bidding and she should have understood that that bidding would also come laced with the lies of Heathwater.

'She is betrothed to Liam Williamson, the Earl of Harrington,' Andrew Milward, her brother's bespeckled emissary, now droned on. 'And no church will sanction the atrocity of taking a woman from her own home.'

Beside him, Father O'Sullivan nodded his assent and fingered a cross. Lifting her gaze, Madeleine focused her eyes upon him, the furrow on his brow deepening as he watched her.

'*In nomine Patris et Filii et Spiritus Sancti…*' The Latin prayer of protection did not go unnoticed in the Ullyot camp. Neither did the strange lines of rainbow light that danced across the head of Lady Randwick. From a single jewelled pin she wore in her hair, it was qualified later, though at the time the soldiers in the bailey had not noticed such. What they did notice was the way she stood. Tall for a woman and straight, her red hair plaited into one long line, the tail of it reaching well down her back.

They also noticed the blood on the hem of her dress and the black circles that smudged the smooth skin beneath her eyes.

'I claimed Madeleine Randwick in the heat of fighting. Were she the prize you are wont to have us believe, you would not have let her wander so carelessly near the battle.' Alexander Ullyot stood against the window, his face shadowed. Outside the clouds scudded across a sky laden with rain and wind.

'She does as she wills, Laird Ullyot. Surely you have seen that by now. She is strong-headed and hot-blooded and her brother is hard pressed to restrain her.' Milward smiled as he caught the sound of murmuring behind him, and, fortified, pushed onwards. 'I have come to take her back, Laird Ullyot, and to relieve you of a problem. I am sure you did not realise when you took her that she was Lady Randwick.'

Madeleine frowned. Drew Milward was clever in his offer of a diplomatic way out of an embarrassing and dangerous stand-off. She was entirely surprised by Alexander Ullyot's answer.

'Tell Noel Falstone that I am keeping his sister. Tell Liam Williamson that I have claimed his betrothed.'

'And the Church? How would you answer the Church, my lord?' The emissary's voice had lost its polite urbanity and sounded to Madeleine's ears far more like the menacing tones one often heard at Heathwater.

'I would say, were Lady Randwick to be the woman you paint her to be, the church should be pleased to have me take her off its hands.'

Maddy smiled and looked down. The Heathwater lies had been neatly exposed, though Milward's next words were more worrying.

'And what of this warrant?'

A parchment was handed to Ullyot and he broke the wax seal and unfurled it, his glance resting on Madeleine as he finished.

'Can you read?'

'Yes.' Surprise and gratitude filled her as he handed the document over.

The decree ordered her immediate release and the threat of retribution was implicit in any failure to comply.

'This order came directly from Edinburgh?' Alexander Ullyot had waited for her to finish reading before he spoke, and Madeleine held her breath, for long had it been rumoured that he was the bastard son of the King of Scotland's uncle.

'No, Laird Ullyot, it was the Earl of Montcrieff who gave permission for the seal.'

The thin voice of the Heathwater emissary quivered. No doubt he too was aware of the whisperings, though Ullyot himself had never claimed Bruce lineage.

'Montcrieff used the seal without the express permission of the King?'

'Pardon, my lord?'

'I speak of the retribution implicit in the decree? The threat to Ashblane?'

Milward's eyes had darkened as he finally saw the danger of insult and tried to find a way to lessen the damage to himself personally. 'The girl practises witchcraft, Laird. Perhaps Montcrieff wanted to level some protection upon you.'

'Protection! My God, you must have trodden on some toes, Lady Randwick.' Alexander Ullyot's tone was menacing as he turned towards her and Maddy watched as Andrew Milward reddened.

'The girl is a whore, sir, and not to be trusted. Anybody will tell you such. And she has bewitched you as certainly as she has so many other men.'

This sentiment, right in line with Alexander's own reasoning, made him angrier. 'Enough. Stop while you still have a head upon your shoulders, for the questionable whims of an earl known for his bad temper can hardly give you leeway to bargain. Quinlan will see you out.'

'Not you, Lady Randwick,' he added as Madeleine made to follow suit. He waited till the door had closed behind the visitors before beginning. 'I would know why

Montcrieff is so concerned over your fate. Was he your lover?'

'No.'

'Your mother's lover, then?'

'Yes.'

'I see.' He upended his cup and poured another drink. 'And why would he want you with him?'

'Enemies are always easier to deal with when they are right beneath your nose.'

'And he sees you as such? As an enemy?'

She shrugged, but did not meet his eye. 'Any woman of substance can be an enemy to a man like him.'

'Especially when that substance hides secrets?' His voice held a note of query and she hesitated as she looked up.

Alex frowned. At this close distance he saw her eyes were like buffed velvet in the play of light. She was beautiful. Probably physically the most beautiful woman he had ever seen. Yet she had been whore to many nobles in both the English and Scottish courts. He placed his cup on the table as he considered her effect on him.

'Lord,' he swore and turned away. To be even thinking this way? Today he was speaking of taking on the combined might of both Montcrieff and Falstone to keep her safe. As well as igniting the wrath of the Church in the process. His eyes scanned her face.

'If these secrets you hide compromise even one person here at Ashblane, Lady Randwick, you would be wise to tell me them now.'

She almost laughed out of sheer nervousness.

One person?

Her secrets would compromise a nation; yet, with Jemmie's life at stake, she could not be honest.

'The secrets, my lord, were those mostly whispered in the heat of passion, and of little accord to anyone come the harsh light of day.'

A complete and utter lie, but a necessary one.

She knew he had heard her words, though he stayed still by the window, a draught of air raising the hair off the collar at the back of his neck, a reddened bruise plainly visible beneath. Like the marks on her brother's neck after he had returned from an amorous time in London. The marks that would enrage Liam Williamson into fury.

The woman Alexander Ullyot had just bedded was passionate, then, and hot-blooded. The thought made her drop her glance and stare at the floor, the image of them happily entwined in his bed strangely disturbing. Finally he spoke.

'Do you remember a soldier you helped who lost three fingers in a battle outside Heathwater? A bright-heided man with a full beard to match? Ah, I can see indeed that you do. He was a kinsman of ours, Jock Ullyot, and he likened you to an angel. *"A heavenly creature inspired by goodness."* His exact words as he lay dying at the end of last winter's reiving. He said you had sworn him to secrecy two years past. Your price for the healing, he told us just before he died, and I asked myself, why would a man as religious as Jock risk his place in heaven by lying to save an English whore? And after that I asked myself, why would a Falstone be interested in risking her neck to heal an Ullyot in the first place?' Crossing the room, he tipped her face upwards, his skin rough against the silkiness of her own. 'Aye, I thought, a whore might take more advantage of a willing paramour. A whore might press her body against mine and use her wiles to gain the promises she could never receive otherwise. And a sorceress would just need to chant a spell to have men founder at her feet. Ye do neither, my lady, and the fact intrigues me more and more.'

His eyes flinted perplexity and another emotion less readable. Madeleine was glad when he set her free.

A powerful, handsome man was Alexander Ullyot. And quick-witted. She could not afford the mix. The royal spies were everywhere and if it were whispered she had lain with the Laird of Ullyot willingly, both their lives might be forfeit. There were enemies she had made who wielded more power than her brother, and the armies of Montcrieff faded against the combined force of those loyal to David and Edward. Two flawed kings and a group of advisors all bedded by her mother. Secrets and lies and whispered confidence. Under the influence of Eleanor's fondling anything could be said. And was.

The sound of his voice drew her out of introspection.

'If I sent you back to Heathwater Castle, what would happen?'

Madeleine tried to mask the fear in her eyes, though she knew he had seen it. 'I should be married by this week's end.'

'Married to whom?'

'Harrington, if you send me back to Heathwater. Any weak noble of note if you choose David's court, and the Earl of Stainmore if it were to be Edward's.'

'A popular choice of bride, then? The whole three are your lovers?' Roughly he caught her wrist as anger exploded.

'Real power comes with spreading yourself around, Laird Ullyot. It is what I am good at. And as the Black Widow of Heathwater I would deem it wise that you stay well away from me.'

If he had not felt her pulse racing or seen the glistening beads of sweat on her brow, he might have acted differently than he did.

Before he could stop himself he bent to kiss her.

And before she could stop herself she kissed him back.

Molten heat flared as his lips slanted hard upon her own, tasting, testing, demanding entrance to her mouth and finding it. Her fingers threaded his hair and brushed across his ruined cheek and everything dissolved into feeling. The beating of her heart, his body against her own, shifting her into the curve of his chest and bringing her closer, the sound of breath barely taken as her whole being heated, coiled and melted into need. She felt his hands across her back and the warmth of him calling. Asking. Needing. Hard against each other and desperate.

It was Alexander Ullyot who broke away first, and the look in his eyes was hardly happy.

'Lord,' he said harshly and repeated it again, swiping his hair from his face and stepping back to leave a good deal of distance between them. 'I have no need for your play-acting, Lady Randwick,' he said at length and softly. 'And know that at Ashblane, unlike Heathwater, your safety is not pegged to sexual favours.' Without another word he left the room.

It was as though she had been struck. She put her hands across her mouth, feeling the place where her lips still burned. Amazement welled up within her.

He was the first man who had ever offered safety unconditionally and she could tell by his kiss that he wanted her. Badly. Could she afford to believe in such a promise?

'No,' she whispered sternly to herself. 'Do not begin to hope.' She had done that before and always she had been disappointed. For now she would see to Dougal Ullyot and then…and then she would try to think of a way of escape for her and for Jemmie.

The sound of returning footsteps made her fight down a rising blush. Was Alexander Ullyot back, this time to take in anger what he had not in passion?

She was relieved to see that it was Jemmie who stood there; the older man she had heard named Hugo stood behind.

'Hugo said he will take me down to see the horses, for a mare is due to give birth at any time and the stable master thinks it will come this afternoon.'

Madeleine frowned. Two men and a stable. Would Jemmie be safe?

'And you will return him when?' She looked directly at the older man.

'Och, in a few hours, I'd be thinking, Lady Randwick. He's but a wean to be stuck in a room for two days solid and the Laird wanted him to be put to some use. The stables are as likely a place as any and the lad has expressed an interest in horseflesh. Gillion may come, too. The Laird's boy, for it seems as if your page has struck up a friendship with the poor wee bairn.'

Shiny brown eyes met her own. 'Hugo said that, was I to prove worthy, I could exercise the horses in the morning sometimes and ride them across the far hills...'

'No.' Madeleine's voice was harsh even to her own ears and she struggled to moderate it. 'No going outside the keep walls, Jemmie. It's safer here. If you were to be caught outside—' She stopped, trying to place her thoughts into some sort of pattern. It was all so dangerous and Hugo was waiting. 'I would prefer my page to be kept inside the walls of Ashblane,' she began, trying to keep the panic from her voice. 'And I would not see him hurt in any way. Horses' hooves can be lethal, Jemmie, so do not go behind any steed and do not frighten them, for they are liable to kick or bite at any noise or movement and—'

Hugo's puzzlement made her stop. 'I shall watch the young lad myself. On that I give my word.'

'Thank you.'

She caught Jemmie's glance, the glint of rebellion sinking hope. Keep safe, she wanted to shout. Stay close to Hugo. Do not speak to anyone. Keep your eyes down. But she could say none of these things. She could only smile and watch them depart, her heart in her mouth and her breathing erratic.

She sat on a chair in the middle of the room and concentrated on allaying panic, hating her weakness, hating her dependence. Had she made a huge error in judgement? Could Jemmie truly be safe anywhere?

If these secrets you hide compromise even one person here at Ashblane, Lady Randwick, you would be wise to tell me them now.

Would she have? Should she have? Trust was an emotion she had never had the luxury of, but she had almost been tempted to confide in Alexander Ullyot.

Almost.

'Ahh, Jemmie,' she whispered into the quiet. 'I do not know the way of safety for us, but your face grows more like mine with each passing day and surely soon someone must notice.'

Chapter Seven

Dougal Ullyot's condition had worsened, she thought, as she placed a wooden stick between his teeth and urged him to bite down. It would at least prevent him from swallowing his tongue and with the lockjaw set she knew she would have little chance of prying his mouth open to retrieve it.

The valerian seemed to be helping, as did the garlic paste. Her own mix of fennel seeds and sage was at least keeping down the fever and the honey and vinegar was doing likewise. But she knew these potions were not enough.

Dismissing the sentry to a seat outside, she pulled a table in front of the portal and placed her hands across his chest. The beat was weaker and more irregular and delirium had claimed him as he thrashed from side to side in the effort it required to take air. Closing her eyes, Madeleine imagined the organ's blood flow emptying into her own, the slow strong pulse of her heart mixing with the shallow quick beat of his. The pressure against her fingers increased, as did the noise in her ears. She would have a headache tomorrow, but still she continued.

Synchronisation and steadiness. His breathing shallowed as his heated body relaxed against the constancy of weight, and the glow of light across his bones widened as she felt the blackness shift and thicken with redness before dispersing. Still she kept her middle finger forced against his right lung, the high noon sun at the window now direct upon her face. Sweat beaded her forehead and ran in runnels between her breasts, the boy's breath coming easier than her own. Roiling redness and the stiffness of disease. She fought for air, straining to untie the knots that crippled them both and transfer them away. Biting her bottom lip, she tasted blood and as she broke contact with the skin of Dougal Ullyot she thankfully fell back.

When she opened her eyes a moment later she saw his eyes upon her, amazement suffused with utter disbelief.

'Who are you?' His voice was hoarse and she knew he was thirsty, but she did not have the strength to physically lift the clay pitcher by the bedside.

'Madeleine Randwick.'

'The Black Witch of Heathwater?' Fright and uncertainty showed bright across his face.

'So they call me.'

'The healing you just did…?' He petered out and Maddy swallowed. How long had he been conscious? She rarely made such mistakes. 'I felt you inside me.'

She laughed and made herself stand.

'Delirium is a part of the fever,' she explained quietly and collected her powders. 'Now you must sleep.' The infusion of chamomile and valerian was strong as she slipped it between his lips. Would he remember tomorrow? She hoped not. Already the room had blurred and was beginning to slide into the familiar orange shadow. Crumbling to the floor, she was glad of the rough felt rug beneath her face and the warmth of sunshine on her back.

The door crashing open made her start, as did the noise of the oak table moving across the floor. Alexander Ullyot's face was six inches from her own, deep-shadowed in the half dusk of evening.

'What is wrong?' His tone was hard as a rough finger touched the tear on her lip. She saw the blood as he pulled away. 'Why has the door been barred and locked? And what has happened to your face? Dougal?' The query was implicit and said dangerously low.

The youth on the bed coughed and sat forward, his cheeks suffused with embarrassment. 'She came over poorly all of a sudden, Laird, and fell.'

'And you left her on the floor?' Nothing in his tone indicated belief and the boy's gaze faltered.

'I could not move from the bed, sir.' He swung his feet around to the floor and stood.

'Yet you do so now quite comfortably.'

Dougal coloured again, even the lobes of his ears ruddy.

'Get up, Madeleine.' Alexander Ullyot's voice was close

as he lifted her to her feet and she stretched against the wall behind her to find a balance, shaking her head to help focus.

He was furious. She could see it in his eyes and feel it in the tension that blanketed the room, though unexpectedly his hand came forward to cup her elbow. Without thought she pressed into him and caught his glance, and his eyes flinted with something she had never seen in any man's before.

Worry.

She was more used to crude lust or the wary alarm of men faced with a woman they had heard to be a witch. These emotions had played on a gamut of faces throughout her life. On Noel's. On Harrington's. At Edward's court. On the faces of the soldiers at Heathwater and the Ullyot retainers at Ashblane. Her isolation from others had been the only thing that had made her safe. She was never present when the tales of her sorcery had swept through the various kingdoms, tearing away anyone who had made overtures of friendliness.

And this morning—had not Alexander Ullyot saved her life and damned his own in the process? Why would he take such risks for her? Nothing made sense. She was about to speak when he caught her beneath her knees and lifted her into his arms, a scowl evident upon his forehead.

'Nay, sir.' Dougal Ullyot's voice. Maddy opened her eyes and tried to focus. 'Lady Randwick is not as everyone thinks. She is a good witch and not a bad one.' He laid one hand on Alexander Ullyot's sleeve.

'A witch? How?' His retort was sharp.

Perplexed dark blue orbs met her own. 'I don't think…I don't know…' Dougal stammered and stood back, the rings of red around the irises of his eyes more pronounced now.

'Get back into bed, lad.' Alexander's voice was kinder. 'And have no fear, for the Lady of Heathwater will be back to tend ye on the morrow.'

Outside the room it was freezing and Madeleine could barely stop her teeth from chattering as her vision blurred and slid into greyness.

'I…am…c-cold…' she managed as he mounted the stairs.

'I ken ye are that, lass,' he answered and continued to climb. The steps he took were wide and steep and the guards were numerous.

The bed in the chamber they finally entered was huge. Muted light dappled the furs of sable that covered the counterpane. A man's room. No accoutrements of a woman's presence. Neat and sparse and without a single item of decoration save for some swords in a corner stacked on timber racks, and a large banner sporting the red-and-gold Ullyot clan standard. *Soyez sage*. The sentiment stuck in her throat.

'Whose chamber is this?' Madeleine began, though she knew the answer before he said it.

'Mine.'

The anger in her welled. *Soyez sage*. Be wise. But how? Tonight she could not protect herself, for her magic was weak.

'Relax, Lady Randwick,' Alexander Ullyot chastened as he took the coverings down before depositing her into the middle of the mattress. 'It's a woman warm and willing I am wanting. Not one half-dead of witchcraft.'

'Dougal will live.' She pulled at his arm as she told him.

'I know. But will you?' He sat down and his eyes ran carefully across her. 'This happens every time?'

'No.'

'Why now, then?'

Exhaustion unravelled caution. 'Because…of the silver…all around you.' She listened to her own slurred words with a detached interest and felt the irregularity of her heartbeat.

'Madeleine.' He took her hand and when she opened her eyes she saw panic on his face.

'I'm…too…cold,' she whispered again, the very fingers of ice invading her bones and sending her teeth to chatter. She could not even find the energy to draw in air.

'Lord, Madeleine. Breathe.' His voice was hard and rough and she tried to focus, but she was sliding into the blackness and it was all too hard. And then she felt warmth along the whole length of her body, touching her feet, her stomach, her breasts and her cheeks. Fire and silver engulfing her, chasing away the numbness. Sighing, she relaxed into the heat and ran her fingers across hard planes of skin. The smell of soap and leather and wood-smoke was calming and infinitely safe and she smiled as air filled her lungs and sleep overcame her.

* * *

He sat with her against him and cursed everything that was happening. Her bastard brother and his pretensions to Ashblane, Harrington's mark of ownership and Dougal's talk of witchery. And as his fingers gripped tighter he felt the soft whisper of her breath against the bare skin at his chest. Damn her. Damn Ian for dying. Damn Edward for turning her into a whore and damn the righteousness of an interfering Church. The last echo of sunlight caught the signet ring he wore and he lifted it into his vision. He knew he could not fight them all and yet to just give her up...?

The evening faded into the gloom of night-time and far away he could hear the hollow sounds of a cutting northerly wind off the heights of the Cheviots. Lord, what was he doing? Ashblane. His home. His people. His land. Madeleine Randwick placed everything in danger and rebellion never came cheaply. He shook his head and breathed in the smell of her. The tinge of fennel and comfrey and sage made him smile. All herbs from the kitchen garden and hardly the oils of a courtesan. Not a witch, either, but a woman badly used by stronger men. And not a Falstone at all in the sense that her brother was, but caring. Dougal's leg, his own arm, the quiet politeness of her relations with the people from his keep. Aye, if she had been a shrew all this would have been easy. But she wasn't.

She wasn't.

Edging away from her, he stood beside the bed and

adjusted the pellets of fur so that they snuggled in warmly against her throat. Already her colour had returned and the blue lines about her lips had lessened.

A healer who set her own life at risk to heal? And a whore with the conscience of a saint? Aye, Madeleine Randwick was a puzzle and a contradiction and, as he looked down, she seemed nothing like the conniving schemer he had always heard that she was.

And yet had she not told him of her penchant for spreading her favours widely and admitted to the slaying of Lucien Randwick?

He scowled again and refastened his sword, schooling his thoughts as his housekeeper bustled in with extra pillows.

'Should I have Ewan move her, Laird?'

He replied quickly, 'Nay, leave her here. I'll sleep in the next chamber.'

'Aye, then I'll see to it that the bed is made up.' Mrs Sim stood for a moment at the head of the bed, watching. 'She's a wee thing really for how tall she is and a braw bonny lass to boot.'

He frowned at the tone his housekeeper used—it seemed to imply more interest than he had intentions of admitting to.

'She's the Black Widow of Heathwater.'

'And well she might be, though it seems to me she's a mite too young to have done half the wicked things that she stands accused of. And Jock once said—'

'Enough!' With one last glance at Madeleine, he let himself out of the chamber.

* * *

He walked to the lake and sat down against the bracken, lifting up some stones and skipping them across the calm dark surface. When he had no stones left, he turned his palms up against the moonlight and ran his fingers across the skin.

He had always been a warrior.

He had killed and fought and slashed across his years until death and dying were all he was left with. All he could truly do. Bowing his head, he ran his hands through the length of his hair and down to the muscles in his neck, which were stretched and sore and tense.

For so long now he had been alone, shouldering the responsibilities of the Ullyot clan, making sure that Ashblane was a keep unassailable and well-aligned. He mused on his return from Egypt and the peace and sanctuary these hills had provided. A home. His first. He remembered the panic he had felt as a displaced child, roaming the outskirts of the nepotistic courts of Scotland, the bastard son of an illegitimate brother of Robert of Bruce. If he were to shelter Madeleine Randwick now, would he be condemning Ashblane?

'Ifrinn.' He swore into the night and closed his eyes, caught between duty and something else entirely. And the anger came because he knew that it would be duty that would have to prevail. Gillion. Katherine. Quinlan. Six hundred families who had depended on him for nigh on ten years. And a home that was his solace. He had no choice at all. He would find a way to see Madeleine Randwick safe and out of his life. And then he would forget her. On the

name of Jesus and the Holy Ghost he promised himself he would, and Isabella Simpson, after all, was both shapely and available.

But she was not strong like Madeleine, not as independent, as unconventional and self-reliant; he found, after years of looking out for others, that these traits were appealing. More than appealing, he said to himself, and felt the hardness beneath his plaid grow at the very thought of her. Angered, he unbuckled his plaid and dived headfirst into the freezing lake.

Chapter Eight

Madeleine awoke to a new day and by the length of the shadows against the wall she knew she had been asleep for at least eighteen hours. She was back in her own room and Katherine Ullyot sat with her, her head bent over a large tapestry.

'Oh, you're awake.' She smiled and looked up from her stitchery. 'I have brought you flowers.' Her hand indicated a pottery urn to one side of the bed filled with a large bunch of wildflowers.

'Where did you collect them?' Madeleine's voice was husky and had the cadence of someone who had shouted for a very long time.

'In the fields this morning with Gillion.'

'And Dougal—how is he?'

'Completely recovered. The folk in the castle are calling it a miracle and Dougal himself sings your praises to all who will listen. My uncle is less forthcoming, though even he admits to the fact that you are very unlike your brother.'

Madeleine blushed—the last time she had seen Alexander Ullyot, she had been lying in his bed hard against his strong brown body.

'Where is he now?' In this state she hoped he would not walk in unannounced. Even the thought that he could do so had her heart racing.

'He is gone with thirty men just these few hours past, though I am not certain why. To see the Armstrongs, I'd be thinking, for it was that way they were heading, but it could be they have gone down to the Grants as their land butts against the Ullyot holdings to the west across the River Annan.'

Maddy was still, glad on one hand that he was nowhere close, but concerned on the other as to the intent of his expedition. Had Alexander Ullyot gone to negotiate a solution to the problem of her being here, or to relay the confession she had made to him of murder? Pushing the covers back, she tried to get up, but Katherine placed surprisingly strong hands across her own.

'Nay, you must stay in bed. Mistress Sim has broth waiting for you and some fresh bread. Ahh, here she is now.'

The housekeeper appeared with Jemmie, and made much of pressing out a cloth on the bed and presenting her well-stocked tray.

'Dougal is my nephew, Lady Randwick,' she explained

as she hovered with a cup of fresh milk. 'And a good lovely lad he is, too. My sister's boy, you see, and she who has passed on left his well-being to me. And Donald his twin.' She brought a large cloth out of her apron pocket and blew on it fiercely. 'So I don't care what it is that they may say of you in the halls of this place. For me I shall always be grateful for what ye did.' Her strong hand patted Madeleine's arm as she left a small offering on the bed wrapped in white linen.

'Open it when I have gone, my lady. It is for your healing.'

With the warmth of the bed to her back and the smell of hot bread pervading the room, Maddy was overcome by a strange sense of homeliness, of familiarity and of belonging. Jemmie looked happy and well-fed, the walls of Ashblane were impregnable and Katherine had brought her flowers.

'Open your gift, Maddy.' Jemmie handed it to her and smiled.

It was a pestle and mortar from the kitchens, well used judging by the marks worn into the sides of the stone.

For your healing, Mistress Sim had said.

Madeleine could not remember anyone giving her a gift before and, listening to Katherine trill on about an upcoming feast day and the worsening of the chaplain's cough, she felt a sense of peace. Everyday concerns were soothing to listen to. Small things that made up the fabric of a proper life.

Safety! It was such a tangible thing. She could feel it in every breath she took here and again she wondered just how long it could last.

She did not see Alexander Ullyot at all the next day or for many days after that. She would have liked to ask Katherine again as to where he was exactly, but hesitated to do so, worrying that she might misconstrue her interest for something else entirely. And question her on it.

To counteract her worries over her future here she had been keeping herself busy, helping in the kitchens, visiting the stables and tending to the castle herb garden. And she noticed as the days rolled on that people did not stare at her, as they once had, did not cross their chests in uncertainty or superstition. More often now people stopped to talk to her about the weather and about themselves and about their many ailments. She began to make her pastes of healing and the scent was so strong that her room reminded her of an apothecary of the type she had seen while in London with her mother. She hung some of the fresh herbs above her window to dry and others on strings before the fireplace to stop the mould. Still others she bottled in boiled water, using wax as her grandmother had shown her to keep it from spoiling in the air. She gathered early green garlic, and pickled cabbage leaves in brine because she found them useful as a base for her poultices. And in a large jug on a shelf by the door she packed seaweed procured from the stores room. A tonic for the blood and a cleanser every bit as strong as garlic.

Jemmie became chattier, too, the dark rings beneath her brown eyes softer now and less shadowed, and often could be seen with Gillion as they ranged across the meadows. Not talking, but gesturing and laughing. The fact intrigued Madeleine—if Gillion could laugh presumably he could also learn to speak. She resolved to leave this problem till a little later, knowing that if Gillion was pushed he would retreat and right now Jemmie was doing a fine job of getting his trust.

Again she smiled, marvelling at her own lightness here at Ashblane. With Jemmie's happiness, Katherine's friendship, Gillion's laughter and Mistress Sim's mothering, all the pieces of her life were falling into place. She raised her arms against the blueness of the sky and breathed in deeply.

Deeply. How long had it been since she had felt like this? Able to breath and laugh and dream.

'What are you doing?' Katherine's voice was threaded with amusement as they walked down the pathway beside the cemetery to the cottages.

'Breathing,' she replied. 'I never could do so properly at Heathwater.'

'Because of your brother?'

She nodded and changed the subject. Today she wanted no questions to remind her of Noel. 'Where is it you are taking me, Katherine?'

'To see my cousin. Brigid is my father's sister's daughter and she is having problems with her labouring.'

Her tone was guarded; before Madeleine could ask more

they had turned into the pathway of a small stone cottage, a thatch of herbs growing abundantly beside the doorway. The cries from inside had Katherine tugging her into the house.

'Come, Madeleine. We must hurry.'

In the smoky warmth of the cottage a man stood, his arm protectively around the shoulders of a young woman whose stomach was swollen with the ripeness of very late pregnancy.

'Thank God you are here, Kitty. I thought you would not come and Brigid is wanting to push.' His voice was burred and husky, the relief on his face changing to wariness as he looked straight at Madeleine.

'Why have you brought her?'

'I do not know the way of these things, Jamie, and Lilliath has said—'

'Are you a midwife, Lady Randwick?' His question was hard-edged and frosty, and dread encapsulated Madeleine. At Heathwater she had never been allowed near the birthing mothers for fear that her black magic would rub off on to them. No child ever approached her. No mother large with child asked her questions or plied her hand for help. And her own barrenness reinforced the fact that she was a bad omen, a hex, a woman who was not a woman but a shape shifter and not to be trusted. The Black Widow. Untouchable.

She could barely, therefore, believe the turn this morning was taking.

'I am not certain—' she began and her voice was strained.

'Lilliath the midwife will not come,' Katherine cut her off. 'She says the child is wrongly formed and bound to a position which is…impossible. She has told us to sprinkle Brigid with rowanberries and amber beads and shoot an arrow from east to west to take away the pain. We tried this, but it has made no difference.'

Maddy ran her hands across her face and stifled the expletive that had come to her tongue. An arrow from east to west indeed and the babe caught fast. 'Hale, then. Where is he?'

'Away at the keep of the Grants. Until this morning Jamie's mother thought she could deliver it herself with me to help, but now… It has been ten hours and the birth comes no closer. We are desperate.'

'Does Quinlan know of Lilliath's refusal to help?'

'Nay, but even if he did he would feel the business to be women's tasks and below his notice. It is the way it is here.'

Women die in childbirth.

The thought was like an unspoken shout in the room. And Brigid was one such woman. She sat herself up now and her eyes beseeched Madeleine. Young eyes, Madeleine thought to herself. Not even yet sixteen if she were to guess her years.

'I will need hot water and clean linen if I am to examine you. And garlic. Do you have that in your garden, Brigid?'

'Yes. At the doorway.'

'Steep it in hot water, Katherine, and we will use it as a cleanser. The colour must be deep or it will not have the strength.'

Rolling up the sleeves of her blouse, she knotted her hair in a tight bun at her nape. She could feel the sweat bead her upper lip, but now was not the time to worry about her inadequacies. If she did not help, then nobody would and Maddy believed enough in her own medicine to also know that the curses at Heathwater had been wrongly reasoned. Good medicine worked for every ailment. She had to believe in that.

An hour later, although Brigid was more relaxed, the baby had still not shown itself. From her earlier examination Madeleine had determined the problem came from the way the child was lying, for she knew it was the head that should have presented first and not the bottom. She had to turn it. But when? The contractions were no further than three breaths apart now and gathering in strength. With determination she made up her mind.

'Jamie, could you step outside please and find more firewood?' She did not want him to see what she was about to do.

Katherine looked at her as she warmed her hands, her eyes under-threaded with a dreadful expectation.

'Will you use your magic?'

The question was barely whispered.

'Healing skills,' Maddy corrected and laid her palms on Brigid's stomach.

Through the width of skin and fluid and behind the pulsating thickness of the birth cord the child lay to the left, its bottom caught in the bag of the womb on its right side. But there was room. Room to move. If they were quick.

'Breathe in, Brigid,' Madeleine said and began to manipulate the little body. Tight, tight, but moving. When the contractions resumed she stopped and waited, her hand measuring the pulse on Brigid's wrist. And when they lessened again she pressed down hard, ignoring the scream of pain from the labouring girl. If the child did not turn, both mother and baby would die. There were times in medicine when strength and muscle were more important than finesse. This was one of those times. Her breath came hard, but still she pushed, and felt a tiny giving, a small bloom of movement. A turning. First the hands and then the feet, and through an orange light Madeleine saw the baby watching her and smiled in a silent acknowledgment of place.

'You will be fine, my little one,' she crooned and moved it around easily now until a rush of fluid drenched the birth canal and Brigid's eyes flew open.

'I can feel it. It is coming.' Fresh hope ousted stale fear and she bore down hard.

The child straightened and was delivered head first into Katherine's waiting arms, its hearty bellow belying the hours of labour, its colour a healthy pink and its eyes wide open.

Brigid began to cry when she took the baby and Jamie rushed in, firewood forgotten and his face marked with relief.

'You are both all right?' His hands clasped his wife's and he looked at his daughter before bending to Brigid in quiet conversation.

But Madeleine could no longer hear anything. The orange of her sorcery was back, claiming her, calling her as she sat at the foot of the bed on the floor and concentrated on breathing, her supply of air as shaky as the tiny girl's had been.

'Maddy!' Katherine's voice, and close. 'What's wrong? Your eyes are bloodshot red.'

'How…is the…child?'

'She is suckling and the afterbirth has been delivered. But you need to stand up.' Worry threaded disbelief, but another emotion overrode them both; looking Katherine directly in the eyes, Maddy saw just what that was.

Fear. Of the unknown.

Fear of something she had seen but could not understand. Her spirits, buoyed by the weeks of acceptance at Ashblane, sank immeasurably. 'You told me once you wanted my magic, Katherine, and now it is time for me to tell you that it does not come easily.' She breathed in deeply, trying to fill her lungs before she went on. 'Sometimes, like now, you pay for it in friendship and blood.'

Katherine shook her head. 'You believe I would think less of you for this? For your bravery and for your skill? For the fright I saw in you when first we came into this house and then your resolve? I love you, Madeleine Randwick, and I swear I will never ever betray you. I swear this on the soul of the Father Our Lord himself.'

Of all the things Madeleine had thought that Katherine might say, this was the very least of them; holding out one hand, she was pleased for the fingers offered back in return. She was a healer and Noel's nonsense of her being tainted and unholy was, after all, just that—nonsense. Strength seeped into her, a core of power as all the preconceived stupidity of the Heathwater prophecies melted away into what was proper and true and right.

And in that unlikely moment a new thought struck her. What if she had a child? What if it could be possible? What if her barrenness had been Lucien's fault, his canker?

Could that be?

She swallowed down the thought and accepted cold water from Jamie as Katherine used a cloth to mop away the sticky sweat from her brow.

Chapter Nine

Alexander Ullyot returned home three days after the birth of Brigid and Jamie's daughter.

Madeleine saw him first as she sat on the stonewall overlooking the fields to the rear of the castle, and when she felt a bright fluster suffuse her cheeks she was pleased that he was so far away. Today he was dressed in a plaid she had not seen before and was giving instructions on the art of war to his younger soldiers, boys of fifteen and sixteen. This morning he had them practising their tilting, the counterweight to the shield they were to aim at being heavy sandbags wrapped in fabric. So far only one lad had managed to stay seated and that boy only by the grace of God, for he had hung drunkenly from the stirrups as the horse had swerved away.

And then Alexander Ullyot had mounted and taken a lance. He wore no helmet or armour, unlike the others, and Madeleine wondered at his safety given the size of the quintain. Waiting against the trees, he was still for a moment and Maddy sensed his pure channelled focus. And then he was off, thundering down the field to the shield hung from a bar, lance held easily in his hand as his thighs guided the horse to an exact position. He hit the target dead centre and the quintain flung across and missed him as he dodged away, lying flat upon the back of his mount and twisting to the right.

In the heat of the moment Madeleine stood up and clapped loudly, her shouts of admiration joining those of the boys, and as Alexander turned she felt her heart slam straight into the wall of her chest. He was sweat-slicked and laughing, the sun reflected from his lance glinting across the fields, and the red-and-gold crest on his shield, of hands in armour, seemed eminently appropriate. *Soyez sage*, the writing above them proclaimed.

The distance between them closed as he reined in his horse. Because she sat on the top of the wall their eyes met level and she saw how he dismissed with a glance the soldier watching her. Today he looked younger, less austere, the shadow of a two-day beard on his cheeks and his hair half-pulled from the leather strap that bound it. In the light it glinted red and gold and corn blond. A mixture of shades as complex as the man himself.

'You enjoy watching the training with the quintain, then?'

'I do, my lord,' she replied, consciously relaxing her grip on the stones beneath her. 'Though I can't help wondering how my stitching is holding up given the pounding your arm is taking.'

'I am right handed,' he countered. 'It was the left one you doctored.'

'And it is better?' He had not allowed her to see to the wound again since the healing in the forest of Liddesdale.

Ignoring her question, he posed one of his own.

'Were you always so forceful at Heathwater? Katherine has been lecturing me on the merits of your medicines and of the wide knowledge you hold about herbs.' His teeth flashed white against the tan of his face as he pulled on the leather harness and turned his horse into the wind, stilling it. 'That was not a criticism, Lady Randwick, and the talk I have heard was only kind. Yet, though it seems you now have many champions, I must warn you that your brother has sent another petition to the King of Scotland asking for your release. Any day a missive from court could come, demanding me to return you.'

'And will you?'

'Why should I not?'

She was silent and his slate eyes flickered. 'Draw me a map of Heathwater. Include the tunnels and the gates and the number of weaponry.'

'I cannot.'

'You cannot?' His own reply was strangely light as he raised his brow.

'I do you a favour, my lord, for Heathwater is as much of a fighting castle as you proclaim your own to be. No matter what intelligence you had about its military capacity, many of you would die were you to storm it. I do not wish to have these deaths on my conscience should the tunnels prove to exist in memory only.'

'Some of us die anyway, Lady Randwick. The cemetery is full of Ullyot souls who would say such.'

'Perhaps then there comes a time for rationality.'

His eyebrows quirked upwards.

'If one of you called a stop...'

Anger crossed his face. 'You really think it to be that simple? How well do you know your brother?'

Colouring, she remembered a time when a truce between Heathwater and a neighbouring property had not been honoured.

'Well enough, I see,' Alexander said softly. 'Well enough to ken that Noel is as deceitful as rumour has it to those who have the stupidity to trust him.'

The humour had gone and in its place stood responsibility and duty. In this light his eyes were the colour of lake water at dusk when the night winds rippled the surface and made it opaque.

Lowering her glance, she tried to think of a rejoinder that would release the tension, but couldn't. Why was it she could not treat this man as she had every other man, with indifference and distance and cold hard censure?

Because she felt a tie to him and had done from the first second of touching him in the woods of Liddesdale. Because beneath the façade he presented to the world she sensed another, softer side, and loneliness. Like her.

The Ashblane keep dominated the land behind him in

much the same way as Alexander dominated the people grouped around him. Not just a physical presence either, though God knows he was tall, but a gracefulness that belied any sense of clumsiness and made one watch him in the same way a hunter would watch a deer running free in the mountains or a fisherman might view a trout swimming speckled-fast in the waters of a mountain stream.

He was naturally beautiful.

The words popped into her head and she frowned heavily, believing for a horrified second that she might have actually said them, but when she looked up again his attention was on two women walking their way and she knew she could not have spoken. He tipped his head as Katherine joined them, a small bunch of late autumn wild-flowers in each of their hands.

'Good afternoon, Kitty. Good afternoon, Meg.'

The other woman beside Kitty giggled and blushed. Why was it, Madeleine thought, that every female in this castle seemed afflicted with a penchant to simper when Alexander Ullyot was about? Including me, she added, and chastised herself soundly.

'We have collected some flowers for Patrick and Ian, Laird. Would Madeleine be allowed to accompany us down to the burial ground?'

Alexander nodded. 'Go no further than the graves and be back by supper,' he instructed before turning his horse around and galloping towards the practising soldiers.

'Jenny McLeod says that he will be married by the end of this year,' Meg said softly when he was out of earshot. 'She saw it in a dream, she said, and as real as though they were standing there.'

'They?' Kitty questioned.

'Laird Ullyot and his bride, of course.'

Katherine sighed. 'What did Jenny say she looked like, then?'

'Oh, now that was strange. She could not see her face for it was covered with a thick veil. But she was tall.'

'You are tall, Madeleine. Perhaps it may be you.' Rolling her eyes, Katherine thrust her bunch of flowers into Maddy's arms and sang a chorus from the bridal tune. Laughing at the gesture, Madeleine imagined what it must be like to for ever live in this place. Uncertainly she turned her head aside, angry with herself for thinking of things she could never have—she was not a young girl in her first flush of youth, and certainly not a woman without reputation, either.

Eleanor had been wrong in her assumptions of protection, for her mother's codicil of land grants had imprisoned her completely. Ever since she was fourteen she had been fighting for her life and she was so very weary of it. And now for the first time…for the very first time she had met a man who was not only strong but also honest, not only powerful but also unflinchingly fair.

The stories about Alexander Ullyot had only ever mentioned his fighting prowess and his military capabilities and his fierce protection of all that he owned. They had not mentioned his intellect or his honour or the way he managed the responsibility of the lairdship with such easy acumen. She sighed and brought the flowers to her face, breathing in the scent. Until now people had always failed her. Apart from Jemmie and Goult and Eleanor, no one else had risked friendship or protection or even just a tepid version of plain niceness.

Because she could so easily ruin them.

Looking back at Ashblane, caught in the light of the afternoon sun, she thought the hard lines of jutted stone beautiful because they promised such safety.

'It was built to last,' Katherine said quietly as she saw the direction of Maddy's gaze. 'It was laid siege to in 1332 and again the year before last when some of the bailey was rebuilt, but Alexander brought in stonemasons from Normandy and good-looking lads they were, too.'

Madeleine laughed. 'Defence and beauty. So synonymous with the Laird himself.'

Katherine looked at her sharply. 'You think my uncle is handsome?'

Meg giggled. 'Handsome is a young boy's domain, Kitty. Our Laird is much more than just that. Every woman with no husband here at Ashblane would tell you so and a few more of the married ones besides.'

Smiling, Madeleine entered into the conversation. 'Then why has he never remarried?'

'It's not for the want of trying, that I can tell you. He was away, though, for a great deal of time with Philip of France and then in Egypt and when he returned he was betrothed to Alice the Fair in a matter of days. When she died he didn't seem interested in anyone else…'

'Because he loved her so much?' A bittersweet emotion swirled in Maddy's head as she waited for the answer, but it was not Meg who spoke but Katherine.

'Alice was fey. And she was timid.'

Maddy frowned. How would that have sat on a man who seemed to have little patience with weakness? 'Timid of the Laird?' Suddenly she wanted to know everything.

Katherine pondered the query. 'Perhaps. Gillion has the same timidity, though in a child it is less galling.'

'You didn't like Alice?'

'I didn't know her well and I was only ten or so when she passed away. She was…distant with children. Distant with everyone, come to think of it. When she died it was as though only a shadow had gone, so little did she ever speak or laugh. And my uncle never spoke of her again to anyone.'

Madeleine remembered the marks of passion on Alexander's neck the evening he had come to her after Noel's envoy had left. Perhaps he was careful to shield his nocturnal activities from his family. She remembered the blond woman she had seen from her window leaning fully against him, the last light of dusk binding their faces together in desire and complicity.

Not just handsome, then, but something far more compelling. Rugged hardness emanated from him in everything he did, every action, every word. And power. Aye, Alexander Ullyot was a dangerous man with his fierce and implacable will and his focused determination. How the fey Alice would have coped with a husband who was so unbreakably strong was anyone's guess. Badly, she supposed, given Katherine's memory of her. And yet one could not help but admire a man who never let anyone get in the way of what he thought was right. It was not arrogance that defined him, she mused, but strength.

Her cheeks flamed at the course of her thoughts and she was glad when the graves came into sight and the enigmatic Laird of Ullyot ceased to be the topic of conversation.

She lingered in the cemetery after the other two had left. A retainer trailed her at a short distance, whether for safety or for surveillance she could not say, but she welcomed his company.

Twelve graves had been dug afresh into the dirt, ten at an angle to the wall and two more centrally placed. With care she walked back over to the graves in the middle.

Ian Ullyot and Patrick Lambie. The names were roughly carved into the tender sapwood. A cairn of stones covered both. She ran her fingers across the face of Patrick's name and bent to one side. Nineteen, the gravestone read. Younger than she was. In the face of a gathering wind and a rain-bent sky, everything suddenly seemed impossibly fragile. Her life. Jemmie's. The future. She picked away the grasses to one side, discovering pennyroyal, the pungent smell filling the air around her as she crushed the leaves between her fingers. Looking up, she noticed Gillion standing in the gateway ten yards away.

'Hello.' She bent her head and gestured for him to come and join her.

His eyes darkened as he sat down next to Ian Ullyot's grave and laid his small hand upon the dirt. Protectively. Lovingly.

'I am sorry.' She enunciated the words with care, wondering if he had the ability to read lips and interpret sounds.

He said nothing.

'I have never properly met you, but I am Madeleine.'

Still no response at all. Reaching for a stick, she cleared a small plane of dirt with the heel of her hand and began to write.

I am Madeleine.

For the first time he looked directly at her. Smoothing the dirt, she wrote another sentence.

Jemmie is your friend.

He nodded and looked up as she handed the stick over. For a second she thought he might toss it away but he didn't.

Instead he wiped away the writing Madeleine had done. And drew. A face. Her face. She recognised her eyes, her nose, and the length of her hair all in the crude medium of dust and wood.

'My God,' she said softly, astonished by his finesse as he finished it and returned the stick into her hands.

Me, she wrote beneath the picture and for the first time the child smiled. Clapping her hands together, she cleared a space in the ground next to his picture and began to draw her own.

A keep formed, the tower high and wide and on the very top she fashioned the armoured hands of Ashblane. Next to the flag she drew two people. *Gillion and Katherine*, she wrote underneath and then gave the stick back to him. Without hesitation he drew in his father behind them, both arms spread about their shoulders.

Papa, he wrote before a movement from behind her had him up on his feet.

When she looked up Alexander Ullyot stood near. He was dusty and tired from the day's jousting.

'You have met Gillion?'

'Your son?'

'Yes.' His hand patted the top of the dark blond curls and she saw the way the child leaned into him before picking up the stick and making off. Behind him she noticed a guard. Not wholly uncared for, then.

'Katherine tells me he has no mother.'

'No. My wife, Alice, died in childbirth.'

'I'm sorry.'

He nodded and watched his son, a smile creasing the corners of his mouth. 'He has had the affliction of deafness for all of his years, and I do not seem to be able to help him.'

It was said almost as a thought voiced aloud and, by the

look of the scowl on his face, she doubted she would hear much more. Yet he had kept the child with him. An impaired heir and his lairdship not directly hereditary. Some men might have found another way to solve such a problem.

'He does not hear anything?'

'No.' He stepped back and ran a hand through his hair. Of a sudden Madeleine saw him not in the guise of warrior, but in the one of father. Marked with the scars of battle and with an authority very few would dare to question, Alexander Ullyot was also a parent who worried about his son.

'And he does not speak?' She regretted the question as he turned away. 'I could help.'

He rounded instantly. 'How?'

'There are ways to talk that do not involve speech. Let me show him these things.' Putting her hands together as in prayer, she faced him directly, liking the smile he bestowed on her when he noticed her method of plea.

'If you could help my son, Lady Randwick…' He stopped and looked up at the guard fifteen feet away, measuring the distance of sound, she thought suddenly. Always checking. Measured temperance and no false moves.

Like me.

The sense of kinship made her turn away so that he would not see what showed in her eyes, and for a second the landscape was blurred. The presence of others also was noted, for Quinlan and Dougal Ullyot were walking down from the high ridge and, closer, an older man ambled with a catch of quail tied to his belt. Rubbing out the words in the dust, she stood.

'Give me leave to practise my medicine openly here and I will look into the affliction of your son.'

'And this will be safe? The sister of Falstone ministering to an Ullyot?'

She felt as if he had hit her.

'I can see the answer in your face,' he added before she could speak. 'A room in the keep will be put aside for your use, though I trust you will take care of the feelings of Hale, for he is old and has been here some time.'

Excitement beat loud in her breast as she listened. This was what she had wanted to do for her whole life. At Heathwater Noel was never prepared to trust her enough to allow her to use her healing powers freely. And now Alexander Ullyot was?

'There may be some failures,' she said quietly. Better to lay her cards out here and see where they fell than be dealt a hand in the upcoming weeks that might floor her entirely.

'Only some?' The humour was back and a spark of teasing. 'What sort of percentages are we speaking of, do you imagine?'

'No more than the very worst cases, my lord. The ones whose injuries have been left to fester.'

'And the women? Will you be seeing to their needs in childbirth?'

Redness swamped her face that a man should discuss

such things with her. 'You know, then, that I helped at the birth of Jamie and Brigid's daughter?'

'A difficult birth, I have been told, with the midwife refusing attendance. I would not like to see that happen again.'

'It will not, my lord.'

'Because you will deliver a baby whether it is in position or no?'

'I shall.'

'Even if it gives you bloodshot eyes?'

'Who told you that?'

'Katherine. She was worried about you and the trace of redness is still there in your right eye. How did it happen?'

'The child was caught in the womb and I needed to see it.'

'As you saw into the body of Dougal, perhaps?'

She was still.

'He said he felt you inside him. Like a warm light. And when you healed me in the forest I remember feeling the same.'

'Valerian is a powerful medicine, my lord. It creates hallucinations.'

His laughter amazed her. 'You will report to me each week to let me know how you fare. If there are problems, I want to know of them.'

He looked surprised as she held out her hand. When he took it she had a sudden and blinding image of him lying with her on his bed fully naked. Shock had her pulling away quickly. A few hours back and Alexander Ullyot had her daydreaming about things that would never come to pass. She hoped he had no idea of the waywardness of her thoughts, but was disconcerted further when his gaze brushed across her own in lazy masculine appreciation.

'I…I need to go now,' she blurted out and turned, glad as an old man mounted the incline and claimed Alexander's attention.

'She's a canny lass, Laird.' Angus Ullyot smiled appreciatively. 'And though it may be said she tricks a man with her magic, it's the softer side of Madeleine Randwick that we've been seeing. My wife Patricia could have told it better, Laird. She had the gift to knowing goodness, God bless her soul. And it was in the eyes, she always said. Gold are Madeleine Randwick's and sad at that. And laced with the carefulness of hurt.' He stopped himself short and doffed his hat.

Alex cleared his throat. 'For a woman who has come to Ashblane as the hated sister of the bastard Noel Falstone she is doing remarkably well. Does not Father MacLaren upbraid her still in his Sunday Masses?'

'Och, nay, for she has overcome his resistance.'

'How?'

'The potions, you understand, Laird. For his cough. She leaves them in the chapel when he is not around to refuse them.'

A sharp bark of laughter filled the air. 'And he takes them?'

'We'd all be thinking so. Last Sunday he coughed only twice and never once did he need to stop his sermon.'

'The Lord moves in mysterious ways then, Angus.' Warmth settled inside him and consolidated. He could hear the sounds of the late afternoon birdsong in the air and the rustling leaves of rowan. From further afield came the cries of children playing within the bailey proper, the high sound of their laughter drifting on the wind and he wished sometimes he might hear Gillion play like that.

The burgeoning hope he had felt suddenly was hollowed. An empty promise, and God knew he had had enough of those. Scuffing his boots against a log to loosen the mud, he turned towards Ashblane, conscious of Angus following him up the incline towards home and of Madeleine Randwick striking out alone towards the castle gate.

Even from this distance her hair looked as though it was on fire, the red gold of her long plait glinting in the thin sun.

Chapter Ten

Madeleine set up her healing room with all the determination of a woman who has waited many years for something and finally got what it was that she desired. She poured her heart into the scrubbing, into the cleaning, into the stocking of jars and the gathering of herbs and when the day came that she was ready, she opened the door with a flourish.

No one stood there.

No line of patients. No one with the ague. No man with a wound needing to be stitched or a woman ripe with the promise of child. Just a quiet and unremitting emptiness.

Jemmie stood beside her. 'Perhaps they are busy, Maddy, and will come when the noonday meal is set, or when they have finished the jousting.'

'Or they will not come at all,' she returned, angry now that she had ever let herself hope. Perhaps these people did not like to be seen consulting her, preferring instead the more clandestine and informal questioning. She bit her lip in anger as she surmised just what this would mean for her.

Jemmie fidgeted with the dried leaves on a bunch of hanging chicory. 'If you could get the Laird to come, they might. Hugo says the men follow him like sheep and he is a good ram to follow.'

Madeleine smiled despite everything. 'Hugo is having a detrimental effect on your language, Jemmie. Though perhaps you are right. Stay here and, if anyone comes, bid them to wait, for I will be straight back.'

Alexander was in a room he used off the main hall. Manuscripts in English, French and Arabic were open on his desk. Did he read these? Were they his? She was astonished. Blotting the writing on the margin of a large journal open in front of him, he replaced the quill pen he was using in a pot of ink and leaned back.

'Lady Randwick. Is there a problem?'

She hesitated, loath to lay another difficulty at his feet for he looked tired, the stubble of a beard on his face making her wonder if he had slept at all the previous night. A half-empty jug of ale stood on his desk and the room smelt of wood-smoke. And then, because he was so obviously waiting for her to begin, she did so.

'I have prepared my healing room and seen no one. No one. Not one of Ashblane's inhabitants have come.'

'And…?'

'And I have come to you to find out why.'

'Perhaps they are all well?' His irony was easily heard.

'Nay. I know for a fact that they are not. Helena told me yesterday of her poisoned toenail and Callum's arthritis is playing up again. And then there's Anna. She has a rash from the reeds she cut yesterday—'

He stopped her simply by holding up his hands and she ground to a halt.

I have become a chatterbox, she thought suddenly.

Never had she been particularly verbose, but at Ashblane the words kept coming. When had that happened? Another change in a personality that had for ever been held in check.

Unabashedly she smiled, took a deep breath and tried again. 'I do not know how to encourage people to come and see me openly. If even one would come, it might…' She tailed off as he stood and walked across to her, the breadth of his shoulders outlined by the shafts of light that angled down from a high window. Her brother was as small-boned as Lucien, slight men with the weight of the world on their sagging shoulders.

Unlike Alexander Ullyot.

Contrasts, she thought. So precise sometimes. And so damned telling.

He stopped a foot away from her and the muscles along the lines of his throat rippled as he swallowed, but apart from that he was very still.

'Why do you want to heal so much when it causes you only pain?'

'I want it because it completes me. Without it there is a hole. Here.' She lifted her hand to her heart and did not look away. The scar on his cheek showed in this light as a pearly luminescent knot.

'My mother was also a healer and I remember her saying the same thing.'

Madeleine was astonished. 'Your mother? What was her name?'

'Margaret Ullyot from the Glenshie. They called her the White Witch.'

'Better than the Black Widow, then,' she returned and caught the quick flash of amusement dart over his features. Desire twisted inside Madeleine and such a need that she felt winded by the intensity of it. She was astonished, for she had always stepped back from anything sensual or sexual. The barren Madeleine Randwick had, after all, little to offer any ardent swain. But here, fully clothed and standing a foot away from Alexander Ullyot, she felt things happening inside her body that had never happened before. A wanting and a weightless throb of passion. A short sharp knowledge of femininity fed by both attraction and circumstance. Scared by the force of it, she moved back. Away. Out of reach. Just in case she laid her fingers across the battered plane of his cheek. And held on. Seeking. Understanding. Knowing. Knowing what it was in him that made the coldness inside her reform and reshape. A woman very different from the one who had always been surrounded by little men.

Lord, even her thoughts were becoming jumbled in Alexander Ullyot's presence, but the sweet true strength of him was like a tonic, like a promise, like a gift wrapped in the threads of some long-forgotten dream of safety—close, real, reachable. Closing her eyes against longing, she took a deep breath.

She was the Black Widow with a raft of lies and deaths upon her hands and a bounty on her head. Vilified. Hated. Pitied. And the Laird of Ullyot had even more reason to hate her than most. The thought sobered her. As did his next words.

'There is something that you could do for me. I have a wound on my leg that needs attention.'

Her sense of dislocation deepened. 'You do?' After he had hurt his shoulder he had never let her near him again.

And then she understood. 'You would come down to the healing room? With me?'

'Yes.' Ground out as if indeed it was the very last thing he truly wished to do.

'I would be most…thankful…' she petered off as he strode past her and out to the Great Hall, his speed belying the complaint he professed.

It was a good hundred yards to the annexe she used for her healing; by the time they reached the small room they had a trail of witnesses. She wondered what Alexander thought of all these spectators, but his eyes did not meet her own and his face told her nothing.

Her table was set up with clean linen and candles. Nervous now, she had Jemmie light the wicks and asked

Alexander to sit. The tails of his long shirt splayed along each side of him and he looked enormous in the smallness of this space. Bending, she lifted the hem and was faced with two heavily muscled brown legs. His leather boots were well scuffed and worn. Not a man with a big wardrobe, she thought, for she had never seen him in anything else but the Ullyot colours and his Highland shirt.

Both knees looked exactly the same.

'Which one is sore?' she whispered, sure now that he did this to help her and not wanting the others to hear.

'The left one.' Leaning down, he pointed out a small graze she had missed. She noticed how he kept his leg turned away from the clan members who had gathered. Noticed, too, how he did not flinch when she touched the bruise.

'How was it hurt?'

'The quintain practice that I supervised the other day. I am not as agile as I used to be.'

'There looked to be nothing wrong with your method from where I was standing, Laird Ullyot. Did you learn your skills here?'

'No. I was in trained in France, under King Philip. Guy de Tour was an ardent knight and times were tough.'

'You were at Crécy and Calais. Katherine told me. She said after that you were some years in Egypt.'

'I was.' A bleak distance was back and, uncertain about continuing this course of conversation, she reached for clean cloths and water. So he had been both in France and in the desert lands, though the Crusades had been over for more than half a century. Why had he gone there and with whom? She remembered the manuscripts in his room. He obviously read Arabic, which implied an intimate association with the culture.

Trying to pry some more information out of him, she carried her thoughts into words. 'I used to wonder and imagine what it must be like to travel. If I had been a boy—' She stopped, flustered by his smile.

'You would have gone to war?' He finished her sentence as a question, and she nodded.

'Be thankful that ye did not go then, for many a lad failed to return and, if they did, they were different from when they left.'

'As you were?'

'Yes.' Maddy got the distinct impression that he wanted no more discussion.

Bathing the chaffed spot on his knee with care, she reverted to silence and, kneeling, ran her fingers down the long line of leg. Sculptured muscle and heavy sinew. And the scars of old battles. As her thumb rubbed carefully across the wound, she caught him watching her. A rising blush stained her cheeks and made her catch her breath as sheer and unadulterated lust bolted through her. Surprising her. Horrifying her. Making her clumsy. The pad of linen she held dropped from her fingers and, pleading an excuse to change it, she was glad for the opportunity to move away. Lord help me, she prayed, as she busied herself at the bench on the other side of the room, trying to banish the breathless rush of want. Let him not divine her thoughts or see in her face the expression she had often determined upon her mother's.

Eleanor de Cargne—a woman who had slept with any man who caught her fancy.

Nay, she was not like that. She was a healer. And she was barren. She would be no man's wife or mistress. She was an outsider and an interloper and the horror of her first marriage had cured her for ever of depending upon anyone.

Walking back, she applied the salve and bandage with meticulous concentration and was pleased when the task was finished.

'You will need to keep it clean and dry. Perhaps tomorrow you could return for another dressing.' She did not look directly at him.

'I shall endeavour to do so, Lady Randwick,' he replied evenly as he stood, and she knew the bandage would be off as soon as he reached his chambers and that he would not be back.

She didn't finish administering to her patients until well into the evening and was just tidying the last of her linens and potions when a message arrived from the hall.

'The Laird says ye are to come to eat now.' The young boy who brought the order was fierce in his delivery and Madeleine followed him, full of well-being and energy. This simple healing did that to her, she surmised, secreting a herbal the housekeeper had given her into the pocket of her skirt for a further perusal later.

There were guests at dinner, which was a surprise. A young man about her age sat next to Alexander and a woman a few years older sat next to him. A lady with gilded blond hair and a winsome smile. The same lady she had seen the Laird of Ullyot with the night Dougal the twin had been brought to her room.

Swallowing her questions, she slipped into the place next to Quinlan, frowning as she noticed the empty space on the other side of Alexander. Had he meant for her to sit there? She caught his glance as he looked up and the expression on his face suggested that he hadn't.

'Lady Randwick.' His voice was as distant as his eyes. 'May I introduce Sir Stephen Grant and his sister, Lady Isabella Simpson? Stephen has been here visiting his uncle, but will take his sister back to London before the week's end.'

Stephen Grant stood and came to take her hand in his, lifting it to his lips. 'Your reputation precedes you, Lady Randwick.'

'Indeed.' She was cautious in her smile.

'I have heard you to be a well-practised healer,' he said above the humdrum of other conversations. 'And Alexander tells me you have set up a room to tend to the sick here at Ashblane.'

Detecting nothing in his tone but sincerity, she relaxed. 'Yes, I have had over ten patients already today.'

'So many?' The Lady Isabella spoke for the first time and her voice was cold. 'Are you here for long?'

The glow from the afternoon's healing diminished somewhat under Stephen's sister's stare. 'No, not long.' Madeleine watched as the woman covered Alexander's hand with her own in a proprietary motion and one that Maddy guessed was designed to warn off interlopers.

'Where will you go after Ashblane?'

'I am not entirely certain, Lady Simpson.' Caution schooled irritation. Did this woman not know that she was a prisoner here?

'According to the gossip, you are betrothed to the Earl of Harrington? A handsome man, and powerful.'

'Yes.'

'Yet you will not return to him?'

'No.'

'I had heard you were a woman of few words, Lady Randwick, but I did not realise how few.' Her long blond hair draped across the sleeve of Alexander's coat and play-fully she pulled it back, re-bundling it into a knot that unwound dramatically the first moment she moved. 'I have also heard that you enjoy entertaining men.'

The interest in Isabella's voice was as easily heard as the anger in Alexander's.

'Enough, Isabella.' He slipped his hand from her grasp and turned to pour more wine, though Isabella was not deterred.

'Lucien was our cousin, twice removed. We played with

him as a child, so I could see why you should look elsewhere for your fun, Lady Randwick.'

Her red lips pouted as she leaned forward and Madeleine caught a good expanse of creamy white bosom and knew Alexander had seen the same. 'We heard that he had died of knife wounds?' The words were formed as a question.

'An accident, Lady Simpson.'

Isabella coughed on her wine, her eyes now full of intrigue, and Madeleine was glad that Alexander Ullyot remained silent, breathing a sigh of relief when she saw the kitchen staff bring in platters of meat and bread for dinner. With resolve she forced a smile and turned to talk to Stephen Grant, liking his friendliness and his kind dark eyes, which were so different to the icy sharpness of his sister's.

An hour after the night meal had finished Alexander found Madeleine sitting against the inner wall of the keep's ramparts, moonlight on her face and Bran, one of the castle dogs, asleep at her side.

'May I?'

He waited until she nodded and gestured to the herbal at her side. 'You have been reading?'

'My grandmother used to say that the most relevant facts a patient could tell you were often the unsaid ones. Signs in the body. Temperature. Rashes. She said that for every ailment on this earth, God had, in his wisdom, made a cure to match it. I would not like to miss anything.'

'And did you? Miss anything of importance?'

'No. Today's doctoring was mostly scrapes and bruises.'

'Like my leg.' In the light of the lamp beside her he saw her soft smile and was enchanted by it.

'Your leg was the easiest mending I did and I would like to thank you for the gesture, Laird Ullyot. Without your help I doubt anyone would have come near me.'

He stayed silent, enjoying the feel of a light wind at his face. A moment or so later Madeleine spoke again.

'Isabella Simpson is very beautiful. Have you known her long?'

He was surprised by her topic. 'Aye. Her husband was a good friend of mine, but he died two years ago. She has been living with her uncle since. In Kimdean, just a few miles from here.'

'And now she would like another husband?'

Her question was so unexpected he began to laugh.

'Isabella was right. You do not mince words, Lady Randwick.'

'I never had that luxury, Laird Ullyot.'

He breathed out and leaned back against the stone wall, wondering what would happen were he to take her hand and bring it to his lips the way he had seen Stephen do this evening. Her fingers looked small and fragile, the nails short and tidy compared with the long talons that Isabella favoured. Around her wrist she wore a knotted string, as if to remind herself of something important. The concoction of a remedy, perhaps, or a potion? He smiled at the thought as she began to speak again.

'I never talked with Lucien, you see.' Her words were precise and quiet. 'He never liked my doctoring or my clothes or the way I wore my hair. There was nothing about me he truly liked. And there was nothing about him that I truly liked, either.'

'You think a good marriage begins with like, then?' he ventured and scratched the nose of Bran as the dog woke and dug his head into his legs.

'Yes. Like is as important as love, I think. You need respect and honour to make a marriage work and I never had that. Did you?'

'No.' He had to be honest and out here in the night it was easy. 'I married for convenience, I suppose, and because I was lonely. Like or love were never a part of it.'

'And it did not grow?'

'No. It lessened, if anything. Alice was nervous…'

'Of you?'

'She was a melancholy woman. I remember that about her. And though I tried to understand her reasons for it, I could not. I think now that it was just her nature.'

'And Isabella? What is she like?'

'Good in bed.' He smiled at her shock and laughed out loud. 'You surprise me, Lady Randwick,' he managed when finally he had regained his composure. 'And that is something few people ever manage to do.'

She was looking at him directly now as his hand caught hers and drew her up against him. In the darkness their bodies fitted together and her fire-hair, draped across his fingers, was muted in the moonlight. Soft and silky, and when he breathed he could catch the scent of flowers. Heather, he thought. And comfrey. A mix of woman and witch.

He frowned as she pulled back.

'Lady Isabella may not like to find you out here in the dark fondling my hair, Laird Ullyot.'

'She has no claim on me, *mo cridhe*.'

Mo cridhe? *My heart*? Lord. He frowned as he realised he had never given such an endearment before to any woman and was glad Madeleine did not have the way of the Gaelic.

'No claim yet, perhaps, although I think she would like to.'

In reply he tipped her chin up with his finger. Madeleine felt anger on the edge of the movement.

'How do you do it?'

'Do what?' She could not understand his drift.

'Make men want you. Like this.' His mouth came down before she had the chance to turn, bleak and hard and bruising. Neither an easy kiss nor soft as he moulded her body to his own, his hands sending shock waves across the bare skin on her arms and his teeth tugging at her bottom lip. A wave of heat spiked through her as she melted into him, the force of his sex between them.

'Kiss me in the way I can feel you want to…here.' His fingers roamed up across the bodice of her kirtle, testing the firm curve of her breast before covering the hard bud of nipple. Close. Closer. The hot lash of his tongue winded her. Delighted her. Opened a place she had long thought of as dead. With a groan she willed him on, wanting what it was he offered even here in the public domain of his keep, her whole being heightened to sensation and hungry for the answering thrust of his loins.

Not asking, not giving, just taking and taking and taking. Around them the curtain of night closed in, breathing softness into the hard hold of reality and making everything easier. More possible.

And then he broke the kiss, his eyes dazed and puzzled. And then angry. Jamming his hands down against his thighs, he moved back. When she looked down, she saw that the knuckles were white with tension.

'I can have you hard or I can have you soft, but mind this. I will have you, Madeleine Randwick. When I am ready and on my terms and without the ghosts of those you have bedded between us or the chance of discovery before I should finish it off.' Roughly he laid the forefinger of his right hand against the racing pulse at her throat, removing it a second before Quinlan rounded the corner, his shock in finding them together in the moonlight comical.

'Isabella sent me out to find you, Alex. I think she would like to retire.'

'Thank you, Quin. And may I ask you to see Lady Randwick to her quarters?'

Without another word he stalked away, though she thought she heard him swear beneath his breath and his gait was laboured as he turned the corner.

* * *

Jemmie was waiting in her room when she returned and was full of the news of life in the Ashblane stables.

'There is another new foal, Maddy. I helped deliver him and it was wonderful. Gillion was there, too.'

Madeleine smiled. 'You like it here, don't you?'

'It feels safe. It feels as though we are a long way from the world and Alexander Ullyot is strong. Stronger than Noel and Liam Williamson, and even stronger than the Earl of Montcrieff, I think.' A pensive look crossed her thin face. 'I wish we could stay here for ever, Maddy. Stay here until we are old and no one was looking for us.'

Madeleine crossed her room and sat down on the bed, drawing Jemmie down on her lap and running her hand through her hair.

Safety. Jemmie had never known it. Not since the first breath of her life, a tiny baby bundled up between the politics of expediency. She had always been dressed as a boy child—Eleanor's way of protection, Maddy surmised—and continued to do so at Heathwater, when the small household had been shifted there after her mother's death. And now, eleven years later, all the old worries still held strong.

'We cannot stay. Noel has sent messages to the King of Scotland and to the church demanding my return. Only my return, Jemmie. If there is no other way…'

'No. You won't leave me. You promised you would not.'

'I would come back for you.'

Tears sprang into gold-brown eyes as the child snuggled closer, and there was silence.

'The Laird of Ullyot would protect you, Jemmie. I know he would. If I got him to give me his word on it, you would be safe until I could return for you.'

'You would have to tell him. About us.'

'I know.'

'He would be cross with us.'

Maddy smiled at the childish interpretation of adult emotion. *Cross?* He would be furious. But, if there was no other alternative, she would have to trust her instincts. And every single one of them said that the Laird of Ullyot was a man who could be trusted.

Bringing her fingers to her lips, she relived his kiss and how the sheer strength of his masculine embrace had been a revelation. Beautiful, beautiful man with anger in his eyes and blood on his hands and the weight of both Scottish and English royalty on his back. And yet he did not waiver, did not take the easier course of sacrificing her as Lucien would have, and Noel. She smiled. His power and sheer arrogance should be anathema to her, given that she had always hated both. But in Alexander Ullyot they were transformed into grace. And underpinned with the certain knowledge of sanctuary. Her sanctuary and Jemmie's. She wished that his hands might have found the soft wet place beneath her skirt that even now throbbed in want. Wished that his tongue had wet the fat swelling of her breasts and suckled them as a baby might. Her sharp laugh made Jemmie look up at her quickly and she shook her head.

'Just a daydream,' she said, angry at the waywardness of her thoughts and standing. She was a hostage with little hope of escape. And he was a Scottish warlord with a long-standing hatred of her brother.

When he took her it would not be in love.

Chapter Eleven

Alexander stood at the window overlooking the bailey and watched Madeleine with her page in the kitchen gardens. Gillion kneeled beside them, laughing when her arm came around his shoulders as he handed her some leaves. Leaning in.

He remembered the feel of her in his own arms last night, easy and loving, her more prickly carefulness lessened under the onslaught of…what? Lust? Desire? Frowning at his musings, he leaned against the wall, a small and slow movement lest she see him.

She was changing him just as she was changing his son! Even from this distance he could see Gillion's furtive fear had been replaced by something akin to the joy Jemmie bubbled over with and often now he caught the two children with their heads together, hatching up another scheme, dark amber against blond.

His eyes flickered across to Madeleine's page. The boy

had filled out a bit in the weeks since they had been here. Still he was a skinny child and his hair next to Madeleine held the same sheen of redness. For a moment he frowned as an elusive thought sifted through reason, but a knock at the door interrupted him. Quinlan stood there with a man he had not seen before. A man covered with the mud of a long ride and wearing the livery of David of Scotland.

'You are summoned to Edinburgh, Alex. King David sent you this and told me that I should wait and ride back with you.'

'Indeed?' With a barely concealed impatience he took the missive and unfurled it. A direct order to attend to the King. Alexander knew that he could not afford to ignore it.

'Send for Lady Randwick, Quinlan. This concerns her. And ready the horses.'

Madeleine arrived in the Hall in less than ten minutes, the smell of herbs and soil on her hands and clothes. Around her neck she wore a clumsy array of shells and nuts threaded on to yarn.

When she saw where he looked she smiled. 'Your son made it for me, my lord, as a present. He collected the nuts in the woods. I am not certain where he got the shells from—'

She broke off as he reached out to touch one. Close. But not close enough, her breasts swelling liquid-warm with the proximity of his hand. Shaking her head, she tried to regain the sense of their conversation.

'They were his mother's. She collected such things.'

'Then I shall dismantle the necklace carefully after I have worn it today and give you back the treasures.'

'No. They were Gillion's to do with as he wanted. He obviously wanted you to have them.'

Madeleine was unnerved by the distracted tone he now used, given her own ridiculous breathlessness, and unnerved further when her eyes fell on the parchment on the desk. Even from this distance the royal seal of Scotland was unmistakable, the red lions rampant against gold.

'David has sent for me?'

'Nay. For me. He asks that I attend him immediately.'

'Noel demanded this?'

'Yes.'

She felt her blood run cold. First the Church and now the King. Her enemies were gathering with a remarkable speed and such an order put everything here at risk.

'If you go, will it be safe?'

'*When* I go I will make certain that it is,' he replied. 'Though there is something I might ask you, Lady Randwick. Is it just familial love that pushes your brother to such measures or is there something else that it might be wise for me to know?'

She hated the colour that flooded her face, but stayed silent.

'I see.' He gathered up the parchment and she could only watch him as he strode from the room.

He knew! He knew she lied and yet still he went, unprotected by the truth. Uncertainty scoured her brow and she swallowed back fear. If anything happened to the Laird of Ullyot because of her…

She could not finish the thought as she balanced her sister's safety against speaking out, and the yarn of the necklace she wore broke under the strain of her fingers, the nuts and shells falling with an angry clatter to the floor.

He left Ashblane with a guard of twenty men and thirty of his best horses. Edinburgh was usually two days' travel away. He reached it in thirty-six hours.

'You will return Lady Randwick to me, Alexander.'

Alex's mouth tightened as he bit down on an answer and watched David pace up and down the bedchamber. At thirty-four David was already an old man. It was the imprisonments he had suffered under the English, Alex reasoned, and the constant threat of Balliol and his southern army. The Bruce blood that beat in Alex's own veins probably also unnerved him, for Ashblane was strong with its three thousand soldiers and numerous keeps along the edges of the Ullyot land. Too strong, some would say. For Alex it was a juggling act to keep it safe and the note of pleading in David's tone and the whisper of something else, which he could not quite put his finger on, unnerved him.

'Why do you keep her, Alexander?'

'I want Madeleine Randwick for myself.' Alex softened the words with a rueful shrug as if he was embarrassed to speak of any intimacy between them. If David thought that he had taken her as a mistress, it might protect her.

'Let your cock talk and the Randwick witch will ruin everything. Edward of England is restless and the Baron Falstone looks for his chance. Nay. Bring her here, to me.'

Alexander's heart thudded hard beneath his linen shirt. David's words were not making sense. Madeleine's presence here at court would not be easy with a monarch like Edward on the other side of the border, demanding retribution for an insult to one of his strongest barons. Nay, given David's self-interest, there had to be something here that he was missing. The expression on her face in the company of Milward and O'Sullivan had also told him a great deal. Whore she might be, but she was also a young woman and afraid.

'She is dangerous to you, Alexander. Noel Falstone wants you dead and the other English barons will follow him if they think that the de Cargne daughter is likely to share her secrets.'

'Secrets?'

'Eleanor's secrets. The ones whispered under the blankets and in darkness. Madeleine Randwick has been able to live under her brother's protection only because he has kept her isolated.'

Alex frowned. Again he had the feeling that something was not quite right here. 'Isolated? At Heathwater it's said she had the ears of a succession of lovers.'

David's face flushed unbecomingly and he stepped back

as Alex determined the reason why. 'She has money, doesn't she?' It was only the promise of wealth that could stir David into any stronger action. The Berwick Treaty Scotland had signed with England had named ransom and David was relying on diplomacy to keep the English at bay. Watching his cousin now, he saw the unmistakable flickers of a weakness that had been the hallmark of his reign.

'The monies of Madeleine Randwick are not your concern, Alexander. They are mine and will continue to be while you hold her here in Scotland.'

'How much money are we talking about?'

'Enough to cut the export taxes on wool and hides. Enough to keep Edward happy for at least a year.'

Alex held his hands as fists by his side and tried to remember the figures bandied. One hundred thousand marks over ten yearly instalments left an annual reimbursement that needed finding. Suddenly he understood. 'And this is why you have asked me to bring her to you? So that you can *protect* her?'

David's eyes darkened. 'Your keeps have been allowed to thrive on the border because you are kin and because whenever I have asked something of you it has been done without question.' His voice carried a touch of irony. 'But, if you want them to continue thriving, I would suggest you bring the Randwick heir to me. After Christmas. I will give you until the first week of January.'

'And who would benefit were she to die without progeny?' He could barely ask the question.

'If Madeleine Randwick were to die without child before she reached twenty-five, the titles of her land would revert to the English King, which would in effect give Edward a direct corridor through the West Marches into Scotland.'

'How old is she now?'

'She was twenty-five on the fourth of October.'

The day she had passed out in his bed, cold and sick after her healing of Dougal. A new thought struck him.

'And what happens after she is twenty-five?' He guessed the answer as he asked it and was already pulling on his gloves.

David laughed and downed the drink in his glass. 'After she is twenty-five, she is fair game, whore or no.'

'And if she dies without an heir?'

David's eyes turned hard and Alex knew the answer that his cousin would never admit. If she were to die, the lands would be restored to the crown. English or Scottish— it just depended on who would be the quicker to claim it.

An expendable heiress. Under the control of her brother until she reached twenty-five. It explained the procession of lovers after Lucien had died.

Mon Dieu! Noel would have wanted the land as much as David or Edward and the only way for him to have this was through his sister's children, though God knows why Edward hadn't demanded Madeleine's appearance at court and killed her himself. Her infamy? he mused. Her reputation as a sorcerer? An unexpected protection.

The blood beat hard in Alex's head. It was already started. First Milward and now this. He trusted his cousin little enough to know what would happen were he to return Madeleine to either court. She would be murdered. By David and his minions. By Edward and his barons. Not marriage, as Madeleine had said, but murder, and by any number of the men who would stand to gain favour from two Kings.

Fuming, he did not stop to gain permission to withdraw as he pulled on his leather gauntlets and strode from the chamber of his king.

Alexander rode for Ashblane as if the very devil was on his heels; only when he gained the Ullyot lands did he slow his flight. Nothing was different. No horses had tracked across the hillocks, bearing a waiting raiding party or the retainers of greedy men. No sycophants of a King prepared to wait no longer.

Madeleine was safe.

The breath he took calmed him, though the implications of his fear did not.

He took her into his room on the evening he returned home. Maddy sensed the danger the moment the slats on the heavy portal fell behind them.

Dusk shadowed his face and bruised the glow of his skin and his sword caught the glitter of candlelight. Raising her chin, she followed the prisms and was struck by the empty loneliness in his eyes. He had been drinking. She could smell it on his breath. There was no glimpse at all of the man who had kissed her less than a week ago.

'Would you like something to drink?' Soft words and good wine and the promise of something else entirely?

'No.' She added a 'thank you' in an unconscious notice of manners and he smiled grimly.

'You may need one, Lady Randwick, in the light of what it is I want to say.'

Again she shook her head and made herself stand still.

'As you know, I have come from King David. He bids me to return you to his court.'

'And if you do not?'

Shrugging, he helped himself to another whisky. 'And if I do not, then I would guess the barons of Scotland and England would rise against me.'

'But that is everyone.'

'The thing to consider, you see, Lady Madeleine, is the fact that you are now turned twenty-five.'

'David told you, didn't he?' She drew in a breath, shakily, and waited until he nodded. 'Did he also tell you that my fortune was entailed only to a male heir? That I will be raped by the first man who can get his hands on me…?' She could not finish. She did not need to.

'Who the hell did this to you? Who decreed it such?'

'My mother.'

Disbelief blossomed. 'Why?'

'It was the only way that she could think of to get me to this age. They had already tried, you see, to kill me twice.'

'Who had?'

'Your uncle and his mistress. Edward and his advisors. The tracts of Harland are like a corridor between Scotland and England.'

'Harland?'

'My father's estate. Through Eleanor.'

'Your mother was not just a pretty face, then?' Alexander mused.

'Nor an easy conquest,' Madeleine continued, 'for she took her own life before anyone could get her to rescind the will.'

'Why are you telling me this?'

'A locked door and a glass of wine. A bedchamber that I have been dragged to in the middle of the night and the mark of your ownership stamped at my breast. What else should I think, my lord? You want the prize as much as your cousin does.' The shock in his eyes made her step back, but this was no time to deal in innuendo. Everything about Alexander Ullyot pointed to the fact that he liked honesty. Disclaiming her fear, she began to fight for her life, though his laughter was not at all the reaction she had been expecting.

'It was protection I was offering, my lady. Not rape.'

'Why?' Gold eyes caught his easily and at her full height Madeleine Randwick was not exactly little.

'Because I owe you a life. My own.'

Shaking her head, she moved away from him, the beat of her heart frantic. 'You owe me *one* life. Not a thousand.

Not Gillion's or Katherine's or Quinlan's. If you keep me here, they will all be in danger.'

'Your summary of the defences at Ashblane is hardly flattering.' A laconic curtness overrode his more normal politeness. 'And, contrary to what you may think, David, Edward or Noel will never assail these castle walls.'

She blushed vividly as he walked to the door and flipped the slat as if in dismissal, though his hand snaked out and held her still as she went to walk by, and the spark of contact that flared between them was unmistakable.

'I am not my cousin, Madeleine, and my domain's surety does not rest on the life of one yet-to-be conceived child or the secrets of a woman harnessed for ever by fear to the mistakes of others. If it is indeed safety that you seek, then perhaps I can offer it.'

She saw the pupils of his eyes widen and felt the quickened beat of his heart in the pulse of his palm, and a new idea began to blossom. Maybe after all there was a way. She took a breath and tried to instil calmness lest he discover everything.

'All safety has a price, my lord.'

With exaggerated care she undid the ties on her kirtle and faced him directly. The rounded outline of her breasts was plainly visible beneath the thin material of her shift.

'I offer you the use of my body and willingly for as long as you should want it in exchange for the life of Jemmie.'

Seeing interest strengthen, she was heartened.

'Send him away tonight with guards to England. To my

grandmother. I can pay you in gold or flesh. Or both.' She was ranting and she knew it. Yet here, finally, was a chance. Swallowing, she placed her hand squarely beneath his plaid and made herself smile. No potions tonight, but a chance. The swollen heat of him pressed against her bare palm.

'Stop it.' He stepped back as he felt a thickening in the region of his groin. Anger and lust. The Lady of Heathwater was turning his whole life upside down; even with the knowing of the men who had boasted of using her, he could not quite find it in himself to join their ranks.

'Get out.'

'You will not—'

'Get out, Madeleine. Now.' His words were softer. Quieter. More dangerous.

If she did not go within the next ten seconds, he knew he would throw her on the ground and have her. Push into her. Consume her with a carnality he had never, in all his twenty-eight years of existence, known could occur. This is what the stories told of. This was the de Cargne sorcery, which twisted minds and made fools of men. Lucien. David. Noel. Williamson. Mad with lust or love or anger or greed—it made no difference. For the first time since Madeleine had come to Ashblane, he wondered if, instead of the swarming and avenging armies of his enemies, she was the one he should truly be fearful of.

He was relieved when she left without looking back, as his thoughts ran to the exchange with Madeleine.

Why had she offered her own life in exchange for her page's? As his blood calmed he began to question. Jemmie. Older than Gillion, yet slight. Small boned. Hands that were soft and fragile.

Lord. That was it! Summoning the guard, he ordered both the newcomers from Heathwater to be brought to his room immediately.

Chapter Twelve

Madeleine leant against the door of her sleeping chamber and laced up her kirtle with shaking fingers. Try as she might, she could not hate him. It would have been easier to hate him.

Jemmie.

If she could get Jemmie to her grandmother, she might yet be saved. A small voice inside her questioned the thought of finally telling the truth. A stronger one disclaimed it entirely. Yet danger gnawed at her reasoning. She had shown her hand and a man like Ullyot must be curious. Crossing to the wall that lay between the two rooms, she tapped softly. A reply came back straight away. Jemmie. Reassured, she closed her eyes and tried to think, but soon loud footsteps in the corridor alerted her to the fact that the exchange between them was not over. She heard the cries of her sister and began to beat against the door with her bare fists, rage and fear overcoming everything. When her own door opened, Jemmie stood there, the fingers of a large, dark-haired man tangled around the material of her shirt and a welt of redness in the shape of a hand across her face.

'Who struck my page?' she demanded loudly, reaching for her wrap and ready to do battle should any more harm befall her sister.

The older man began to laugh and his hands wandered across the swell of her bottom with more than a passing caress. She turned on him immediately, scraping her nails down the side of his cheek, and backed up against the wall, pulling Jemmie with her.

'Where is it you are taking us?'

Everything was dangerous. It was after midnight and, for all that he lusted after her, Alexander Ullyot was angry. What was his intent? Had he given orders to simply dump them outside the castle? She breathed in a sigh of relief as she recognised the stairwell to the tower. Alexander Ullyot's room again? Please God, let it be to him that they were taken.

Alexander was still contemplating the motives of his beautiful captive when she burst through the door of his room, hair half-down and a cape draped across her shoulders barely hiding what he now knew to lie beneath. And she did not come quietly, but demanded their release loudly and authoritatively.

'If you must summon me in the dead of night, Laird Ullyot, at least you could use guards with hands that do not wander—'

'Quiet,' he said and was surprised when she obeyed him. Indeed, she seemed almost glad that it was in this room they were now deposited.

His retainers stood uncertainly, giving Alex the impression that they did not trust any Falstone, especially one with long red hair and dimples. Motioning them gone, he shut the door and crossed to the window.

The boy lingered at the back of the room. Alexander watched Madeleine turn to see where he was, amused as the Lady of Heathwater then placed herself in his line of vision and obscured the other entirely.

'Why are we here?' The brash confidence of a few moments ago seemed badly eroded.

'I have changed my mind.'

'Pardon?' He saw her swallow and pale noticeably.

'I will take up the offer of the use of your body, Madeleine. Disrobe.'

Horror, embarrassment and fury flowed simultaneously across her features.

'May we talk of this privately, my lord?' she said coldly, though he could see the hand she gestured with shook.

'Oh, I think not, Lady Randwick. Jemmie's freedom for your body. Is it not fair that he should know of the consequence?'

Without waiting for her answer, he summoned the lad forward. In this light he was amazed that he had not noticed before what he saw so plainly now.

'Get into my bed, Madeleine.' He untied his own shirt

and threw it aside on to a chair. 'Jemmie, help your mistress undress.'

'No.' The boy looked perilously close to tears.

'No?' He heard the anger in his voice as if from a distance.

'He means no, he cannot help me, for he has trouble understanding the workings of a woman's gown.' Madeleine sounded quietly desperate.

'Is that what you mean, Jemmie?'

'No.' The child's top lip began to tremble.

'Come here.'

'Stay where you are.' The voice belonged to Madeleine as she moved in close and he glanced down at the dagger in her hand, shaky but sharp. Feeling the prick of it at his chest, he was still. Knowing that he could hurt her easily, he stopped himself from retaliation.

'I am the only one who can help you, Lady Randwick. Kill me and both you and the *girl* will die.' He felt her stiffen and deliberately leant into the steel. More blood welled before she let the blade drop, the only noises in the room the hollow whir of the turning shaft and the smaller sobbing from the child.

'Who is she?' he asked quietly, the shock in Madeleine's eyes almost causing him to smile.

'My sister.'

He had not expected that. 'Eleanor had another child?'

'Yes.'

'And her father?' he asked, almost knowing the answer before she supplied it.

'King David.'

The ground moved beneath him. 'Your mother was his lover in London?'

'As a woman she was known to be persuasive. She visited him in the Tower after the Battle at Neville's Cross and Jemima was born in 1347.'

'That's her name, then? Jemima? And you have been hiding her all this time?'

Jemima's sobbing increased, supplying him with an answer that made him run a hand through his hair.

'Enough, Jemima. Have the courage of your sister and stop crying. I will not hurt you. Who else knows of this?'

'My grandmother and Goult, our uncle.'

'Not David?'

'No.'

'Not your brother?'

'Nay. If he knew who she was, he would use her name for his own means. Heathwater. Harland. If they are the beginnings of his quest for more, how much easier would it be to dangle an heir before a childless King? Dressing Jemmie as my page was the only way I could think of to both protect her and keep her with me, and Eleanor was adamant no one should ever be told.'

'Can this Goult be trusted?'

Her slight hesitation told him the answer. 'Lord.' An old man and a secret that could tear apart two nations. Madeleine Randwick had promised once that her past would not harm them here. And now?

'If you could supply us with horses, we will leave—'

He did not let her finish. 'And what? Fly over the heads of an avenging army?'

She was quiet. He watched her take Jemmie's hand and hold it close.

'If you could help us get to the border, Laird Ullyot, I promise you the rewards would be substantial.'

He did laugh then. Loudly. 'Substantial wealth when one is dead is no wealth at all, Lady Randwick. And the delivery of a Princess of Scotland to the court of David would be simpler by half. More lucrative, too, for the clan of Ullyot.'

His grim mirth silenced her and for a moment she wondered what the truth might have cost them. Still, she could not afford to let him see her fear.

'You would think to profit from the death of a child? For that is what will happen should you take her to Edinburgh. Robert the Stewart waits his chance to rule, as does Balliol and the sons of Edward the Third. Grown men with armies at their backs and power in their eyes. My sister would be a pawn to them all and she would not stand a chance.' Bringing Jemmie's cold fingers into her own, she pulled her closer and summoned logic. The whorl of a cowlick at the base of Alexander Ullyot's hair caught her eye. Once Eleanor had taught her how to kill a man by pressing down on such a spot. Looking up, she saw he watched her.

'I would think to hold my clan safe, Madeleine, just as you have held your sister's safety above those at Ashblane.'

'I did not ask to be brought here.'

'No?' He swept up his shirt from where it lay against a chair and roughly put it on. 'And why should I believe that? Why should I believe that you did not wish to escape Heathwater in the light of what you have just told me? Would it not be prudent on my part to think you were making a bid for freedom when first I found you at the edge of a battle before your brother could regroup his men? And then, should I not think that a woman of your wiles would also be clever enough to choose her man? One with the men at arms and the means to protect a sister whose very name would endanger anyone associated with her, and say hang the consequences.'

'No. No, it was not like that. I would not lie—'

'Enough, Lady Randwick. You lie as easily as your brother does, and perhaps more often. And right now Ashblane and those in it will not be thanking you for the jeopardy you have placed them in.'

Madeleine stayed silent. All he accused her of was true in the way he would see it. And if one life in Ashblane should truly be lost because of her… She could not finish the thought.

'Where is the army of my brother?'

'Why?'

'If I could get to—' She stopped and swallowed before starting again. 'If I could get my sister to Goult, I could—'

'No.' Jemmie threw her bony wrists around Madeleine. 'You promised, Maddy. You promised you would stay with me.'

'And I'm trying to do that, Jemmie,' she said desperately, bending to the child and laying her cheek against her sister's. 'Goult can take us to France where we could just disappear. No one else need know…'

'Stop.' The voice was Alexander's. He was furious. 'You think this aged uncle can protect you from an army of twenty thousand greedy men? It's seventy miles to the Firth of Forth. Across clan land to which you have no allegiance. The Scotts. The Hays. The Ramsays. There are eyes everywhere, Lady Randwick, and your chances of passing through unnoticed are about as remote as finding this uncle. You will die within a day of leaving and women in these parts do not die slowly, even given the meagreness of their years.' He looked pointedly at Jemmie, the flickering fire reflected in the slate of his eyes. 'And as for you, Lady Randwick, surely the past years have given you some sense of the world outside? Your shape and face would be infinitely captivating to men long starved of the finer points of a feminine form.'

He was suddenly tired of his careful words. 'Understand this. An army of any persuasion will tear you both to pieces before you could last out a night.' Blunt. Raw and honest. Frowning, he saw her face pale noticeably.

His lips moved, but she heard only the sharp gasp of suffocation and, groping her way to the bed, sat down. The softness of a fur pelt beneath her hands calmed her and a little air got through.

Closing her eyes, she centred on her body, small in this room, smaller in this world, and breathing. The noise of Jemmie's sobbing and Alexander's quiet voice brought her back.

'Breathe, damn it. And slowly. That's better. And again. Do as I say. Again.' His hand stroked her shoulder and she felt the whisper of worry on her cheek. Drawing her head against his chest, he took her on to his knee and loosened the ties of her kirtle.

The darkness receded into light as her body relaxed, the air she took finally her own and deep. In an anguished embarrassment she sat still and refused to look at either of the others.

Alexander shifted her away and stood, his hands falling to his side. In her stillness and silence he recognised himself after a battle. Needing aloneness to survive, and shunning the company of others. Pulling Jemmie up from where she kneeled, he led the child to the door and hailed a servant.

'Take the boy to the kitchens and find him some supper,' he said quietly. 'The Lady Randwick will stay with me for a time.' Shutting the door, he leant against the lintel. Waiting.

Fifteen minutes later she raised her eyes to his. Uncertainty punctuated by anger.

'I have attacks of the breathing sickness.'

'Badly,' he said. Not as a question, either.

'I have had them since I killed Lucien.' She needed to

tell him what she had never told anyone. 'It's the curse of St Helen, my patron saint of honour.' She wondered if he could hear the beating of her heart.

'You think you lost your honour when you killed Lucien Randwick?'

Brown eyes filled with tears raised to his, then the tears overflowed down her cheeks. She had not cried when he had chained her on the cold flagstones of a dungeon or marked her breast with the sharp edge of his knife. She had not cried when Patrick of Jedburgh had been slain before her eyes in the Great Hall or when Milward had called her a whore in front of a hundred of his men. Nay, she had stood firm, proud and unbreakable, until now when there was a question of honour.

Her honour.

'Would you do it again?'

'What?' For the first time in twenty minutes she looked at him properly.

'Kill him? Kill Randwick?'

Brimming eyes hardened as the muscles along the fine lines of her jaw flexed. 'Yes.'

'You would kill him again?' he reiterated.

'Yes,' she said more loudly this time as she got to her feet. Certainty clouded fear as anger chased hard upon its heels. 'Yes, I would. I would kill him again.'

'Then you have your answer, my lady. Sometimes honour is a luxury only saints can afford. In the real world it is eminently more expendable.'

'And the afterlife? What happens after death to those who are dishonourable?' She whispered the question as if to even voice it was a sin.

'We meet an omnipotent God and explain.'

Incredulity blazed in her eyes. 'You believe this? Who taught you this heresy?'

'An Egyptian from Alexandria. He called him Allah and said that the one God goes by many names. I came to believe him when we were blown off course in a storm off Dumyat and the boat overturned in the middle of the night. Kamil called out for Allah and a boat bound for France bore from its course and threw us a rope. We'd been swimming for three hours, you see, and what little strength we had was quickly diminishing. That night, drinking the wines of Burgundy and sailing again for Scotland, I vowed I should never see the world quite the same again and that the taking up of other idols was not the equivalent of the hell that narrow-minded Christian folk may believe it is. Perspectives, Madeleine. And amenity. Honour has not so tight a form as you may believe and it comes in many shades.'

'And your chaplain here? He knows of your beliefs?'

'The good pastor MacLaren endorses and encourages debate. A forward-thinking man handpicked by me.'

Ridiculously she began to laugh. 'Do you never doubt yourself, Alexander Ullyot?'

'Not in matters of honour, Lady Randwick. It's a quality too easily misinterpreted and hallowed. The price of life is never so easily paid as that of death.'

'Yet you survive? Alone?'

He hesitated for a moment before answering. 'Ian was always there…' he said quietly, but did not continue as he walked to the window. The draught brushed his hair in waves around his shoulders and Maddy found herself speaking with the man and not the legend.

'I saw you. In the battlefield before you captured me.'

In one quick movement he turned, eyes threaded with a guarded wariness.

'I was in the trees,' she continued, 'waiting to see whom I might need to heal.' Tightening her fingers in the material of her skirt, she summoned calm, for the aura around him was strong.

'And did you often heal your brother's men after a battle?'

'I did.'

'Rumour has it you watch rather than heal.'

'Rumour has it you never shed tears,' she returned and stood her ground.

Unexpectedly he smiled. 'I would prefer that particular rumour to stay intact,' he said and relaxed when she nodded. 'What else does rumour say of me?'

'That you have no family. That you can fight off ten men unarmed and still be unbeaten. That when you were a child a wild dog marked your face with the sign of the devil and that you are a bastard cousin of the Scottish King.'

'Comprehensive,' he remarked.

'But not all true?' she returned.

'The scar I carry here was from Cairo and as for family…I have Gillion and Katherine and Quinlan.'

She noticed he said nothing of his royal connections, nor did he elaborate on his fighting prowess and she liked him for it. Whatever he was, Alexander Ullyot was not vain. Measuring safety, she continued slowly.

'Rumour, you see, is a thing that can grow. Take my own situation, for instance. Witchcraft. Sorcery. The sensual arts. There are many who would say I practise these.'

She moved towards him. He noticed both the way her hips rolled seductively and her sultry woman's smell.

'My brother imprisoned me, and I was allowed to speak with no one save for several of his hand-picked friends. At first I thought he did this because he hated me, and then…and then I thought it was something else.' She did not elaborate on this other reason, but a blush crept into her cheeks. 'Discredited, I was able to stay on at Heathwater, an easy conquest with a supply of healthy young men…not all young,' she amended and stood her ground as Alexander whipped her wrist into his hand and tugged at it without gentleness.

'Why are you telling me this?' he said savagely.

'Because what you hear is not always what you can believe.' Pulling her wrist free, she raised herself to her tallest height. 'With powder and potions a competent healer can make a man believe anything. And I am competent, Laird Ullyot.'

Her eyes caught in the light from the fire and the skin

at the nape of Alexander's neck prickled. He did not doubt it. Not since first she had cured him.

'Why are you telling me this?' The cadence of the question was different now, more puzzlement than anger.

'Because you did not kill my sister. Because you have not thrown us out. Because you told your serving woman to take *the boy* to the kitchens and feed *him*.'

A feeling unlike any he had ever had tightened Alexander's chest and in self-defence he moved back.

In the half-light of his chamber it would have been easy to slide his hand across the line of skin that disappeared into the hollow of her throat, to feel her beating pulse and touch the flame that was her hair. Yet he was wary. And cautious. Something of another world hung in her eyes and around the full shape of her confession. A witch, a dream taker, a soothsayer. Aye, all had been said of the Lady of Heathwater at one point or another and well he could understand why.

'You're telling me you are an innocent?' The jibe was pointed.

'Hardly,' she countered in the same tone. 'Lucien was eighteen when we were married and I was fourteen. My brother had a vested interest in seeing the marriage was consummated, though after determining it as a fact he left. Lucien himself seldom troubled me again after the first year.'

'Why?'

'He was afraid of me, even then. And his sexual tastes were…unusual.'

'Lord.' The expletive was said solemnly. 'And the procession of lovers?'

'Oh, that was a more recent thing. After Lucien's death my brother wanted me with child for Eleanor's will had stipulated an heir. The money and lands would have been his to control legally if I were to produce a male heir, at least for the time it took for the child to reach his majority.'

'So Noel came up with an alternative?'

'I was not the right gender for Harrington's tastes and my brother, despite all his other faults, always drew the line at incest.' Amazingly she smiled. 'In Scotland men fear you, Laird Ullyot, because you are strong and ruthless. Well, the de Cargne sorcery protected me as surely, though sometimes there were men I could not control.' She pushed back her sleeve and the mark of a brand showed, burnt black into the soft skin of her right forearm. 'Lucien was at least more manageable than some of Noel's "friends" and that was something to be grateful for.'

Not all potions and competency then, he surmised, the proud strength of the Lady of Randwick more honourable again in her honesty, but something about this story bothered him.

Madeleine said she had killed her husband, yet he doubted she could have done it had Lucien been the character she was painting him. Removed. Distant. Fearful. But why would she lie?

'Where was Jemmie when all this was going on?' A

sharp flicker of anger had him guessing. 'Lucien knew Jemmie was female?'

She did not answer, but turned away. He could see the thin line of sweat beneath the heavy swathe of her hair and he suddenly had it.

'Lucien Randwick liked young children?'

'Yes, damn him.' Fire and ice ruled the lines of her face and her breathing was fast and furious. 'He liked young, young girls and boys. I was fourteen when first we were married and already within the year he had tired of me.'

'And Jemmie was what, nine or ten, and he was interested?'

'Nine. She was only nine.' She shouted the words and turned away in fury, remembering everything.

Remembering Lucien tearing at the ripped clothing of her hysterical little sister, remembering the surprise on his face when he saw her gender and then the expression of self-interest as he understood what such lies might be covering. And how much more this secret could be worth to him. She had brought the knife from her pocket and embedded it in her husband's throat even as he prepared himself for rape. Then she had stood beside him to make full sure that he had not lived. The blood beat so loudly in her ears she almost did not hear what next he had to say.

'He deserved it, then.'

'Pardon?'

'The bastard deserved a knife in the back or wherever you planted it. I hope it was slow.'

'It was.' She suddenly smiled, lightened by his certainty.

'If I'd have been there, I would have cut off another part of his anatomy, too.'

'I thought about it.'

'Good for you.'

Suddenly she laughed. It felt so good to talk about all this with someone. For two long years the deed had festered inside her, eating at goodness and grace. And now to be offered a form of absolution. Her smile faded noticeably—nay, absolution was impossible without honesty.

'Lucien carried no weapon.' She waited for his shocked reaction.

'Carried no weapon? Was he not five times stronger than you were and ten times stronger than Jemmie?'

She nodded.

'Weapons lie in sheer brute force as easily as they do in the wicked sharp heft of a well-honed blade, Madeleine. And had you let him use her as he willed, what then?'

'Yes,' she cried and looked directly at him. 'I have thought of that, often and often,' she added raggedly, 'and yet…' She was quieter now. 'His was still a life.'

Crossing the chamber, he tipped her chin up to his. 'Jemmie or a mad amoral rutting bastard, Madeleine. I would have thought the choice simple.'

'Simple? His blood ran across my shoes and into the hide of a rug on his bedroom floor. I could have stopped the bleeding. I could have covered his throat and pushed down hard. I am a healer…'

'But you didn't?'

'No.'

'And neither would have I.'

She was still, the only sound in the room that of the wind against the leather that hung across the window.

'Have you ever killed a person in cold blood?'

He laughed. 'Your dealing to Lucien Randwick was hardly in cold blood, Madeleine. Cold blood is creeping upon a man who is only doing his duty and ending his life before he has the chance to report anything out of the ordinary. And this I have done many times.'

'In defence of your home?'

'Defence of one's home under the auspices of war is often as much of a fable as the romantic vision of a young husband handpicked by a king. No, your valour in seeing to the safety of your sister was not nearly as questionable as mine has often been.'

'You do not mince words, Laird Ullyot.'

'Thank you.'

'That was not the compliment I think you perceive it.'

'Nay?' He smiled and Madeleine felt her insides curl into heat.

It would be so easy to love this man.

Shocked, she turned away. Ashblane was unassailable and well defended, a place offering a temporary shelter while she sifted through the options for herself and her sister. If she stayed here, everyone would be in danger— any number of her enemies would see to that.

She made herself stand still, shuttering the longing in her eyes and clenching her hands together to stop herself from reaching out to touch him. Not in one word or gesture would she betray herself. For the first time in a long time she felt honourable.

He watched her draw into herself, the whitened knuckles of her fingers telling him of some other struggle she now battled with. Her hair fell in molten waves to her hips, which were softly rounded against the candlelight. He remembered the dusky pinkness of her areolas and the feel of her hand beneath his plaid when she had offered him her body. And in her eyes a minute ago when she had teased him, he had thought to see something in them that smacked of a softer emotion. Shaking his head, he crossed the room and opened the door. A guard stood outside.

'Take Lady Randwick to her chamber, and stay by her door to make sure that she stays safe.'

He turned away before she had the chance to thank him.

Chapter Thirteen

Her uncle arrived at noon the following day. Standing beside Alexander, Madeleine watched him ride in, though his hand stopped her from rushing forward as Goult came through the bailey and into the courtyard proper.

'Wait.'

She stiffened at his command, but obeyed it. With trepidation she felt the cold prickling of danger radiating from him. His fingers rested lightly on the hilt of the sword he wore at his waist.

'Welcome, Aidan.' He greeted the soldier at the front of the column and gestured for him to dismount. 'Were there problems?'

'Nay, Laird. Falstone is in London.'

'Why?'

'To petition the English King this time, seeing as David is not listening, and to demand the return of the Lady Randwick through royal channels.'

Alexander felt a rising anger as he looked at the old man on his white horse. A proud and craggy visage returned the surveillance. Fleetingly he felt a resurgence of hope.

'You are Goult of Kenmore?'

'I am.' Opaque eyes watered in the cold air.

'Welcome to Ashblane.'

'Thank you, Laird Ullyot.'

'Bring him to my chambers, Aidan, once he is ready, and let his niece bid her kin welcome in private.' His hand slipped away from Madeleine's and let her free. Without reserve she ran to her uncle, who had dismounted and now held out his arms.

Alexander watched as her fingers traced the lines of his face as she held him close. A bond of love, then, and more than expediency.

It would be interesting to talk with a man who had known Madeleine Randwick since childhood.

'You have spoken to no one about Jemmie's parentage?' Alexander's question to Goult an hour later was quietly asked in the privacy of his own chamber with only Madeleine present.

'I have not.'

'And did Noel ever question her presence?'

'Once he did.'

'Once recently?'

'Yes.'

'But you told him nothing.'

'Nothing.'

'Where was the child born?'

'In Vorpeth. At the home of Josephine de Cargne.'

'Your grandmother, Madeleine?' Flint-hard eyes locked on to her own.

'Yes. She lives with her second husband, Lord Robert Anthony.'

'Anthony.' He mulled over the name. 'From the battle of Halidon Hill?'

'Yes.'

'A decent fighter, then?'

'Yes.' She tried to keep the worry from her voice and failed. Alexander looked up.

'You think he could not defend his home?'

'No, my lord. It's just that he's old now and my grandmother does not wield the influence she once may have had.'

'Influence?'

'She was lady-in-waiting in the Court of England until ten years ago. The royal connections protected her.'

'And now don't?'

'She was found with a necklace belonging to Queen Phillipa and was accused of theft. Fortunately, given her years of service, the whole thing was hushed up and she was merely dismissed.'

'You believe she did it?'

'I'd like to say no, my lord, but Grandmama liked pretty things. Sometimes she took my mother's jewellery.'

'So she is a thief?'

Madeleine bowed her head. In the cold light of day the crime took on a significance it had always before lacked in her mind. And she was sorry it should be Alexander she had to tell. Her grandmother was a thief, her mother a whore and her sister a love-child whose very existence threatened everything. The muscles in her stomach tightened as she saw Goult take breath to speak.

'Noel wants his sister back and I have heard it said that he swears nothing will get in his way of retrieving her.'

'Nothing save for me.'

The humour in Alexander's voice was apparent and as Goult smiled Maddy felt a strange joy. It had been so long since she had seen her uncle smile and she blessed Alexander Ullyot for the small favour before soundly admonishing herself.

His next words were surprising. 'I would like for both you and Jemmie to promise not to walk outside the walls of Ashblane for it may bode ill for you if any were watching.'

'Sometimes there is doctoring to be done down in the cottages. If you are worried, perhaps a guard could accompany me.'

'No. Have those who are sick up to the castle.' The sentence was given in a tone that brooked no argument.

'You are doctoring again, Lainie?'

Alexander looked up at Goult's mention of her pet name.

'I thought you would not keep her from it for long, Laird Ullyot, such is the gift she has for it.'

'Indeed. I was her first patient. My arm was dislocated in the battle at Heathwater.'

'Yet you allow her the practice of healing here in your keep? Noel could never abide the magic so close to home. Too little a man, I think. Too closed a mind. He allowed her to tend to his men in the battlefield, but that was all.' Goult's eyes narrowed. And Maddy knew why. She started to worry even as his old eyes shifted to Alexander.

'Perhaps, Laird Ullyot, we may have a talk?'

Alexander nodded.

'Without my niece,' Goult added and waited.

'No, I want to hear what it is—' Maddy began, but as both men turned to her she was silenced. Pure male will sliced through argument. With a twitch of her skirts she left, making sure that the door was not quite shut.

Goult patted down the bristles of his long white beard before he started with a question. 'Who was your father, Laird Ullyot?'

No one had ever asked him that directly before and Alex could barely believe he had heard the old man right. He stayed silent.

When Goult saw that he would not answer, he continued. 'Lainie's grandmother holds a letter that identifies Jemima as the King of Scotland's offspring. Were it to ever find its way into either court, her life would be forfeit.'

'How long has she had this letter?'

'For eleven years. Since the child's birth. But she is ill

and not expected to live through this next winter. And when she dies her effects will be sent to her oldest grandchild, Noel Falstone.'

'Hell.'

'My thoughts exactly, Lord Ullyot, but there is also another problem. No Scottish force of any size could travel unnoticed so far down into England. You could only send a few men to retrieve the letter and they would need to be completely trustworthy.'

Alex ignored the old man's words. Goult was English. He would not understand the insult he had just given and as such it was better to place the criticism of his men down to national ignorance. He changed tack completely. 'Does Madeleine know of this letter?'

'No.'

'Don't tell her, then. She's damnably impulsive as far as the welfare of her sister goes.'

Alex detected a smile and didn't like its implications. He knew what Goult was about to ask even before he did so.

'Could you get the letter? And destroy it?'

'It would be dangerous.'

'I would not expect you to do this for nothing.'

'Indeed?'

'Nay, I would pay you well with land.'

Alexander laughed. 'You promise me the same riches your niece at one time did. I told her a dead man has no need of material wealth.'

'And what of the wealth of sheep?'

'You have sheep on these lands?'

'Indeed I do, my lord. A flock to rival that of the Hungerfords on the rolling chalk ridges above Sarum and a lively market for the broadcloth on the Continent as well. If you went tonight, you could be back before a sennight. I will watch over Madeleine for you and guard Jemima.' He stripped off a medallion he wore at his neck. 'I will write down the directions to Vorpeth for you to follow, but, to make her believe that you are who you say, you will need to give Josephine this. Tell her Goult has sent you and that you have Eleanor's daughters safe at Ashblane.'

The smile Goult gave him was as worrying as his next words.

'I have heard you to be an honourable man, Laird Ullyot. And, indeed, if Bruce blood flows in your veins, Jemima would be your cousin of sorts. Had you thought of that?'

Alex frowned as he reached out for the medallion. Cousin or not, he could not allow the wolves of war to pull a child to pieces under the banner of protection. As Goult nodded his head, he realised the wiles of an old man had outwitted him completely. And he knew also it was not for the promise of the wealth of broadcloth that he had agreed to go.

Quinlan fair shivered in front of him, the image of his disbelief mirrored in the blade that he honed with a loadstone.

'I canna believe this is your wish, Alexander. She's an

English whore with half the armies of every enemy we have after her and the scorn of two kingdoms, and ye'd be thinking of protecting her. She's cast a spell, that's what she's done. It's the bloody de Cargne magic and you're the victim this time. Can't you see that? And now this journey down into England, to accomplish what exactly? To see her grandmother because she is ill? And if we cannot defend the keep with you gone, what then? Does Gillion die and Kitty? Do you expect the men and women of Ashblane to lay down their lives for that of the enemy's sister?'

'No. David will not come until after the Yuletide. He has given me that time.'

Anger mixed equally with puzzlement in Quinlan's voice. 'And if you die?'

'Then you must hold Ashblane till David comes.'

'And if the others come first?'

'Hold them off and wait for the King.' He wrenched off his signet ring and handed it over. 'Give David this with the deeds of Ashblane and swear allegiance to him, for he would not destroy an army that is loyal in the face of the wrath of both Edward of England and the church.'

'I can't believe you would think to do this. It's everything we've ever—'

Alex did not let him finish.

'I would hold you to a promise of keeping Madeleine, Jemmie, Gillion and Katherine safe.'

'So it's Jemmie now, too? The page?' Raw anger threaded his face, but Alexander ignored it.

'I have never asked you to do anything that was not important to me, Quin. Believe me when I say this is vitally so.' He was relieved when the man before him nodded. 'If all looks lost, send them through to France, with the largest band of soldiers you can muster.'

He said the words quietly as he ran his hands through his hair, knotting the length through a leather tie he held at his wrist.

'Lord.' Quinlan stalked around the room. 'Lord,' he repeated. 'Could we not just hope that they will tire of laying siege for a single woman, Alex?'

Alexander thought of Jemmie and the easy whisperings of treason. Greed, power and land. And two women who could legitimately call up the disenchanted masses of Scotland's enemies and lay threat to the seat of the Edinburgh royalty. He could not allow that.

Slapping his palms against his thighs, he stood, catching his reflection in the mirrored glass above the hearth plate. In this light the scar that crossed his ruined cheek was plainly seen and he wondered again at the fact that Madeleine Randwick seldom stared at it the way most other women did.

He'd given little quarter to the wiles and ways of women in his life. Alice had been his wife for four years and yet he had barely known her, and any other liaison prior to his marriage, and since, had been transitory and expendable. He smiled to himself and brought his knife out of his boot, taking the liming stone from the mantle and sitting down to sharpen it.

Truth be told, the times he had spent in the company of the opposite sex since Alice's passing had been negligible. He'd almost been a saint for damn near on five years, save for the few meetings he had had with Isabella after she had come to Kimdean. War had taken his energies and the lonely isolation of Ashblane had underlined his position. He hadn't wanted to take the girls of families he lived with as consorts; though sometimes he had welcomed the advances of the village tavern wenches, the times were far and few between. And he never felt satisfied afterwards.

Celibacy and loneliness. The double-edged sword of a warrior.

Until now.

Madeleine.

His knife slipped off the stone and cut into the flesh on his left hand. Swearing, he dropped the blade in his lap and brought the gash to his mouth, pressing it against the butt of his tongue and waiting for the blood to stop flowing.

Madeleine?

What was he to do with her? Even the mention of her name in his mind had the lust running to his loins and filling the spaces of emptiness, the safety of his keep pressing against his own needs as a man.

Keeping her here until he saw what the English barons would do might be the wisest option. Perhaps if they saw his intentions they would back off, give him the space he needed to see her and her sister safe.

England.

God, how he hated the damp lowness of the place. And he was due to depart for it within the hour.

Chapter Fourteen

Madeleine tailed behind Alexander at a good distance, knowing that he would see her if she got too close. Sometimes she lost him completely and then she would see him again cresting a hillock or as a far-off flash of green and white between the boughs of trees. He wasn't travelling fast. For that she was grateful. And then she could no longer see him at all, not even from the high ground that she had ascended, with the wide valleys around the River Esk spread out before her.

'Damn it,' she muttered to herself and looked around. She had seen no sign of habitation for the past two hours and did not even know if she still stood on Ullyot ground as she travelled west, the sun in her face and the faint stir of air at her back. The danger of it all left her breathless. Should she press on or should she turn around?

Someone hit her broadside, flinging her from her horse and to the ground in one fluid movement and, as the breath was knocked out of her lungs, she felt the sharp prick of a well-honed knife at her throat. Alexander Ullyot's pale eyes above her radiated with shock and fury.

'Madeleine. Hell. Madeleine.' He could barely splutter her name as he sheathed the knife and rolled away, the muscles in his cheeks grinding though he stayed silent, their heavy breathing the only sound around them.

'Why have you followed me?' he said at length, his voice strained and over-polite.

'I knew you were…going to get…the letter…for Jemmie…' She was still winded and every word was hard to say.

'Goult told you this?' he asked incredulously, as if revising his good opinion of her uncle downwards.

'No, I listened at the door. I overheard your plan and came to help. I know where the letter will be kept and if my grandmother becomes difficult…'

'Where is it?' He prickled with impatience. 'The letter,' he added as he saw her puzzlement.

Suddenly she knew his game. 'If I tell you, you will make me go back.'

Rage made his eyes blaze. 'Where is it, Madeleine?'

'I think it will be in a carved box she used to keep beneath her bed. There is a secret cache in the bottom, opened by pushing the sapphire on the side. Josephine showed me once.'

She had had plenty of practice in her life to be able to tell when a man was at the very end of his tether.

'Good.' He threw her reins across the head of her horse and turned it around.

'I can help you get them,' she began desperately. 'I can gain us entry as a granddaughter.'

'No. It's too dangerous.'

'Not this way. It's much more dangerous to just charge in. The Earl of Anthony has a considerable number of re-tainers, and he—'

'I was hardly going to just charge in.'

'Jemmie is my sister, Alexander. This is my duty, too.' He flinched at her use of his first name. She had never said it before and he liked the sound of it off her lips, with her prissy English accent and her husky voice. He felt himself losing ground.

'It will take three days to get there and we will be alone. Do you mean to stay with me alone at night, Lady Rand-wick?' Perhaps he could scare her off.

Colouring, she remained quiet and he knew she would not answer when her teeth worried the skin on her bottom lip. The nervousness angered him unreasonably. In woollen hose and jacket and with her hair jammed beneath a straw hat, all obviously borrowed from a stable hand, Madeleine Randwick looked magnificent. His eyes ran across the rounded swell of her buttocks and the long lines of her legs.

'If you come, you must obey me implicitly. We'll be in and out. No more. If I say run, you run. If I say go, you'll go. If I say ride, you will ride. Understand?'

'Yes.'

'Are you armed?'

'I have my knife.' She retrieved a small dagger from her jacket pocket.

'And can you use it?'

She hesitated. 'I know the weak points in a body. In my surgery…'

'Lord. Do you know how to use it? To defend yourself?'

'I think so.'

'Give it to me.'

She handed it over promptly and he took her hand in his own as she did so. 'Show me how you hold it.'

She took the knife and held the shaft tight in her fist, the blade curving upward.

'No, like this.' He turned the grip around in her hand. 'You will not be strong enough to bring the blade up from below. A stab down will be much more effective, especially with your weight behind it.'

She smelt the wool of his tartan as he came closer.

'Now come at me.'

'Pardon?'

'Use it on me. Practise on me.'

Raising her dagger, she brought it down, carefully, so as not to hurt him.

'Properly!'

She tried again and almost fell over as her balance tilted.

'Keep your weight on your front foot. Like this. If you need to move back, do this.' Fisting his knifeless hand he showed her the angle at which to attack.

She copied immediately.

'Better. Now come at me like you mean it.'

She missed him again.

'If you can't do better than that, I'm putting you on your horse for Ashblane.'

She lunged.

'Still paltry, Lady Randwick.' But the lights in his eyes danced as he feinted away. 'With a defence like that, anyone could take you. And will.'

'Try it,' she shouted at him, angry now both at her ineptitude and his laughter, and he did so, moving with the grace she had become so accustomed to, the knife knocked from her hand as his big body pinned itself against her own.

'Now do you see your frailty, Madeleine,' he whispered in her ear, 'and the danger that it could cause us both?'

'No.' Bringing up her knee, she kicked him, though amusement was the only response until she bit the exposed skin on his arm near his wrist and he let her go. Reclaiming her knife, she raised it and circled, staying on the balls of her feet in the way that he had shown her, and feinting to the left and right. The blade went through the sleeve of his jacket, the heavy wool ripping and pulling her full up against him as his evasion tipped her balance.

'Much better,' he said quietly, though there was an edge to his voice she had not heard before. Questioningly she looked up. Alexander Ullyot's hair was loose, his face unshaven, and his eyes were dark and dangerous. She felt his arms tighten across her back and the hard ridge of his manhood thicken. For a moment she wondered what would happen were she to lean into him, turn her lips towards his, run her fingers through the gold and corn of his hair. But she could not do it. Not with the anger vibrating between them. She was both relieved and saddened when he let her go and handed her back the knife.

Panting, she pocketed it and sat down against the trunk of a tree. 'Are you not afraid to instruct your enemy on the finer points of knifemanship, given it may be you to feel the prick of my blade in an unguarded moment?'

'*Are* you my enemy, Madeleine?'

'No,' she whispered.

As the sun glinted in his hair, Maddy felt overwhelmed by the danger of her situation. He was not a man to be trifled with. She could see this in the strong lines of his body and in the hard planes of his face.

'You'll take me with you, then?' She injected as much coolness into the question as was possible, wanting distance to survive.

'Yes.' His reply was given in much the same tone, eyes flat now and guarded.

They rode for two more hours before stopping and Madeleine clung to the saddle for support as she dismounted. If Alexander Ullyot had not been so near she might well have dropped to the ground and crawled over to the grassy mounds he had indicated as a place to sleep. All she wanted was stillness and rest. The fire he started was warm, though, and as she recovered her equilibrium she wondered at the wisdom of such a beacon.

'You are not worried the flames will attract visitors?' she queried when he handed her a piece of bread and beef.

'Nay. This is Turnbull land. We've no enemies here.'

'When did we cross out of the dangerous lands, then?'

'This afternoon, at the Woodhill stream.'

And yet they had seen no one all day. Testimony to his ability to pass through unnoticed, she decided, wondering when and where he had learnt his art of warfare.

'Why did you come?' she asked suddenly. 'Why did you not send others to do this task? You would still have Goult's promised lands if others from Ashblane were successful.'

'Because your sister is, in effect, my cousin. I felt a bond.'

The implications of his statement sunk in. 'Then you acknowledge you are the cousin of David?'

'Yes.' Staccato. Abrupt. Angry.

'I heard it whispered as a truth when my mother and I were at the court of David, though I never saw you.'

'No.'

'Where were you?'

He grabbed at a stick and fed it into the fire, piece by piece. She noticed the leather straps about his wrist to give added strength to the wielding of a sword. She noticed also the way he held the wood, his skin white against the knuckles.

'I was in France for a time.'

'But I was only twelve when we came to the Scottish court. How old would you have been?'

'Young enough to think myself invincible and old enough to be able to wield a sword. There's a difference, mind, in the thinking of it and the doing of it when you've just fifteen years.'

He lifted his head and their eyes met across the fire. And in his she glimpsed the core of the boy he must have been once. Vulnerable and lonely. Surprised, she looked down.

'Were you hurt?'

'Aye, many times. The knight I served in France was a man who thought that every battle against the English was preordained to end in our victory. There were some that did not.'

Maddy was caught up in this fascinating cameo of a younger Alexander Ullyot. And because he so seldom let her know what he was thinking, she pressed on with her questions.

'You told me once you were in Egypt? When was that?'

The look he gave her was guarded as though he were weighing up the purpose behind the question.

'After the siege of Calais.'

'But I thought no prisoners were taken in Calais.'

'You thought right. After Edward spared the lives of the city we caught a ship to Scotland and hit a storm off the coast of Ireland. When a merchant ship from the city of Alexandria offered aid, I took the opportunity of accepting it—the court of Scotland had always been difficult for me and the promise of adventure was…' He stopped and tried to find the right word. 'Exhilarating.' He laughed and looked directly at her. There was no humour in his eyes. 'After discharging our cargo in England, we went on to Alexandria where the hospitality of Al-Nasir Muhammed dulled my purpose for travelling home, although after a year or so the newness of everything waned. And waned again when I would not convert to Islam.' His fingers felt along the raised skin of his cheek. 'I got this in a fight in Cairo during the second year of my travels. For a while I thought I would not see the green hills of Liddesdale again, for it festered. Badly.' Chucking the last of the wood into the fire, he was quiet.

'Obviously you recovered.'

He grinned. 'The haemorrhaging in my skin meant my face never returned to what it had been, but I learnt a lesson that day that I've never forgotten.'

He stopped and Maddy prodded him on.

'A lesson?'

'Home is the only thing worth the fighting for, worth the dying for. Home and hearth and family. So when I came back to Scotland it was'na to the court and its politics that I went, but Ashblane.'

'Your mother was there?'

'Nay. She died when I was young. Up at the foot of the Glenshie in the Highlands where I was born. But her own people were.'

There it was again, that sense of lonely distance. And here was part of the reason. He had had even less of a family life than she had.

'And your wife. Alice?'

'She was Ian's sister and young. Her husband had been killed a month or two before I came home and I felt a duty to her.'

An arranged marriage, then, and not a love match. Madeleine was surprised at the sense of relief she felt and was pleased Alexander was lying on his back and looking up at the stars.

The fire between them burned warmly, throwing shadows into the undergrowth and above them the heavens seemed endless. The first night in a week when it had not rained, though a ring of clouds circled the moon. Tomorrow it would be colder.

'When I married Lucien, I thought that we would have children and live happily ever after. That we would have a home and that the people of Heathwater would be as family to me. It was the first home I had truly had, you see, for with Eleanor it was always a constant move. So when Noel, under the auspices of Edward, arranged the marriage and offered me a place, I went. And then—' She stopped and caught her breath.

And then I knew that I was barren. Barren.

The word said even in her mind was jarring, tearing away possibility and hope and future.

The barren Witch of Heathwater.

How often had Noel called her that? How often had he taunted her with the codicils of her mother's will and brought forth yet another of his friends to try and make it different?

She remembered the procession with an ache. Men who would wake in her bed in the morning with the illusions that she had planted there. Just illusions, although once or twice, before the effects of her draughts had taken shape, her would-be swains had become violent.

'And then?'

She smiled as she watched the sky, remembering that it was Alexander Ullyot who had told her of the name Scotland knew her by.

'And then I became the Black Widow.'

He laughed, a low rumbling laugh that warmed the coldness in her and chased away the anger. Catching her hand to his, he held it across the small space between them, his tongue caressing the skin of her palm before he let her go. The wetness chilled against the air and made her shiver, a thin pain of want and need threading through caution.

If only he would come closer…

'I'm thinking the name "Black Widow" does not suit you, Lady Randwick. You are too soft and shapely.'

'What would you call me, then?' Madeleine became braver.

'I would call you a puzzle,' he returned quickly. 'And if others call you a witch, then maybe there's some truth in that, too.'

'Did your mother mind being called a witch?'

'As I was only four when she passed on I can't say that I remember. You remind me a lot of her, though. Not in looks, but in the core of strength you have. From all the stories I have heard of her, she had that, too.'

Madeleine blushed. 'I thank you for the compliment, Alexander Ullyot.' There was pleasure in her voice.

'Many women would have taken that as something else entirely, Lady Randwick, and acted upon it. For a widow you are remarkably innocent.' The gleam in his eyes was easily seen by the light of the fire, the pale silver shot with flame.

Innocent? When she longed to throw herself at him and run her fingers through the living gold of his hair? Skin to skin, breath to breath, bone to bone. It took everything that she had to keep her hands still. He would want a barren woman as little as her husband had and she knew that she could not bear to see in his face what she had come to know well in Lucien's.

Pity.

Nay. From Alexander Ullyot such a thing would break her heart. Better to feign distance and keep respect. At least that way when he left her she might weather it. She would not daydream of what could never be. She had Jemmie to consider and Goult. An old man and a child and hundreds of miles between her and safety. There was no point in weaving baseless hopes into happy endings.

Rolling over towards the darkness of the woods, she stretched out the muscles in her legs. Her brother had never encouraged her in the use of horses from his stable and Eleanor had always had a lively dislike of anything equestrian. The freedom of today was exhilarating. Alexander Ullyot was exhilarating.

And forbidden!

Smiling into the darkness, she closed her eyes and listened to the sounds of the night.

Alexander waited until she was asleep before he stood. He never slept well. Not since he had sold his soul to the brother of the merchant he had been boarded with in his second year in Egypt. He smiled, struck by the irony of it all.

…at the court of David, though I never saw you. Where were you?

Madeleine's words floated back and he tensed.

Where were you? Where were you?

Lifting his left arm into the moonlight, he traced the tattooed mark on the fleshy part above his elbow and prayed to God that Madeleine might never find out about his lost years in Egypt.

Seventeen. You did things at seventeen to survive that you would not have contemplated later. Images of blood, death and screams overrode the peace of this night and he pulled up his sword to hone the notches of it to smoothness against the glow of the fire. One day someone would tell Madeleine Randwick the full extent of his sins. He wondered if perhaps it should be him to broach the subject first—that way at least there would be some truth amongst the lies. *Not yet*, his conscience whispered. *Not just yet.*

His glance travelled across her face, the fire burnishing her hair as its shadows and light played across high cheekbones and porcelain skin. So delicate, so fine. His glance slid lower to slender legs easily outlined under the plaid. Tomorrow he would ask her to put on the skirt that he had seen in her bag, for the tight hose she wore were too distracting.

He smiled as he mulled over her reaction to his compliment. She had blushed beet red. And he had wanted to give her more. Wanted to take her hand in his and pull her across to him and show her just exactly what he meant by it.

God, and just what did he mean by it?

The sky was tinged with the first tendrils of pink before he finally fell asleep.

Chapter Fifteen

They saw no one at all the next morning as they tracked through the broad sweeps of countryside. By mid-day all Maddy wanted to do was to stop and get down off her horse, but Alexander prodded on undaunted, backtracking sometimes along the higher ridges. For protection, she was to think later, though he never explained any action he did or did not take. Indeed, he was unbearably distant. Focused on survival and flight and camouflage, he moved purposefully through the hills, stopping every ten or so minutes just to listen to the sounds of birds or look at the way the dust whorls lay on the track. He took nothing for granted and held his hand ready above the hilt of his sword at all times. Stealthy. Dangerous. Alert. She felt his channelled power, and marvelled at it.

And then, as the sun lay just above the far-off hills, he led her down into a glade backed by stone and she wondered why they had left the track. Ten minutes later she knew, as a dozen men trailed down the ridge opposite them.

'They are the Kerrs,' Alexander said. 'This is their land we cross before we reach England.'

'You knew they were here?'

'They've been shadowing us all afternoon.' He took a leather strap from his bag and tied back his hair. A knife was jammed into his shoulder pouch and another she had not seen before was hooked into the belt of his plaid. With the claymore at his back and the crossbow and falchion tied to his saddle, he was well armed and showing it. She noticed the position where they waited, his horse before hers and the cliff behind them. Quickly reaching into her pocket for her own knife, she jammed the hilt between her fingers.

'Keep your blade out of sight,' he cautioned. 'And don't speak. I will keep you safe.'

She wished she had left the woollen hose on and wished too that she had worn her hat. The Kerrs all watched her closely as they filed into the hollow, and Alexander waited until one older man came forward from the others.

'Brian Kerr. I trust you are well.' Alexander's tone was mild. Why, he acted as if he were riding down the street and had come across some old acquaintances.

'I am that, Laird Ullyot, though I am also curious to know what brings ye across our lands?' The look in the man's eyes was watchful. Something else lingered there, too, for his hand trembled as he held it out.

Alexander's handshake was stronger. 'I am bound for England.'

'With this woman? We have heard rumours of the sister of Falstone…'

Alexander Ullyot hesitated for a moment, slate eyes slashing across her, the colour darkening as he seemed to make up his mind about something. Leaning over, he placed her right hand in his left one, threading their fingers together and raising the joined fists. 'Lady Madeleine Randwick is my wife, by handfast.' The pressure of his clasp strengthened as she went to argue. *Handfast?* She had heard of the custom from Katherine. It was a betrothal of sorts. For a year and a day. But why should he think to even say such a thing? And then she understood as more than twenty of the Kerr riders lined up behind them. Only bravado and authority would ward off challenge and Alexander was vulnerable. By himself he may have risked the chase, but with her…

She swallowed back protest and nudged her horse closer.

'Handfast, you say.' The old Kerr watched her closely, sizing up the situation. She did not dare speak and was glad when he looked away and called forth the allegiances of shared kin and allies.

She felt Alexander relax as he did so, answering him name for name with the supporters of Ashblane, and when the Kerr leader lowered his weapons and called for the others to do the same she let out the breath she hadn't realised she was holding.

'We will part company on the morrow, Ullyot, but tonight will you consider joining us in some food and wine?'

'We would be grateful for it.' Alex sheathed his own sword, though he kept his knife visible as he dismounted and turned towards her.

Usually she got down from a horse by herself, but today she let him help her; indeed, stood close as he removed her steed's bridle and saddle. The group of thirty men, who all looked as if they had seen neither bath nor bed for at least a month, were unnerving to say the least and the diminishing light added to her worry. Where would they all sleep? As a wife she could hardly be seen to make up her pallet on the opposite side of the fire to her husband. And in this company she certainly would not want to. The problem was solved as Alexander drew her to one side and prepared a bed against the base of a large stone and a little out of the way of the others.

'We'll leave at first light,' he said softly and laid his arm across her shoulder. Startled, she began to drag it away.

'Pretence, Madeleine,' he qualified as he held on tightly, 'is as important as the bravado. As a sorceress you should at least know that.'

'That's why you told them we were handfast?'

He nodded and rolled out his plaid. 'If you had been an unattached female travelling alone with me, I should imagine Brian Kerr would see it as his right to share the favour. This way they know that, if they touch you, I would have to kill them.'

'Yet he has heard of me?' She was shy in her query. The reputation she had suffered could be often seen in the leering eyes of strangers. She had seen it in Brian Kerr's and knew Alexander must have, too.

'Who has not heard of the bad and dangerous Lady Randwick?' he countered and laughed. 'But tonight your reputation helps us.'

'How so?'

'If the Kerrs cross themselves when you look at them and see the sorcery of the de Cargnes in your every glance, then it is a protection. For whatever you have heard of my fighting prowess, my lady, let it be known that even I could not hope to ward off single-handed the serious attack of thirty men.'

So he too had wondered as to the motives of the Kerrs. Yet not in a glance or a word or a gesture had he betrayed his thoughts.

'You think them dangerous?'

'Out here everything is dangerous,' he replied obliquely and began to rub down the coat of her horse.

A fire was started and a whisky keg, belted to one side of a large black stallion, cut free. Beef and bread and surprisingly good cheese added to the feast and Maddy was pleased to sit beside Alexander and eat.

Now the talk turned to campaigns and battles and Brian Kerr was not one to beat about the bush.

'The Baron Falstone does not make an easy enemy, Laird Ullyot, and word has it he wants his sister back.'

She felt Alexander stiffen.

'And what do they say of David's reaction to Noel's demands?'

'They say he will wait until after the New Year to make a decision. To give you time to sort out your own house, it is said in some quarters, though others speak of a rebellion should you not see fit to bring Madeleine Randwick to court. A land question, I think. Something of a corridor into England?' Speculation was evident in his questions. 'Many of the barons are unhappy, Laird Ullyot. They could be cajoled into open revolt should you lead an uprising.'

Alexander upended his drinking horn. 'Revolt would rip the clans to pieces, Brian, and Ashblane has always answered to the King of Scotland, no matter how misguided his edicts.'

This sentiment relaxed things considerably and rumbling laughter shook the bellies of the men around the fire. Not true converts to the power of royalty or rebellion then, Madeleine thought and thankfully took a sip of her whisky. Pure uncut fire raced through her veins, welcome in the coldness of night and after the length of the day. Finishing the horn of whisky, she was promptly handed another, the smoke of the fire and the burn of the drink making her comfortably weary.

She leaned against Alexander and did not remove his arm as it lay across her shoulder. Let them believe that I am his wife, she thought. She could smell the heavy dampness of wool on him and the dusty odour of horse. But

it was the underlying scent that had her closing her eyes
and reaching for an elusive familiarity. Pure masculinity
and a tinge of lye soap. Not a man prone to perfumes or
herbs. She blushed and pulled away at the errant train of
her thoughts, setting some distance between them. If he
noticed he gave no sign of it, merely shifting his own
position to accommodate hers and taking up another horn
of whisky until she caught his eyes across the small
distance between them and everything stilled. For a second
Madeleine felt something stronger than her magic, something more real, some dancing life-filled thing that hung
about the clearing and breathed in the silvered essence of
him.

And was then gone.

She broke the contact and turned away, shock claiming
her composure, as want, lust and need all drove through
her in a welter of emotion, skinning the edge off everything
else. If they had been alone, she would have taken him then
in the way her mother had taken her lovers, without thought
or worry for the future. Taken her fingers and run them
down the red-gold pelt on his chest and then run them
lower. She smiled at her ridiculous thoughts and placed the
whisky away from temptation. She could well imagine Alexander's reaction to such a blatant invitation and especially with Brian Kerr sitting next to him with his thirty
men behind.

A shout from the forest changed the mood in a moment
and Alexander was on his feet, sword in hand, dragging her

up and shielding her with his body as a group of Scotsmen broke from the trees.

Brian Kerr was the first to fall, a clean slice to the neck, his bubbling cries for help making the skin on Maddy's neck crawl. There was nothing she could have done anyway, save hold him. Already the glazed opaqueness of death clouded his eyes. Alexander had stepped back and taken her with him into the covering of the trees. Hastily he forced a hole in the bracken and pushed her into it. 'Stay here. If anyone comes, scream. I'll hear you.'

He was gone before she could answer, his sword swiping with finesse at the band of men before him. This was the man of the legends and well she could see how they had grown. Gone were the measured moves of the mock battles on the fields outside Ashblane. Here the raw hard strength of muscle was blindingly evident. As was his grace, when thrust and counter-thrust were easily thwarted. At fifteen he might have been vulnerable; at twenty-eight he was untouchable. She could see it in the stance of his body, utterly relaxed in graceful menace. How paltry her efforts at self-defence must have seemed to him yesterday when today, with just a single swipe, his blade felled grown men. Always before she had seen battles at a distance, had not experienced the noise or the smell or the sheer blinding force of them.

She had closed her eyes against the chaos for a moment when a sound to the left had her frozen with terror. She could see the silhouette of a man poised above her, his sword raised against the night. Screaming, she rolled out into the open and away from him, bringing her dagger up against his leg and nicking it even as he kicked hard at her arm to dislodge the blade from her fingers. A keening cry from Alexander had them both turning and everything changed into slow motion. The sword coming down across her leg. Her own cry as the pain hit her. Alexander's dive at her attacker. The blade of his sword crossing throat midair and the heel of his foot breaking the neck as he landed. Time suspended in pain and blood and breathing until Alexander was above her, his eyes tender in the moonlight, and worried. No noise was left save silence.

'Ah, love,' he crooned as he bent down to her. 'Stay still while I see to your leg.'

'No.' She tried to crawl away, tried to see to it herself, but everything was shaking. Her hands, her head, her teeth, chattering in the sudden cold of the night. All around she could see the countenances of the Kerrs as their faces faded in and out of vision. Alexander Ullyot was the only one who truly seemed to be there, his shimmering silver aura blackened at the edges.

'I used my knife like you said…'

'Shh.' His whisper was husky as he lifted her hand into his. 'Don't talk. You'll need your strength.' She felt the light brush of his lips against her wrist.

Savage anger consumed Alexander. He could not believe one of the Haigs had got past him and found Madeleine. He never made such mistakes. Never. Until today.

Until now. Until knowing that she watched him from behind the bush, he had become cocky and compromised his fighting skills with vanity.

And this was the result.

With his free hand he bent to lift up the material of her skirt. She pulled it down and tried to move away. Her blood flowed through the material of her dress, soaking redness with a scent of iron.

With a bellow he grabbed her good arm and anchored her to the spot, flipping the skirt up easily and scowling at the sight before him. The wound was long, slices of her dress material and dust caking the slash.

Pressing his hand down where he could see the pulsations above the wound, the flow eased considerably. What now? he thought wildly. What the hell would Hale have done next?

'Don't burn it…clean it…' Maddy was having trouble speaking.

'Seal it…use whisky…a poultice of whisky, and then bind it. With clean cloth. Use my petticoats.'

She clutched at his hand with her good one and held it close to her face, tucking it beneath her chin and leaning into it as he touched her leg. When he felt wetness against his skin he cursed again. She looked so damn little and hurt. And above her knee she wore silken rose ribbons to hold up her stockings. Fragile. Feminine. Gentle.

Loosening the garter, he rolled down the stocking on her right leg, ruined from the blade of the knife and blood. A dainty band of plaited gold adorned her ankle, a small womanly vanity. His frown hardened as he heard the collective sigh of the Kerrs. They saw her as the others at court did no doubt. A fallen woman with loose morals and questionable ways. He would kill the first man who voiced these thoughts aloud. He swore it.

'You'll bring her home to our place then?' Andrew Kerr, Brian's brother, met his glance as indecision swamped him. Alliances were easy to break and he did not want to be trapped with Madeleine alone in the Kerr keep. Nay, better to weather it outside, for here in the forest he retained a small piece of control. A tug on his hand brought his eyes up to Madeleine's face.

'If I take the fever and die, Alexander, will you promise to bury me at Ashblane?'

He jumped back as if he had been stung. Did she have some premonition of her own death?

'Please,' she added shakily, misinterpreting his fright as anger. 'I was happy there…safe… I could stay with you… for ever…safe.'

'Stop it, Madeleine. You are damn well not going to die.' His fingers pressed down upon the artery on the inside of her shin and he counted the rate of her pulse.

'How can you know that?'

'Because I bloody well won't let you.'

She smiled and fainted away.

She came awake in a forest filled with shadows. Alexander was beside her, slumped against the trunk of a tree, eyes closed and the dark growth of a long day easily seen on his face. Across his lap lay his sword, unsheathed and ready, and in the quiet of the night she could hear his breathing. She raised her arm and reached towards him, the movement bringing him awake, though he had to focus momentarily as if to remember where he was.

'Water.' She could barely say the word.

Leaning forward, he used his arms to lever her up and her world spun as he offered her his bottle. When she gripped tighter, his worried eyes searched hers.

'Where are the Kerrs?'

'Gone to scour the land for Haigs.'

'Haigs?'

'The clan that attacked us. Their holding is just to the north.'

Her fingers crept into his and she was pleased when he made no move.

'Why did they attack us?'

'God only knows, for I don't.' The warmth of his hand reassured her in the shimmering cold of night. 'They signed a treaty with the Kerrs last summer. That should have put them as friends.'

'And the battle? Were there other casualties?'

'Brian died along with five of his clansmen, but Andrew Kerr will flush them out or run them off. They will'na be back.'

'Who bandaged my leg?'

'Me.'

Wriggling her toes just to make sure that the feeling was still in them, she felt immeasurably better. Even the pain was minimal. 'You have some skill.'

A curt nod was the only reaction and unexpectedly she coloured. She remembered flashes of the hours gone by. His arms around her as they had sat here alone and the quietly whispered encouragement that, in a different situation, might have doubled as love words. And what might she have said back to him in her state of compromised rationality and especially given her earlier thoughts?

'When a person is in shock they ramble. If I said anything…'

'You didn't.'

Unhappily, she blushed. She could not in all honesty leave it at that, for she did remember telling him to bury her at his home if she died, and on his land. Looking away, she began again. 'I have spent the last ten years of my life uncertain about whether or not I would wake up in the morning. At Ashblane I felt…' she floundered for an adjective '…safe. I felt safe. With you I feel safe.' She looked at him directly now, a thick lump in the back of her throat. 'You are the only person who has ever made me feel that way.'

Please let him understand. Please don't let him laugh.

'Lord help me, Madeleine.' His voice was husky and the silence of midnight beat down upon the spaces between his words. 'When I see your brother next I shall kill him, not for what he has done to me and my clan, but for what he has done to you.'

Her smile was wobbly. 'See that you do that,' she whispered and was surprised by the intensity of anger in his eyes. Obsidian grey. And dark. And something else was there, too. A pain of longing pierced her deep inside and snaked up through her stomach to blossom warmly around the edges of her heart. This was the feeling the ballads spoke of and the jesters and minstrels.

She could barely take in enough air though it was not the breathing sickness that robbed her of breath, but wonder, not pain that held her still, but amazement, for she had fallen in love with Alexander Ullyot despite every warning not to.

Reaching up to his face, she stroked a finger across the raspy hardness of his cheek, her heartbeat accelerating as his hand caught at her hair and brought her mouth slowly into his own.

He was not gentle and she was glad. His lips met hers in a searing blistering explosion of lust, weeks of wanting sandwiched between this very moment and a future stretching only into difficulty.

His tongue forced open her lips and plundered the softness inside and she felt her body buck up against his own, wanting, asking, needing. Stretching her hands around his neck, her fingers caught at his hair, freezing as he tugged at the straps of her shift.

He stopped then as if in question and she wordlessly answered him, her hands bringing his head down towards her, all thoughts of shyness dispatched by his expertise. At this moment there was no pain, no damning arguments of impossibility, no Noel, no Eleanor, no kings. Just this feeling of safety mixed with love and an aching longing to hold the warmth of Alexander Ullyot close. To know his strength, his scent, his body beneath her fingers. To know what it truly felt like to have a man like him hold her, love her, touch her. She frowned when he drew back.

'I would not wish to hurt your leg.' Not quite a question. She felt like crying. It was not pity she was after. For years she had been sequestered with a weak and puny husband, whose few forays to her bedroom had ranged from disappointing to violent, before ceasing altogether. She had never known what it was that other women sometimes whispered about, the light in their eyes telling Madeleine of an undiscovered secret she had not been privy to. And now here she was with the one man in all of the world who held the ability to show her, and he remarked on her sore leg.

Frustration suddenly overwhelmed her and she batted away his arm. Perhaps she was never to know what she wanted, perhaps he did not wish to show her, perhaps the feelings that consumed her were completely and absolutely unreturned by him, though her breath caught again as his fingers banded about her shoulders and he looked at her closely, and not indifferently. Whereas Lucien had preferred little girls, she could see in Alexander's eyes that his preference was for a woman.

For her.

Holding his glance, she pushed the straps of her under-garment aside and felt the cold air harden her nipples.

Alex's heart slammed into the wall of his chest, for the invitation he could see in Madeleine's eyes was not difficult to miss. Neither was the outline of dusky pink nipples on top of full rounded breasts and skin that glowed satin soft in the moonlight. Wetting his forefinger, he reached out and drew it across her top lip, liking the way her head went back, the corded veins of her neck attesting to her trembling emotion.

Lord, he breathed out. How long was it since he had felt like this? Never with Alice. Sometimes with the whores of Alexandria as they did things to him in the night-time places of the cushioned salons in the old Palace of Kala'un. And now with the Lady of Randwick with her de Cargne sorcery and her molten red hair.

The mark at her breast beckoned him and he touched it first with his thumb and then with his lips, coming down on one nipple and tugging hard. She gasped and he tugged again.

'Alexander.' Her fingers slid into his hair, no soft touch, either. He felt the ramrod stiffness of his sex with a groan. She went to pieces on a whisper, felt her body reaching for something she had not known before, the cold and lonely Witch of Heathwater melted in a single moment of careful loving by a man who was a master. On and on the waves of pleasure brushed across her body. Heat and warmth and promise.

And finally horror.

He sat there fully clothed and smiling, his eyes on the

hard nubs of her nipples and the sheen of perspiration that covered her.

Embarrassment roiled across everything else. He had barely touched her and she had gone up like a flame, like a living spark, like a wanton woman.

Like her mother.

'I am sorry.' She barely knew what to say. Lucien had always been angered by her coldness. And now here with Alexander she had disgraced herself with exactly the opposite.

'I have never been good at this….'

'This?' There was a catch in his voice.

'This lovemaking,' she qualified. 'Though usually I…' She made herself continue. 'Usually I feel nothing.'

There, it was said. Out. He could take it as he liked.

'I am barren, you see. A lot of land and gold, but no chance for an heir. It is the final irony, I think. Eleanor codiciled me to the promise of an heir and then she used a curse to for ever bind me to barrenness. For protection, she argued then, though now…'

She swallowed, hating the tears that pooled in her eyes.

Hating the thickness in her throat and the aching, aching loneliness of being exactly who she was.

His answer came as a caress. A small twist of his hand across her stomach settling at the line of her hips before falling lower.

The shift she wore was discarded easily and then she wore nothing as he lifted her across to him. Carefully. His shirt he had off in one quick movement and she noticed the blue of a tattoo banded around his left forearm. Intricate and foreign. And edged with newer scars. He jolted as she touched it. He has secrets, too, she thought, and tilted her head in query.

'Egypt,' he whispered. 'I think I told you once.'

'And they hurt you?'

'Yes.'

From a man who never admitted to any weakness or pain to a woman who had told him of her barrenness. There was a wholeness there, and a trust. A giving and a taking of secrets.

Her fingers splayed out across his chest, wide and muscle-strong with a fine sheen of gold hair etched into brownness. His nipples hardened as she ran her fingers across them.

'This is nice?'

'Aye. Verra nice.' His accent was thicker than usual.

She circled a nipple with her fingers and tweaked it as he had and then she laid her mouth against the smallness and sucked.

'Ifrinn.'

The expletive in Gaelic made her smile. She could affect him in the same way as he had her? Looking up, she saw that a fierce hunger dwelt, dark and powerful, in his silvered eyes. She felt the push of him from beneath her as he brought his fingers into the soft folds of her femininity, knowing her, exploring her and reassuring her when her whole body jolted in surprise.

'I would not hurt you.' His words were soft and yet he

was hard and big and ready, his heaviness pressing against her as he waited...for what?

For her, she was to think later. For her to be less afraid, for her to relax into a man who would love her well. His fingers probed deeper and she arched, the scent of her between them.

'You are a witch, Madeleine,' he said as he raised up her hips. 'If I did not know that before from your magic, I would do so now with your loving.' She felt him between her legs and groaned as his free hand caught her chin and turned her face to his. In it she caught all the desire she knew must be reflected in her own face. And yet it was not easy.

'It's been a long time since Lucien,' she offered simply and tried to move back, but he would not let her.

'Shhhh.' He gentled and pushed forward. Hard. She felt his fullness as a pain and opened further to adjust to the size of him, and the breeze that wrapped them in its chill was no match for the fiery heat of their bodies.

Sheathed in Madeleine, Alexander tried to calm his wants, tried to slow down, tried to still himself before he drew back and began again. But stillness was not an option and as she circled her hips he slid deeper and deeper until white-hot lust consumed him. Kneeling, he took her with him to the forest floor, the hard coldness of the flora making her gasp. She lifted her back as he slid the warmth of plaid beneath her, a barrier against the coldness and joining them even closer.

And then it started again as he built up a rhythm, his fingers fondling the hard nub of her hidden flesh, his manhood stroking a place never reached before.

'Is it here?' he asked and she saw his teeth white in the moonlight. 'Or is it here?' He shifted just slightly and her stomach clenched.

'Yes,' she breathed into his mouth and dug in her nails, bringing him closer, higher, tighter, until the crashing waves of fulfilment drowned out all uncertainty.

'Yes!' she shouted as she came and came and came again, her voice hoarse against this night-time silence, rolling shifting pangs of pleasure until he cried out too and held her very still. His heart thudded between them and as he tipped his face upwards she saw in the light of the moon a terrible joy, teeth clenched and eyes shut and the beads of perspiration full across his brow.

Afterwards he lay there stunned, his heart thundering in his ears like a drum of war. With Madeleine he could hold back nothing, and this feeling was new, for always had he kept a part of himself hidden.

When at last he had his breath, he rolled her to one side and anchored his hand across her bottom so they stayed joined as he shifted the weight off her sore leg. Their breaths mingled, a small island of heat amongst the coldness of the forest.

'Thank you,' he said quietly and she smiled, trying to push her hair back as he took a molten curl in his fingers and brought it up into the moonlight.

'Your hair burns as brightly as you do.' His voice was strained as though he had been running for a long time. 'When first I saw you I was surprised by the colour. No one had told me it was red.'

'Red-brown,' she qualified.

'Pardon?'

'Red-brown. Not red.'

'You don't like red.' Amusement laced the question.

'My mother's hair was red and I am not like her.'

He sobered. 'You think red hair affects your character in some way?'

'I do.'

'In what way?'

'Red hair makes a woman wanton. I have heard it said many times. Eleanor herself told me it was so.'

'And you don't wish to take after your mother in that way?'

'No. Of course not.'

He began to laugh in earnest, though he stopped as his movement threatened to separate them. 'How I hate to be the one to break the news…'

He smiled as she nudged him. 'What news?'

'It's my guess you could have given your mother lessons in wantonness.' He stilled her as she went to pull away and laid her hand across his heart. 'That's a compliment, sweetheart. I swear it. And if the beat stopped at this moment, I would die a happy man.'

He meant it. No teasing, this, but truth; for the first time in her life Madeleine saw herself as the woman she had always wanted to be. As strong as he was. And as free. And although there had been no talk of love between them as he had kissed her, there was for now something that she needed more. Respect. Admiration. Honour.

She could see it in his face and had felt it in his hands, and the shadow left by her years with Lucien Randwick frayed around the edges to a quieter hurt and a more distant memory.

Here in Alexander's arms she was safe. She liked the way he held her, his thighs hard across her own, her body fitted into his. But as his thumb rubbed across the scar upon her right breast she shivered.

'I claimed you once in blood and again in the ritual of handfast. Now I claim you as my own in flesh.'

'Nay, it is too dangerous—'

He stopped her by the simple act of placing his fingers firmly against her lips. 'I claim you as mine, Madeleine Randwick,' he repeated and she was still.

'Against all of Scotland and England?'

'Yes.'

'Against David and Edward and Noel and Harrington?'

'Yes.'

'Against the church and its bishops?'

'Yes.'

She held his forehead to her own. 'You are the only man in Christendom whom I believe could actually honour such a promise, my lord, and I thank you for it.'

'But you refuse?'

'If you claim me so, you will be thrown into the middle of a war.'

'Nay. By claiming you I might be able to stop one.'

'I don't understand.'

'The lairds are uneasy and David is a king without heirs, which is why they look to me to lead them. If it is seen that there is an alliance between us, with David and Edward's agreement, and that your lands are equally divided between the English and Scottish crowns, they may well think of playing a waiting game and leave things as they are. The status quo.' He ran his hands through his hair. 'It may be enough. God, I hope so, for another civil war in Scotland will rip the clans to pieces and England under Edward is volatile.'

Madeleine was speechless at the intensity of his argument. *Politics*. It all came down to politics.

And she was as compromised here as ever Eleanor had been. A pawn in a game she had always been a part of. And now continued to be. She pushed his hand off her hip and slipped free, gathering her clothes and standing. She saw his eyes brush across her body, saw, too, the easy rise of his manhood.

But he had made no mention of love.

'My mother was compromised by men who decided to use her body in the pursuit of peace, my lord, and, watching her juggle their greed and weaknesses, I can tell you that the promises were always empty.'

'You think that of me?' He had not stood, but was

leaning instead back on his arms, a splendid study of naked masculine beauty.

'I do not know what to think of you. You are a wild card in the power struggles here, a gatherer of men who would lay down their lives for you and a King who would make certain that they did not. And now you think to claim me for political reasons. Well, I have walked that road once before with Lucien and look how badly that turned out.'

'What is it you want, then?'

She hesitated just for a moment and then she took a chance. 'Love. It is love I want from you.'

'Ahhh.' Said in a way that made it sound like such a trifling and feminine thing. 'I am a warrior, Madeleine, and have been for ten years or more and I am not certain…' He shook his head and stood, shrugging on his long Highland shirt and belting it. 'I dinna' know the way of love.' Genuine puzzlement was thick in his voice.

'Then, Alexander, I must teach you.'

The remainder of the ride into England was a quiet one, and Madeleine, on her horse behind Alexander, was glad of the silence. It was as though they had crossed to a different place in their relationship and neither knew the way on from here. Alexander in his honesty, and Madeleine in her promise. *Then, my lord, I must teach you.* She shivered as she remembered her words.

How?

How did one teach a man like Alexander Ullyot to love

when he had told her that this was an emotion he did not
know the way of? And how did she, with her record of only
one fulfilling sexual encounter in her entire life, and this
with him, think to know the answer, anyway?

She sighed and tipped her face up into the warmth of
the day, small thrills of pleasure passing through her body
as she rekindled the memory of their tryst. As a lover she
doubted him to have equal in all of Scotland. Indeed, the
lesson had been so wonderful that she would like him
again now. Right now. This minute. In the glen with the
noonday sun upon their skin. Perhaps this was the way to
it? To sneak up on his wanting of her as a woman and hope
to catch his heart?

She spurred her horse on and rode along beside him, deliberately coming so close at times that her undamaged leg
brushed his.

No response.

She pulled the hem of her skirt up across her shin and
made sure that a good measure of bare calf was easily seen.

No response.

She loosened the laces of her kirtle to show her thin shift.
With the difference in height between them his view should
be bounteous.

And he was looking.

'These are lands foreign to me, Madeleine, and dangerous. I need to be watchful.' The knuckles on both hands
showed white, and there was a taut edge to his voice.
'Besides, your leg—'

'Feels a lot better,' she finished for him. 'I made a salve of herbs this morning.'

When he ran his fingers through the heavy blond of his hair she smiled.

She was beginning to get through to him.

She could feel it in the tension all around them and see it in the pulse at his throat. When the path forked half an hour later, he led her down to a small river.

Dismounting from his horse, he came across to help her, his hands coming full around her waist and bringing to mind the loving of the night before. She grimaced as she put weight down upon her leg.

'It pains you?'

'A little,' she replied, frowning as he knelt before her and lifted her skirts. His fingers were cold against the heat of her leg and the skin on her arms goose-pimpled in pleasure.

'That feels so very good.' Her hand fell to his hair.

'And this? How does this feel?' His fingers skimmed her inner left thigh and rode higher, parting the swollen flesh of her sex and pushing inwards.

So easily done.

She opened her mouth to speak, but found that she could not. And then they both wore nothing and the wildness of their night-time coupling was replayed again into the day as he laid her down on the soft grasses beside the river in the sunlight and showed her again what heaven was made of.

* * *

Afterwards they lay together, spooned up under his plaid, with the quiet sounds of twilight all around them.

'Did you ever love Lucien Randwick?' His question was unexpected.

'No.'

'Harrington, then?'

'Never.'

She caught his smile through the dark.

'And yet you think to instruct me on the ways of love, Lady Randwick? You with no experience of it at all?'

'Until now!'

He was still, but she was tired of being careful.

'I love you, Alexander. I have waited for you for ever and I will love you for ever.'

In answer he turned her over, entering her in one quick stroke of possession and the ragged sensuality of his breath sent goose bumps along her spine.

Chapter Sixteen

They reached Vorpeth by nightfall of the next day. Her leg ached now with the relentlessness of the ride and, although she had removed the bandages in the early afternoon and re-poulticed the cut, she wished she had hot water to soak it properly. To soak the soreness from her shoulders and neck, too, and the sticky dampness of Alexander's seed from her thighs. He had barely said a word to her since her confession by the river. She thought he had wanted to at times, thought perhaps there was something in him that demanded saying, but he looked away when she caught his eyes and went steadily on, as vigilant as ever and as distant.

At her grandmother's house they were ushered into the front hall by a servant and she felt a fierce pride. The English clothes Alexander had changed into accentuated his tallness and his hair had been drawn back tightly by a leather thong, the thick waves of gold and red plastered darker away from his face, which made the scar across his cheek more easily seen. He looked to her like a man who could protect her from anything and anyone. And would.

Her grandmother was in bed when they were taken up the stairs. Bending down to kiss her on the cheek, Maddy was aware of her familiar scent, though it had been six years since last they had met at Heathwater Castle.

'Madeleine?' Josephine's voice was croaky and thin, her faded blue irises now ringed with whiteness, but the most surprising thing of all was the shock of white hair that framed her face like a cloud. An old lady who has buried her only child, Madeleine thought, and had had little contact with her grandchildren. A woman whose love and time had always been bounded by the men she had married. Three men. Eleanor's father and now the Baron Anthony. Her first husband had been a sixteen-year-old boy who had perished in battle in the Holy Lands.

'Let me look at you, Madeleine. All grown up and here for Jemima's letter, I would wager?' Relief wreathed her face. 'I knew you would come. I saw it in a dream.'

Maddy smiled, the clairvoyance of her grandmother a remembered thing and not at all threatening.

'Goult came to Ashblane. He told us the story.'

'Us?'

Alexander stepped forward and handed her the medallion. 'I am Alexander, the Laird of Ullyot, and Goult of Kenmore sends you this. He said you would understand the message.'

Josephine sat up further, her thin arms straining against the movement. 'Oh, indeed, Alexander Ullyot, and I have heard of both you and your castle. The unassailable Ashblane. Yet you stay loyal to the King of Scotland?'

'That I do.'

'What are you to Madeleine?'

'Her husband, Lady Anthony.'

Madeleine started. It was all very well to tell the strangers a lie, but her grandmother? If Alexander was going to keep to this handfast, she wanted him to mean it and not use it merely as a political ploy. Nay, she wanted the love words from him, wanted to see in his eyes the same thing she knew he would so easily be able to fathom in her own. She began to protest, but he stopped her with his hand as she moved forward and the scorching heat of the tiny contact left her mute. Just a brush of skin against skin and her whole body rose up to his. Such an unexpected joy, his touch and her reaction. She felt like dry tinder next to live flame.

Her grandmother's words brought her back into the moment. 'I should have known. He has the silver, Madeleine. All around him. But there is blackness there, too. And sorrow. Old sorrow tempered with new blood and the baying hounds of conscience. They will eat him up in the end if you let them.'

She saw that Alexander stiffened and stepped back, but Josephine was not finished.

'Your mother always disappointed me, Madeleine, but I think you will not, for I have been praying for guidance and now you have come. It is the fulfilment of my dream.'

She was getting tired. The colour of her skin was sallow.

Age and grief. These things were written into the deep lines of her forehead and into the vertical marks between her eyes.

'How long can you stay, Laird Ullyot?'

'One night. We will leave at first light. If I could have the letter…'

Josephine interrupted him. 'Tomorrow.' Her eyes narrowed at his impatience.

'It would be safer now.' All he wanted to do was to get his hands on the evidence and destroy it.

'No. You must not destroy it…it can help you…'

Alexander looked up sharply. Was mind reading another of her gifts? And yet in what political reality did she inhabit to think that a document labelling her grand-daughter as the progeny of a childless king could be helpful? Still, she was old and he did not wish to alienate her. He nodded and held his peace.

'Tonight there must be a dinner. Matthilde is here. Just my husband and Matthilde…must be careful. I know.'

'Matthilde is my grandmother's sister,' Madeleine qual-ified as Alexander's eyebrows rose in question.

'The fewer people who know about our coming, the safer we will be. We shall be gone from here come morning.'

He stepped back, suddenly consumed by an inexplica-ble dread. He wanted to be in Scotland where he under-stood the language and the landscape and the weather. Already outside cold rain had swept the fine blue day away and replaced it with greyness. Two seasons in a single day. The weather was like the English, changeable and dangerously fickle. At least in Scotland when it rained it stayed raining. His fingers clamped hard around the knife in his pocket and he fingered the intricate filigree on the hilt. One night only would they stay. He swore that was all.

He came to her in the late-night hours after the dinner had finished and when the house had settled into silence and the banked fire dimmed her room to a dull ember. She heard the door click and watched as he leaned against it for a moment, listening, never trusting, always alert. What had made him like that? she wondered. She pushed the bolster behind her up against the bed-head and sat.

'Your grandmother is quite a woman.' His voice was husky as he bent to the fireplace and added another log. 'And wily. I think she has kept the letter to make sure that we did not flee the place tonight under the cover of darkness.'

He removed only his sword belt and took a chair near her bed. Not touching. Uncertain. As if he would speak, but had no place to start the conversation.

Finally he began. 'Josephine said that the baying hounds of conscience would eat me up. And she was right. I do not know how she could know this but…she was right.' He repeated the words and she felt a rising tension. Tonight emptiness lay across him, a lonely distant burden that lent fierceness to his eyes. 'When I told you I was in Egypt, I told you only a little of the story.'

He ran his fingers through his hair and stopped for a moment, his face remote. 'I was eight when my father sent me to France to the court of Philip to train to be a knight, and England under Edward was rampant. Guy de Tour was a hard man, but to give him his credit he knew that only hardened trainees would ever return from battle and God knows he tried his best with me. For nine years I learned the art of warfare in France against the English and then I went to Alexandria.

'At first it was a place of wonder. Al-Nasir Muhammed was a sultan who believed in both charity and patronage and his palace was home to many historians and poets. And books.' He smiled, remembering the first time he had seen the madrasa library of the school at Alexandria. 'I was wooed at first by the learning and scholarship of the Mamelukes and then by the fighting ways of their soldiers. The Karimi merchant who brought us down to Alexandria had a brother who was head of an army regiment in al-Qahirah and he took me beneath his wing when he saw the extent of my interest. His name was Talib ibn Abi Hakim and he was a man who hated anything to do with the Christian faith. There was a cross in purpose, you understand, for I was a seventeen-year-old Scottish boy who still thought of anyone not Christian as an infidel.'

He shook his head and kept on. Madeleine could see a fine sheen of sweat on his brow. 'Before I turned eighteen I went with Talib to Cairo. Away from the calming influence of Al-Nasir Muhammed he became different. Angrier. Less interested in teaching and far more interested in punishment. He set up a fighting school and began using me as his bait, a white-skinned foreigner with the mantle of Christianity firmly around my shoulders and ten years of intensive training in the martial arts of both East and West shining as beacons from my eyes. Aye indeed, seventeen is a foolish age and I became the willing entertainment for a good deal of gold. Money and position—the two things I had never had the luxury of as the bastard son of Bruce progeny in Scotland. I was mesmerised at first and then just as quickly disgusted, for the opponents I was up against were boys like me. Boys as young as fifteen who had barely begun to understand what it was they did not know…would never know… I broke their necks…easily. Like saplings. The older ones were more difficult, but it was me or them and I was damned certain that I was going to live.'

He looked over at her and in the light his eyes were flat grey shadows underscored by something akin to shame.

'Yazid, a friend of mine there, said I had no choice but to do it. He said that by taking Talib's gold I had in effect sold myself to him. And yet I did have the choice. I could have stopped eating and wasted away. I could have refused to fight and accepted death as a way out. But I…I could'na bring myself to even start such a thing. I wanted to live, ye understand, above everything. And when I did live I found that there was something in me after all that had died. If Alice were still alive, she would have told you what she so often said to me.'

He faltered, stopped, the muscles in his cheeks shifting

in the candlelight. 'She said that Cairo and Talib ibn Abi Hakim had taken my heart. She said that in the dark watches of the night I should ever be reminded of the souls of the bairns I had killed. Lord.' He stood suddenly. 'I was but a child myself and fifteen did not seem at the time so much younger than eighteen. And yet her words have stuck, grown…' Pale eyes met hers, and the sheer depth of sorrow within them broke Madeleine's heart.

Covering his lips with her fingers to stop him saying more, she stood before him.

'If you had refused to fight, what would have happened?'

'To me?' He did not look at her. 'I would have been put to death. Talib had no qualms in dealing with the dishonourable.'

'So in his terms fighting was honourable?'

'Yes.'

'How long were you there? In Cairo?'

'Eleven months and five days.'

So precisely known. Her stomach turned against the horror of it all and she brushed his arm, lifting the loose fabric of his shirt.

'And this tattoo?'

'He gave it to me as a gift. For the fighting.'

'A gift that you have tried since to erase?' The curling scar tissue along the thin bands of indigo was easily seen.

He nodded. 'When I returned to Scotland I burnt it off until I could stand no more. Alice said it was my penance.

My shame. She said I should leave it untouched to for ever remind me how I had sinned.'

Quietly Madeleine laid her hands around him, hating his long-dead wife with an increasing fervour. The beating of his heart was frantic. She could feel the coursing redness of blood beneath her fingers and the black-edged sorrow of which her grandmother had spoken.

'Your wife sounds like a righteous woman, but a hard one. If she had stayed but one day in Cairo, I doubt she would have been so certain, for bravery is easy to feel when you are a thousand miles from danger. You made your choices and you lived by them. Others made their choices and died by them. It is not your fault that Talib did what he did.'

'I could have stopped him.'

'Now you could have, maybe. Now at twenty-eight you could have made a fist of it and stopped him. Perhaps. But at eighteen…'

Seven years older than Jemmie and thrown into hell. The dreadfulness of it leached through her like a poison.

'Eighteen-year-olds are not much more than children in anyone's language. The shame was not yours, Alexander, just as the shame of killing Lucien was never mine. You showed me that, told me that. We were both the pawns of others.'

'God, you are so unlike Alice…' he whispered softly and wound his fingers through her hair.

'And I give thanks for the fact that I am,' she returned.

The beat of his heart had slowed now, though it spiked sharply as she pulled off his shirt and laid her finger across one nipple, flicking the skin with her nail. Hard. She smiled at her secret woman's power and leaned into him.

'Will you stay? Here with me tonight?'

She saw his answer in the smouldering passion of his eyes. Bringing his hand up across her heart, she held her own across it. 'This is what is real now, Alexander. Your heart did not stop in Cairo because it heard the call of mine. Listen.'

She placed his other hand against her breast and breathed in. 'Two living beings as one for ever joined and wrought together by sadness and loss. But saved by love.'

The beats came together in perfect harmony so that each could barely tell where one began and where the other one ended. And as his lips slanted across hers she could speak no more.

In the early hours of the morning Alexander lay with his eyes open and his arms around Madeleine. For the first time in his life he felt as if he had found a home. Not in a pile of stones after all or in the glory of battle, not in the court of David or in the bosom of his clan.

Nay, Madeleine was home. This was what it felt like to truly belong.

This is what it felt like to be vulnerable. If he should lose her… He made himself stop and carefully eased out of the bed. At the window he laid one palm against the unfamiliar coldness of glass and frowned when the imprint of his hand left a momentary outline. A fleeting shadow of his being there.

He hoped it was not an omen, this transitory shape of himself fading into oblivion even as he watched it.

The Baron of Anthony tried to detain them the next morning and Madeleine could see that Alexander was wary.

'Your cousins should be here in the mid-afternoon. Will you not at least stay for that?'

Alexander's curse was succinct. 'I asked you not to speak of us to anyone.'

'I did as you bid, Laird Ullyot. It was not London I sent the message to. Merely the country estate of Franklin Moore. Matthilde's husband. Surely there can be no harm in a simple family reunion?' He had been standing in the corner by the window as he talked, but suddenly took up his hat and left. Madeleine was pleased to see him go, for she didn't think her grandmother would mention the letter with him in the room and when she sat up and beckoned her over she felt a quick thrill. This was it. The moment of finding the paper that threatened Jemmie's safety.

'Jemima's letter is tucked into the back panel of that painting, Madeleine.' She gestured to a landscape near the window and they watched as Alexander tipped the frame forward and extracted a parchment, shoving it into his shirt without even glancing down, his whole stance giving Madeleine the singular impression of high alertness. The shout outside explained everything.

Betrayal! She could see the thought mirrored in her grandmother's face.

'Go out through the back,' Josephine whispered, pointing to a door on the other side of the room even as Alex drew his sword. Nothing hidden. No pretence of intent. Pure-bred Scottish warrior. And undisputedly furious.

'What sort of man is this Franklin Moore?' His tone was sharp.

'I don't know. I have met him only a few times.' Maddy could barely remember his face.

'Then he will have no particular care for your well-being, and, if David is keen to get a corridor into England, it will also damn well work the other way around with Edward.'

She nodded, feeling the tightening in her chest as they wound their way outside into a courtyard she had not seen before.

'Stop it, Madeleine,' he said suddenly. 'Breathe, damn it.'

Later, she was to think that all that happened next was her fault. Had Alex not had her to deal with and worry over he would have easily heard the soldiers surrounding Vorpeth Manor. Had he not been distracted by her sickness he would have taken flight and melted into the countryside in that particular way she had already seen him to be so adept at. But by the time she had garnered some control over her breathing it was too late and the company of King

Edward's men around them were well armed and purposeful. She saw that Moore stood with the newcomers. Not apolitical, then. And not indifferent to an inheritance that could be cut were her grandmother to include her name on any will. Greed and the promise of land made fools of both kings and men. And Matthilde's husband was no exception.

'Are you the Lady Randwick?' A swarthy man stepped forward, the marks of a captain on his uniform.

Looking at Alexander for guidance, she saw that he nodded.

'I am.'

'Why are you here at Vorpeth?' Impatience creased his brow.

'My grandmother has been ill. I wanted to see her before…' She stopped and glanced downwards in an effort to look grief-ridden.

'And the Scottish Baron?'

'He insisted on bringing me. For safety. We were just leaving. Going home.' Everything was an effort. Breathing. Speaking. Trembling. She hated the weakness. Would it be as Alexander had guessed it? Would King Edward demand an audience and sanction the ceremony of handfast, or would he decree her betrothed to any baron he had the most control over? She could see irritation in the eyes of the English captain and a still menace in Alexander's.

'The King wants you brought before him. You are to come with us now.'

'And you think you have the means to take me?' Alexander's voice was dangerously calm. Did he think to brazen out the encounter here in the same way he had in the glade with the Kerrs? For a moment she could not comprehend his methods and then it hit her. Already in the face of his insult the ring about them had broken, the two soldiers nearest him walking forward, giving him the only chance that he needed.

Within a second Alexander was through them and on the pathway to the chapel. The letter, she thought suddenly. He has it in his coat pocket. It was not for his own sake or hers that he ran, but for Jemmie's, and suddenly she knew that he would be caught. Caught after the time it took to destroy the document and make it appear that he had only used the chapel as a throughway.

'No!' she shouted and began to follow even as the heavy oaken door of the prayer house slammed shut and the arm of the captain circled her waist. Shaking him off, she rounded upon him.

'He is the Laird of Ullyot, an independent Scottish Baron and you have no right to waylay him like this. He is David of Scotland's cousin, for goodness' sake, the son of Robert the Bruce's brother, and if you are not careful it will be war your actions incite.'

Her whole being centred on the noises coming now from the chapel. A bellow of pain and shouts of victory. When the captain seemed bent on doing nothing, she changed tack. 'Call them off, please,' she begged. 'It is me that you want and I will go without force. I promise you this as long as you do not hurt him.'

The man opposite her smiled. 'A touching sentiment, my lady, but unenforceable, I expect, given what we have heard over the last moments. Ah, here they come now.'

The door opened with Alexander in the midst of at least ten English soldiers, his head bloodied and his left cheek swollen. Beneath the cuts and dirt, grey eyes clearly caught her own and winked. He had never meant to fight or flee. His courage calmed her, and she waited to see just what he would do next.

'Bring the Scottish Laird here.' The English captain's words were clipped and Alexander was hauled before him. Standing face-to-face, they were of much the same height.

'Give me your name, sir.'

'Alexander James Ullyot, Laird of the Ullyot clan of Liddesdale.' He blinked rapidly as a run of blood from a cut on his forehead filled his left eye. With his hands caught behind him he could not wipe it away. 'What is it you want?'

No diplomacy now. The raw anger of his words was plain to hear.

'Lady Randwick has been asked to come to court, Ullyot. And you have waylaid us. The King does not look kindly on such insolence.'

Madeleine stepped forward, suddenly and desperately afraid for, unlike her, he had no land in the Marches to barter his life with. 'If you let us go, I could pay you in gold.'

The captain lifted his hand to stop the chatter of his men

behind him. 'A servant of the King does not take bribes and it would be wise not to refuse the dictates of your liege lord.'

'She is his no longer, captain. My wife is a citizen now of Scotland. You may tell Edward we were made handfast three days ago in front of thirty witnesses.'

'You wed her?'

'Handfast and binding.'

'Where?'

'On the border of Scotland in the stronghold of the Kerrs.'

The benign expression on the captain's face was now replaced by a mask of rage. 'King Edward will be furious when he finds out. My orders were to bring the widow Randwick to London.' Turning, he struck Madeleine hard across the cheek and all hell broke loose.

Alexander shook off the grip of the man who held him and rammed a fist into his nose, flooring him before the soldier behind charged, then balancing on the balls of his feet to deal with the next one. A third man stepped forward, the sword in his hand bright and Madeleine screamed in warning. But it was an easy enough disarming. One kick with his foot and a wicked slam with the base of his hand and the man fell senseless.

Two more soldiers circled on each side though Alexander had them both in the time it took to lay his hands upon the base of their throats and squeeze. Maddy wondered if they were dead, but small movements told her that they were not and she was relieved. A beating, if it was to end in victory for the men of King Edward, would afford Alexander less of a punishment than a killing.

She blanched as he looked up and caught her eyes. Pale arrogance coated silver irises. And humour. He looked as if he was enjoying this. How could this be when fear coursed through her own veins as at least twenty soldiers now joined in the fray? She knew that there was no way in the world that Alexander could actually win this battle and he was tiring. She could hear it in his breathing and see it in the colour of his cheeks and the fast-racing pulse at his throat. The circle around him had widened, but there were knives out now and bucklers.

He shouted at Madeleine to stay back when she came forward, the blood on his face flowing down on to his white shirt and plaid. And then he found the English captain, ramming the arm he had hit her with up and out and breaking it easily. Behind Alexander another soldier cracked something down hard across his skull. He fell heavily, his face kicked again by the boot of a soldier without any redress to fairness, though as the others moved forward she was pleased to hear the soldiers call a halt to it. Not for common decency, she suspected, but more for the fact that the Laird of Ullyot's death here in the backwaters of England might cause King Edward problems. A relative of the Scottish King. The leader of a clan in the dicey borderlands. Care and protocol had to be seen to be observed, even if it wasn't. She closed her eyes briefly in prayer and then, running to him, she held her finger to his wrist, counted his pulse against the moment.

* * *

'Damn you,' she whispered as she used her petticoat to sponge the caked blood from the corners of his eyes and out of his hairline. His blond hair was pink now and wet, the long tendrils curling softly against a face as hardened as hewed iron. 'Why did you do this?'

'They hurt you.'

She could not suppress a faint smile. 'Not half as much as they hurt you, Alexander.'

'Where are we?'

'In a camp a good hour's ride from Vorpeth.'

She laid her fingers against the broken skin under his left eye and frowned. 'You should have left them to do as they willed. Noel and Lucien pushed me around far more than they were ever about to and I survived them.'

Absolute disbelief seeped into his eyes. 'I am the Laird of Ullyot and you are my wife. It is my duty to protect you.'

'Against thirty armed soldiers and you already hurt? It was madness. You could never have won.'

'But I did,' he answered softly as she lifted her brows in silent question. 'I stopped them from hurting *you*.'

Her fingers closed around his and a lump formed in her throat. Beneath his nails she could see traces of dried blood and on the back of both hands there were new grazes and cuts.

She had spent half a lifetime with men who said they cared for her and didn't. Her brother with his heavy fist. Liam Williamson with his caustic words. Lucien with his madness and anger. Well, Alexander Ullyot had made no pronouncement of love and yet in his every action she saw his intention to provide protection and safety.

I stopped them from hurting you.

She could barely keep the tears from her eyes as she bent over his cut hands.

'What did you do with Jemmie's letter?'

'Burnt it. There were candles at the altar. Which road are we on?' His quick question surprised her.

'The London road.'

'And how many soldiers ride with us?'

'At least fifty. More joined us as we left. From Stainington, I think. It's a town not ten miles from here.'

'And Anthony? Where is he?'

'He says he will come to London to petition the King to see what can be done.'

Swearing in Gaelic, Alexander came up on his haunches before stumbling and sitting back, hands wrapped around his head.

'If you could find me water.'

She held a flask up to him and he drank deeply, flinching as he moved his jaw against the mouth of the bottle.

'What did that English bastard hit me with?'

'A buckler. There was a swelling, but I have seen to it.'

Unexpectedly he smiled and took her hand in his. 'If we stand firm in our resolve, Madeleine, we can brazen this out. If you are taken alone to the English King, tell him you will cede your land on the border to him in return for safe passage to Ashblane. But take care with your words—there is no one who combines the qualities of ruthlessness and treachery as well as English royalty. If Edward will not listen to what you say, then barter my life for your own...'

She cried out and shook her head.

'Listen, damn it. Say you refute the handfast. Tell him I made you do it, forced you into it. A promised betrothal to a puppet baron should give you time at least to escape back to Ashblane and collect Jemmie. Quinlan will help you from there.'

'No!'

'Only with me gone is it possible for him to marry you off. Money, land and favour. The King will be appeased.'

'I won't do it, Alexander. I won't betray you.'

He laughed, the white of his teeth startling against the tan in his face. 'If you are with child from our nights together, Madeleine, you will betray me more if you do not do this.'

'Nay, I am barren. I told you. It is the least of our worries.'

'You were barren with Lucien. You will not be so with me.'

She smiled at his arrogance but a small worm of hope turned. 'If I carry your child, I would not have him fatherless before he is even born.'

'If you carry our child, Madeleine, then it is your responsibility to have him born.' He stood, bowing as the tent roof came against his hair. She saw that he was careful not to touch her.

'As it is your duty to die?' Her fingers wrung the wet rag in her hand. 'Is that what you are telling me?'

'No, I am saying that Edward is a king not to be trusted under any circumstance. He would think nothing of killing a child if it gained him the sort of lands you may bring to the English monarchy. Or murdering the mother. Especially when the land in question is in the Marches.'

'Then let us make a run for it here. Together.'

In reply he wrenched off the ring he wore and took her hand, placing the warm gold band on her third finger. 'With this ring I thee wed,' he said simply. 'With my body I thee worship.' His knife sliced into the fleshy part of his thumb and hers and he brought them together. 'With this blood I bind my life to yours and ask God to bless our union. For safety,' he added as he saw her astonishment and held her wound to his mouth, sucking hard until the pain left and the bleeding stopped. 'And if it all goes wrong, Madeleine, I would have you remember this. Remember me.'

The tears in her eyes blurred his face as she turned towards him and held him tight.

'I could not lose you, Alexander. I could not lose you and live.'

'Shh,' he crooned and trailed his fingers through her hair. She felt the heavy mass of it lifted before he placed a kiss on the tender skin beneath. 'Edward will want the land. If we can make him believe that we are amenable to this, then we have a chance.'

The sound of footsteps made him stop and he rose up and placed Madeleine behind him as an older English soldier came into the tent.

'You are to go with Baron Anthony to London, Lady Randwick.'

'And Laird Ullyot? What of him?'

'He stays with us.'

Wild terror spiralled, leaving her dizzy, and she found Alexander's hand and held on tight. But he was prying her fingers apart even as the guard moved forward.

'She will go with you now, though I ask for your oath on her safety.'

'You have it, sir,' the other man replied and turned towards the door flap, giving them a private moment in which to say goodbye.

She felt his hand against her cheek and closed her eyes briefly so that she might burn the feel of him to memory. When she looked at him, she was surprised by the humour on his face.

'This is not the end, my Madeleine, I promise.'

As her tears spilled down across his arm, she felt herself pulled away and then he was gone.

Chapter Seventeen

King Edward of England was furious when Alexander was hauled out of the dungeons in the Tower of London and brought before him.

'Lady Randwick has told me that you are handfast, Laird Ullyot. Handfast in front of witnesses, she said. Thirty witnesses to be precise and all Scottish.'

'We were on a journey south, your Majesty, and met up with the clan Kerr. It was the only way I could think of to protect her.'

'Well, think again, Ullyot, for I swear to you she will be dead by nightfall if you cannot conjure up some way to undo the state of handfast and have her happily married off to a man of my choice. I do not want difficulties, you see, Baron. I have enough of those with the King of Scotland's border issues and the squabbling of the clergy. I want Madeleine Randwick's land and most especially the tracts in the Marches. Dead or alive I could take them, but it would be far simpler and less messy were she to happily acquiesce.'

Alexander began to sweat.

'Acquiesce?'

'Marry one of my trusted barons before the end of the month. And without a whisper of reluctance.'

'I see.'

And he did. Unless he could convince Madeleine that the King's plan was in accordance with his own he knew that she would never do it. And then she would die.

How long was it now since he had seen her? Three weeks? Longer? He had lost track of his days in the dark damp of the tower where he had been since his arrival. Sometimes he had had word of her. She was lodged in the Savoy Palace in a series of rooms overlooking a courtyard. Baron Anthony had told him this when he had visited on the second week of his confinement. Alex had sent him away and made him promise not to come back or to tell Madeleine where he was. Only in distance did he have any chance of keeping Madeleine safe.

His whole body roiled at the possibilities as they presented themselves. Madeleine dead? Her lands in royal hands again? Such a small and easy order for a King who thought himself inviolable.

'Is Lady Isabella Simpson at court, my lord?'

'Yes.'

'Then perhaps after all there is a way.'

He was throwing away his own life to save Madeleine,

but at least here was a chance. Ignoring the heavy beating of his heart, he began to outline a plan.

The beautiful Lady Isabella Simpson came to see her in the fourth week of her captivity in the Savoy and Madeleine saw the quick flicker of something akin to triumph before she could hide it.

'Thank you for receiving me, Lady Randwick,' she began, her voice as glacial as Madeleine remembered. 'I have come to ask you to release the Laird of Ullyot from whatever vows he made to you. Handfast, was it not...?' The sentence tailed off but the tone made clear the scorn with which she held such a notion before she continued. 'I have already had an audience with the Laird of Ullyot. He has been told of the child that we have conceived.'

The room whirled and Maddy steadied herself against the high back of a velvet chair. For a second she could not quite comprehend what had been said.

'A child? It is his?' She remembered the passionate marks she had seen on Alexander's neck.

Isabella was short in her reply, the haughty woman she had met at Ashblane well on display. 'Yes. It is only early yet, but I would like the blessing of the church on this union and Alex did promise to marry me when first we were intimate.'

Madeleine blanched. 'I don't believe what you are telling me. I could never believe it. Alexander has made you say this to protect me. He has made you lie...' Her breathing began to tighten and she turned away, hand at her neck and horror-stricken.

'I feared that you would not believe me, but Alex is here to see you to tell you the story himself. Could I ask him in? The King did give his permission.'

'The Laird of Ullyot is here? Just outside?'

'Yes.'

Madeleine's heartbeat trebled and she felt a rising ache. A minute or two in his company and all this would be cleared up. Turning to the doorway in anticipation, hope died as she watched him enter. It was in his eyes, in the line of his body, in the way he walked and bore himself. She could see that everything Isabella Simpson had told her was true.

'Lady Randwick.' His voice was tight and he did not use her Christian name.

She cleared her throat and tried to speak. This could not be happening. Outside the day was blue. The world the same as it had been here before everything inside her had fallen to pieces. It had to be a charade. A complex charade to protect her. Had he not intimated as much on the road to London? Whispering his name beneath her breath, she summoned courage and began to fight.

'Isabella has told me, my lord, that she is pregnant with your child.'

He glanced across at Isabella and nodded before meeting Maddy's glance directly for the first time. She gasped. His left eye was black and the corner of his bottom lip had been split wide open.

'Is it true?'

He hesitated before answering.

'Yes.' One word dragged from bleakness.

'Then it seems you have a problem, Laird Ullyot.'

'It seems I have,' he answered and inclined his head towards a jug of wine that sat on a cabinet near the window. 'May I?'

She watched as he sloshed a good quantity of the wine into a glass and brought it to his lips.

His hand shook.

Badly.

A sign? A clue of his being forced into this confession?

'When did you know of this? This child?'

'Just in the last week. I did not know that Isabella was with child from our union, but now with the knowing of it I feel a duty to be father. I hope that you might come to understand that.'

Duty. A child. It was the only argument he could have used that could make her believe. One hand wandered by its own accord to her barren stomach as tears filled her eyes. With exaggerated care Maddy helped herself to some water. She held the goblet so tightly that for a moment she wondered what might happen were it to shatter. Like her own strength. Into a thousand million pieces and each one of them loving Alexander. But she could not let that happen. Nay, she had to hold herself together and pretend. Pretend, as she had a hundred times before and would again, now that any promised safety had been denied her.

'And Edward has sanctioned this union between you both?'

'Yesterday.' He looked her straight in the eye. 'Ashblane is a fighting keep, Lady Randwick, and the Ullyot clan needs heirs to make certain that it does not fail through the lack of a male line, for Gillion cannot rule if his deafness prevails.'

'So the child Isabella bears protects Ashblane.'

'Aye, it does that.'

Fathership and the safety of his castle. In just seven words she knew that she didn't stand a chance.

The air she took was strangled but she forced a gaiety into her voice for there were things she wanted to know.

'Where is it you have been staying in London, my lord?'

'King Edward has given me rooms at the Palace of Westminster. But he has given me leave to travel home.' He crossed the room and took Isabella Simpson's hand in his own. 'We will go tomorrow.'

'And the marks on your face. How came they there?'

'I have been jousting with the King's guards and they unseated me several times before I was able to get the feel of the horse I rode.'

Madeleine lost her last bit of hope. Not the dungeons in the Tower of London, then, or a gaoler who had been too fond of his job. Whilst she had been languishing in the guise of what could almost be considered a prisoner at Savoy Palace, Alexander had had the freedom of this town and a suite at Westminster. An adaptable man who had seen his main chance and gone for it. Just like every other man who had professed to an interest in her. Her mind was made up.

'To become handfast was indeed a silly thing to do and under these new circumstances of course I relinquish any claim.' She turned to face Isabella and made a show of bravery. 'It was said on a whim to protect me from some other travellers we had met on the road, you see. There was only the Laird of Ullyot and myself and thirty Kerr soldiers.'

'You were *alone* together coming south? You travelled without a chaperon as an unmarried woman?'

Hearing the censure in Isabella's voice, Madeleine quickly worked out how she could use it.

'I have been married before, Lady Simpson, as well as having a succession of lovers. Did you not know? They came to Heathwater and paid for my services. I am really quite famous…'

'Stop it, Madeleine.' Alexander banged down his goblet and the grey in his eyes was so desolate and unending that for a second the ache in Madeleine's heart threatened her resolve.

But not quite. There was a child involved in all of this, which made everything different.

'Stop what, my lord?' She smiled at him and tipped up her chin. 'Stop using my charms? Stop enjoying the company of men? Why, I have already released you from any custodial rights you may have once felt bounded to me by, so now you cannot think to instruct me as to what I can or cannot do. That is a husband's prerogative and you are hardly mine.' She hated the anger in his eyes, but she could no longer worry. If Alexander Ullyot could not protect her from what King Edward would now undoubtedly demand, then her own poor reputation still might. After all, what right-minded baron would wish to be betrothed to a self-confessed whore even given her wealth of lands, and a small hesitation might be enough.

Isabella Simpson smiled as she crossed the room. 'I am so pleased we have had this little talk, Lady Randwick.' Her fingers threaded through the lapel of Alexander's jacket. 'Perhaps you might even consider standing in as a godmother.'

The sharp twist of pain must have been reflected in Maddy's eyes for a flare of sly triumph crossed the older woman's features. 'Do you not agree, Alex? After all, the story of your handfast is bound to resurface one day and when it does we can say that love mellowed into friendship. Well,' she added, egged on by Alexander's silence, 'that is if one presupposes that there was any love there in the first place.'

Madeleine felt the thin veneer of protection that she had woven around herself eroding, although years and years of being bound into lies heartened her purpose and she struggled to find strength. Strength to have Alexander Ullyot out of the room and out of her life before she broke down and threw herself at his feet to beg for what had been lost.

Lady Simpson sighed loudly and drew herself to her full

height. For a second Maddy thought the woman was going to hit her and she moved across towards Alexander. On instinct, she was to think later. His fingers curled around her own, though he dropped them the instant he realised and shifted away.

'You will not see us for a few months, however, Lady Randwick, as we have passage to France. Normandy has always held a fascination for me and Alex has promised to take me there.' Isabella giggled as her hand fanned her stomach. 'We shall return, of course, before the child's due date, will we not, Alex?'

'We will.' The voice barely sounded like his and Maddy looked up, surprised, but his eyes were hooded. Whatever it was he felt he was keeping it close, and this time his hand was at Isabella's elbow.

And then they were gone. No private conversation. No explanations.

Pure undiluted grief roared through her, the indifference and the relief he was bathed in a potent indication of his betrayal. And when the gilded door banged shut and she was once again alone Madeleine crumpled to the floor, hand held against her mouth to stop the cries that gathered from the pit of her stomach.

'I hate you,' she whispered into the emptiness of the room, but even as she said it she knew that it was not true.

Chapter Eighteen

Alexander stood in his cell and punched his hand against the brick wall as hard as he could. Again and again until the raging anger he felt was under control and he could trust himself. The Palace of Westminster and jousting and a trip home to Scotland tomorrow. Lies, lies, lies, but at least Madeleine would stay safe and alive. At least the King of England would not have her killed.

Marriage and deceit. Better than death. Safer than truth. For now.

The arrival of a visitor brought him out of his reveries: Baron Falstone. Years of hatred simmered between them as he stepped into the light.

'I have been given leave by Edward to tell you that my sister is to be married to Nigel Mummington within the month. The Earl of Stainmore. He is a particular friend of mine. Perhaps you have heard of him?'

Alexander had. He was reputed to be a weak and greedy

baron with more than a passing fondness for men. Noel's friend, he surmised, and pliable. Just the sort of man to sacrifice Madeleine to. A groom as malleable as Lucien Randwick had been, and as expendable.

If the fastenings had not been around his ankle he would have taken Noel Falstone by the throat and killed him. As it was, he could only stand still and quell his desperate anger.

Come closer, he thought, measuring the distance between them against the length of his chains. The bindings allowed some movement and he had broken men's necks before with just the whisper of a chance.

Noel Falstone stopped. 'How much do you love my sister?'

A different question than Alex had expected. He looked up.

'Mummington is a man who has disposed of one wife already when she did not produce him the expected heir. And we all know Madeleine's problem.' He laughed as the accusation of barrenness hung between them, unsaid. 'So like my sister to make everything difficult.'

Red anger consumed Alex as he pulled at the chains and wrath spiralled down into dread. Falstone was Edward's man and with the stakes so high he could not afford to give an inch.

Tempering his voice, he looked away and summoned calm. 'Why are you here?'

'To see you die, Ullyot. To see the spirit of who you are

die and to tell you that there will be nothing left of you save what lives in the broken heart of my sister. Nothing left but the smouldering ruins of Ashblane and the legend of a Scottish Laird who was put to death in the Tower of London.'

'Why?' Alex had to know what made the hatred of a man like Noel so virulent, so all consuming.

'Why?' The question seemed to fuel him anew and his dark eyes glowed with hatred. 'You of all people have the nerve to ask me why? The constant reiving. The border battles. A thousand cattle one year and half that number the next. Our lands have never easily met; yet, before you came back, it was I who ruled the area. It was my prowess people admired. My wealth. And now it is your fighting skills that have turned the heads of men who were once in my pocket, and I can see the fear in their eyes when I mouth your name. And then you took my sister and lost me Harland in one foul blow. Harland.' He almost spat out the word. 'Rich land I could have made something of, become something from. Now Edward cedes me a small holding in the west country and he thinks he does me favour.' His hand came down hard upon his thigh. 'A favour when, but for you, it could have all been mine.'

Alexander had had enough. 'It was not Madeleine's fault that we took her at the side of the battlefield. She came unwilling and angry, yet, if you do this thing you speak of, it is she who will suffer.'

'Nay, Laird Ullyot, it is you who will endure the suffering—even from this distance and in this darkness when you speak of her I can see plainly the marks of love on your face. You and your men took my future as certainly as I now will take yours. An equal hurt.' He laughed suddenly, the high and unstable cackle sending threads of unease through Alex's body.

My God, he was mad. Dangerously mad. How much contact would the King allow him to have with Madeleine while she was here in London?

'Where do you stay here in London, Baron Falstone?'

Alex asked the question without expecting a reply and was surprised by Noel's sudden candidness.

'I am quartered with Baron Anthony at the townhouse of Josephine de Cargne.'

'And she is there? The Baroness is there?'

He could not keep the interest from his voice.

'She will not help you, Laird Ullyot. Her magic is not what it was and she ails by the day. Madeleine protects her with letters full of lies, but the pain she suffers on her chest keeps her indoors. Soon she will die.'

'Because you will help her on her way?'

He laughed. 'What are grandsons for but to ease the final years of passing?'

Alex had heard enough and his eyes sought the guard outside the door as he beckoned him forward.

'The Baron is just leaving. You may escort him out.'

He could not bear another moment in the company of Noel Falstone or watch the thought of murder light up his eyes. Especially when he knew that, as her brother, he would be given automatic access to Madeleine.

When Noel's footsteps were only a noise in the distance he cursed. Loudly.

If Noel was telling the truth Madeleine would be heading straight into a trap, and here he was bundled in the Tower of London with gruel for food and the damp of an English winter seeping into his bones. And not a thing he could do to help her, for he knew that his own life was hanging by a thread. King Edward would never allow him to marry Isabella Simpson because he did not trust him. Far easier to kill him and have no word of any of this reaching David's ears or Madeleine's. Until she had produced an heir at least.

An heir? And she was certain she was barren.

He turned to the wall, wild fear coursing coldly through his body as everything he had tried to set in place to keep his wife safe crashed into pieces around him. She would die at the hand of either her brother or Nigel Mummington. Lord. The gamble with Isabella Simpson was lost as death stalked them both. Stuck here in this place, with chains around his legs and a sturdy lock on the door, he had run out of options. Or had he?

When the prisoner opposite caught his attention, a new idea burned into his thoughts and, seeing that the guard was momentarily occupied with Falstone, he removed the medallion from his neck and rolled the leather strap that held it into a tight ball. Facing the man directly, he called out to him through the bars of his cell. Anything was worth a risk now.

'Do you often have visitors?'

'Sometimes, sir.' His voice was guttural and uneducated with a hint of wariness on the edge of it.

'If you could get a message out of this place for me with one of them, I would reward you handsomely.'

'What sort of message?'

'I need this medallion delivered to a friend. He will be worried.' He tried to make light of the task. 'Would twenty gold sovereigns be sufficient recompense?'

'Sufficient what, sir?'

'Payment,' Alex returned as impatience blossomed.

Alexander knew he had got him the moment he mentioned the money.

Stephen Grant came to the Tower two days later with Anthony and a man Alexander did not know at all. By the reckoning of the marks he had scrawled upon the stone floor it was almost the end of November. As they came into sight Alex heard his friend tell the guard to fetch tankards. The clink of coins completed the transaction and then they were alone.

Shivering against stone, he tried to install some warmth into coldness. He had a cough and a fever and his head hurt like hell. The sores on his legs had festered and wept and the fingers on his left hand where the guards had stamped on them felt broken. All in all, he thought, he was in a worse condition than he had been in Cairo after the débâcle with Talib ibn Abi Hakim. And at least there it had been hot.

'Stephen.' He got to his feet and tried to stop the shaking that had consumed him since yesterday morning when he had been doused with a bucket of freezing cold water in lieu of a bath. 'I am glad to see you, indeed.'

Stephen Grant moved forward and stripped off his own jacket, anger marking his face as he placed the garment around Alex's shoulders. The warmth was welcomed.

'How is it possible that you have been allowed entrance?' Alex asked. 'And so easily.' All his senses were on alert for another trap and he stiffened as Baron Anthony produced the medallion from his pocket.

'Grant sought my wife's help in the matter, and I have strong connections here.'

Lord help us, Alex thought, and looked across at Stephen, the quick query giving him answer as he determined the shape of a dagger in the folds of his shirt. Interest flared immediately though he quenched it as Anthony spoke.

'Josephine bids me to return this to you and to also say "remember the magic."'

'Remember the magic?'

'Just that. I think her mind is now lost under the onslaught of her sickness, so perhaps I would not take too much note of such a prophecy.' He placed the medallion in Alex's hand.

'And Madeleine. Where is she?'

'She has gone to Mummington with a number of women from the court. Her wedding is to be within the month. I would, however, counsel caution in your bid to see her. She has the notion that the betrothal she is set in is somehow your fault. The mention of a woman, I think. Isabella Simpson, if I were to remember rightly.'

'My sister.' Stephen spoke sharply. 'She's gone now to France, Alex. You never could see a woman in love, even when one tripped over you. Though in your defence at least you were unremittingly honest and the gold you afforded her was generous.'

Alexander nodded and cut to the point. 'Are you here to get me out?'

It was Baron Anthony who answered. 'When you leave here, Ullyot, you will find four horses outside beneath the overhang of the Red Lion tavern. The man who holds them has swords and knives. And medicines for your sores.'

'And you…?' Nothing made sense. Anthony was a minion of Edward, a King who would not forgive any perceived betrayal lightly.

'That is why we have Jack with us.'

The hooded man removed his cloak and the face of a fighter was uncovered. The bunched keys of the jailer were in his hands.

It took him less than a moment to release Alex and knock Anthony out cold upon the stone floor.

A ruse. A protection. A well-thought-out plan, Alexander decided as he followed the others, stopping only briefly to tell the prisoner opposite where he would deposit the twenty golden crowns for collection.

And then they were outside, the smell of night and smoke in the air. Alex breathed in the cool dampness of November as he followed the others.

Chapter Nineteen

Madeleine sat, well wrapped, in the covered gardens at Stainmore Castle and listened to the small trill of birds in the ashes and oaks. It was peaceful here and quiet and the nightmares that might have been were as nothing. It was her lands that Nigel Mummington wanted and the lands that he would get. An easy solution. Quiet, binding and legal.

No one visited Stainmore. And no one left. No one, save for Eileen Birmingham, the dark-haired mistress of Nigel Mummington and a woman that Madeleine had come to like, for she was as caught up in the politics of it all as Madeleine was.

Today Eileen sat with her, the woman's hand resting on a stomach that was well rounded with the swell of an advanced pregnancy.

'Another four months, Lady Randwick, and we can both be free. When Nigel claims my child as the heir you will be able to leave, I swear it.'

Madeleine smiled. 'You endow men with too much honour, I fear. He will kill me the first chance he gets. A christening and then a murder.'

'Nay, I shall not let that happen. He has not touched you because I asked him not to and he will do this for me, too. Especially when I present him with a son.'

Maddy had to concede the point, for she had only seen Mummington once here with Eileen Birmingham and that from a distance. His manners had been impeccable, and his love for his mistress obvious.

'Mummington may want to do as you wish, Eileen, but it will be Edward who will be pulling the strings. And he will not let me live.'

Eileen's tears surprised her greatly, although Madeleine knew that pregnant women were often highly emotional. Suddenly she just felt tired. Tired of hoping, tired of wanting, tired of wishing every single thing in her life different. She had sent a letter to Jemmie, telling her where she was and how she was, but nothing had come back in return. She wondered if it had even been taken to Ashblane, though the housekeeper assured her that it had, and she seemed like a woman who would not lie. Then why would Jemmie not write back? How was she? Where was she? Was Isabella kind? Was Alexander happy?

Alexander. My love.

The words turned around and around in her heart and she closed her eyes, imagining him. Where was he now? In France with his wife perhaps, the beauteous and fertile

Lady Simpson, or at Ashblane thanking his lucky stars that Madeleine Randwick was no longer a threat to his keep.

If only there had been a child.

She shook her head. That was nonsense. There would never be a child. Not for her. A single tear coursed down her cheek. It was as though she had faded into another life. As though Ashblane had never been. Jemmie would miss her, but she knew that Alexander would honour his promise of guardianship. And eleven was too young to hold on to sadness for ever.

With care she stood. The bruising at her hip was sore from where she had thrown herself against the chapel door on Sunday, hoping that the catch might work loose and let her escape that way. Escape to what? Escape to where?

But Eileen was not so easily dismissed.

'I can help you, Lady Randwick, to an extent. With this child I cannot risk anything too much, but perhaps with a little help you could leave and go far from here—'

Madeleine interrupted her. 'Could you get me sulphur and saltpetre and potassium?' Her heart skipped a beat as she quantified the possibilities of success.

'These are potions used in the making of weapons?'

'Yes.'

'If you hurt Nigel…'

'I promise you that I would not.'

'Are they hard to find?'

'Nay, the arsenal at the castle would hold such things.'

Eileen nodded, and for the first time in weeks Madeleine clung to hope.

The sun coming out from behind large clouds mirrored how she felt. If she used her head she might yet be saved.

The sounds of horses broke the peace of the day and, hurrying to the side of the castle, Madeleine saw her brother Noel's standard flapping above the heads of a hundred horsemen.

War.

It had come to this place.

Quickly she helped Eileen Birmingham to her feet and shepherded her inside, all other thoughts forgotten.

Chapter Twenty

∼∽∞∾∼

Alexander rode into Stainmore ten days after his escape from London and with a hundred of Ashblane's best soldiers. The Ullyot banners of red and gold streamed behind him, *soyez sage* bright in the gathering breeze, though he saw nothing of this for his whole being was fixed on Madeleine and her safety. If she had been hurt he would raze this place. He promised himself that on the soul of his mother.

Six soldiers rode out to meet them. One Alex recognized as Mummington. Hatred flared.

'Why are you here, Laird Ullyot? This is England. You have no jurisdiction here.'

Alexander ignored the thinly veiled threat and got straight to the point. 'If you have hurt my wife in any way, Mummington, your life will be over. Now, where is she?'

Something flickered in the dark eyes of the man before him.

'Edward has promised her to me, Laird Ullyot, and I think you will find her happy with things the way they are. She is English, after all, and this is her King's will. If I were you, I would ride away from this place and be glad for your life.'

Stephen Grant shook his head, but Alexander stayed still. Something was not right. Nigel Mummington was petrified. He could see it in the racing beat at his throat and in the lines of his body. His fingers went to the hilt of his sword and stayed there as the Earl showed them through into the bailey.

'I will send food and drink out to your men,' Mummington said as they gained the main door to the keep, but Alexander was barely listening. Madeleine was close, he could feel it. Tiring of social niceties, he stepped forward into the hall and into the swords of fifty Falstone men. The sharp tips of steel pressed against his back and he was still.

A trap.

He gestured to Goult, Quinlan and Marcus to keep their hands away from their own armoury. They would have to bide their time until they saw where Madeleine and her brother were. Then he could take his chances.

As if on cue, Noel Falstone swaggered to the front of his men and the look on his face was hardly friendly.

'I hoped you would be dead by now, Ullyot.'

'It takes more than hope to kill me, Falstone. How did you know I was coming?' Noel was a man who liked to boast of conquests. This one would be no different and it would buy him some time.

'Baron Anthony. He's as much Edward's man as I am.'

'And it is easier to kill me here than as a prisoner in the Tower of London?'

Noel almost smiled. 'You have it exactly, Laird Ullyot. Much less fussy. And with Grant involved, seemingly legitimate.'

Stephen went for his sword and a dagger was quickly at his throat.

'I'd advise you to drop it, Baron Grant.'

'Alex?'

'Drop it.'

The clang of metal punctured silence before Alexander began to speak. 'Let my second-in-command take Madeleine back to Ashblane. I ask for her life in return for my own.'

'You are hardly in any position to bargain, Laird Ullyot. All the cards lie in our favour. It's a clean sweep I want.'

'We have a hundred men camped outside your castle. If you kill us they will lay siege to this place.'

'You are trespassing in England, Laird Ullyot. How long do you think Edward will allow you to do so?'

'Long enough to take our own number of English soldiers to the grave and more. Long enough for the Church to become furious at the attempt to dismantle my legitimate marriage to the Lady Randwick.'

Now Noel did laugh, loud and long. 'Handfast, was it not? By the grace of what God were you joined together? A single vow in the middle of a forest in the middle of the night and before a clan that is as unlawful as your own. I think, Laird—'

A scream stopped him as a woman ran into the hall babbling of witches. And behind her came Madeleine, dressed in a light kirtle of deep purple and swirled in blue smoke. Power and magic cloaked her and her hair in the candlelight was the colour of rowanberries in autumn.

'Let him go, Noel.'

'Madeleine?' Alex's bellow of rage shattered her trance and she turned to face him, relief, desperate longing and an unfettered worry all etching her brow in a quick succession of emotions.

'Madeleine?' His voice did not sound like his own. His wife and men caught in the scheming clutches of Noel Falstone and the smell of blood and betrayal in the air.

'Let him go.' She had come into the Great Hall armed only with her words and magic. 'Let the Laird of Ullyot and his men go, Noel.'

Her brother began to laugh.

'You are more like Ullyot than you may think, Madeleine. But I have fifty men, sister dear, and licence to murder from the King himself. I would hardly be tempted to let him go simply because you asked.'

She moved again, taking Noel's anger with her.

'No.' Alex tried to step forward, barely able to believe that Madeleine would have the temerity to barter against a madman with nothing. The tangle of arms that clutched at him held him back, his sword long gone and the Falstone retainers immobilising all movement.

'Let them go, Noel.' Madeleine again, and stronger.

This time she raised her fingers and blue smoke swirled, distancing her from everyone in a cloud of turquoise mist.

Lord, she really *was* a witch, Alex thought. And she had never looked more beautiful. Power and certainty cloaked her. She stared at the swords in her face without the slightest show of fear and as she brought her hands up the man before her slithered to the ground.

'Shall I kill him, Alexander?' she asked then. Softer. Quieter. More dangerous.

'No.' His thoughts raced as to where she was heading with this, and Josephine de Cargne's words rolled around in his memory.

Remember the magic. Could it save them here?

'Should I kill them all?' she repeated and picked up the sword of the soldier who lay writhing on the ground. White light radiated from the blade, falling across the faces of a hundred men. Disbelief turned to something else entirely.

'No, do not kill them, Madeleine.' He injected as much fear into his voice as he could manage and walked towards her.

No one stopped him.

As he reached her he saw what he had not from a distance. A red band of bruising licked across her cheek and into the hair at her temple. She felt hot, as though the smoke and fire of her hair had transferred itself to her body and created a glowing candle of her skin.

'Are you hurt, my lady?' he whispered, and was pleased to see the quick shake of her head. Bringing her behind him, he turned to face her brother, who, recognising showmanship when he saw it and also the turning tides of his own fortune, strode forward, sword raised.

'Kill them,' he screamed as Alex squeezed the hand of his wife.

'If it's a witch ye truly be, Madeleine, now might be the time to use your sorcery. Is there another trick?'

In answer she took a handful of powder and threw it into the air. A rainbow hung across the ceiling, touching timber, and now the anger of the Heathwater soldiers was threaded with caution. Men moved back, swords drawn and dangerous still, but at least a little more distant.

'She can hurt you,' Alexander yelled above the noise of the soldiers, 'and so can I. Curse you and hurt you and send you to hell.' The sword he had taken from her cut through the air, underlining the danger. Ribbons of white light still bathed the room. The smell of sulphur was strong.

'Kill them.' Noel Falstone's cry went up and he advanced on his sister, but Alex was quicker. He had his blade on Noel before anyone could stop him.

'If even one of your soldiers moves towards us, Falstone, I swear I will slit your throat where we stand.' And this time nobody doubted that he meant what he said. 'Now move back.'

Alex laid his fingers to his lips and whistled and the arrival of the retainers from Ashblane was almost simultaneous. Boxed in by the men of the north, the Englishmen loyal to Noel laid down their swords, resignation and uncertainty scrawled across every face. But there was also another emotion, Alex thought.

Relief.

There would not be a bloodbath today, for the causes Noel Falstone embodied were not fully embraced by his men. Or Mummington's. And life was more sacrosanct than dying for a lost cause.

Carefully he dropped his guard, but only enough to let Noel Falstone reach for his sword. Exactly as he had wanted it, for it would save him killing him in cold blood.

'No.' Madeleine's shout was heartfelt as the first clashes of steel rang out around the room, and he gestured to Quinlan to pull her back. The Baron of Heathwater was reputed to be one of the best swordsmen in England and the confidence that showed on his face in a galling smirk faltered somewhat as Quinlan rounded up behind him.

'You would play this unfair, Ullyot?'

'As unfair as ye played Ian. If I fail to kill you, I promise that my men will not.'

'Ian?' The tone of Falstone's voice changed. 'Ian? Ian the Red. The big man who would not die on the hills overlooking Heathwater. Ten stabs it took and each one deeper. He howled like a baby.'

Roiling fury blanketed sense as Alex came forward, but as Falstone countered with finesse he made himself think. It was a ploy, and anguish made him vulnerable. Keep calm. Breathe deeply. The rapid beat of his heart slowed, all his energies centred on the blades between them.

'Now when the odds are even and I am not chained to the wall of an English prison I will kill you, Falstone.'

Noel's returned sneer fired Alexander's resolve and sparks flew as metal hit metal and the battle was engaged. A quick swipe of Falstone's blade whistled past his left ear. Then a double lunge. Alex felt the passage of wind and smiled. Parrying against the dip of the other sword and a wicked upward thrust, he moved back and waited, playing with the moment until Noel committed himself and came in. Feinting to the left, he watched as Noel struck down, his expression changing to disbelief as he saw that his blade had not only not connected, but had stuck true into the wooden palings around the door. Falstone's knife was out of his belt quickly and he cut across the flesh on Alexander's right hand.

Pain slashed through adrenalin as he surveyed the damage. Deep enough, but not too much of a handicap. He saw Madeleine step forward and shouted to Quinlan to hold her, for this was his fight and he did not need the distraction of seeing to her safety. Noel had rounded to the left now and Alex found his reasoning. The soldiers from Ashblane were thinner at this end of the room and there was a doorway to the kitchen thirty yards from where they stood.

With care he placed himself along the escape route and withdrew his own knife, throwing his longer sword to one side and bending as Noel came at him with the confidence of one who had drawn blood and now expected to draw some more.

'Come on, Falstone,' he muttered, 'let's finish this.'

The blades clashed as each drew inward and as Alex came in hard he felt again the clip of Noel's blade. On his neck this time, but deflected by the brooch he wore to clasp his plaid. But an opening had been left, and one large enough to finish the fight entirely. Putting all his effort into the thrust, he drove his blade. The shirt Noel wore parted and deep red blood gushed out, disbelief glazing fury as the Englishman slid to the floor.

'I curse you, Ullyot. I curse you and my sister and the whole house of Ashblane.'

Alexander just laughed.

'Empty words, Baron, and unwise ones, too, I'd be thinking. A confession of sins may bring you more hope in the afterlife, though when Ian finds you there I doubt even a penance will suffice.' Wiping his blade, he sheathed it and watched Madeleine's brother die.

Behind, the soldiers from Ashblane raised their weapons, but the retainers of Heathwater disbanded, falling back from the hall as quickly as they could, leaving Mummington and his paltry few soldiers to face the enemy.

The end of a dream.

The end of a tyranny.

The beginning of a new age born from the ruins of the old. In every face Alexander could determine confusion. No one came forward.

'Go home, Ullyot.' Mummington's voice was tired now. Older. 'And take your wife.'

A woman heavily pregnant came to stand at the top of

the stairs and Nigel Mummington moved back to the railing where first the balustrades began.

Protection. Alex recognized the action in his own as he faced the Earl of Stainmore. 'Tell Edward that I am keeping Madeleine *Ullyot*. Tell him that Heathwater can be his for the bride price, for I want nothing more to do with the place. And tell him that if he crosses the border into Ashblane, I will be waiting for him with ten thousand soldiers.'

The slight bend of Mummington's head was all that could be seen to show he had understood.

Carefully Alex withdrew, and only when he was outside, mounted on his horse with Madeleine safe in front of him, did he let out his breath.

Noel Falstone was dead. He could barely stop himself shouting with the joy of it. Ian had been avenged and yet to Madeleine he was family.

'If ye ever loved your brother, then I am sorry for it,' he began softly.

As she shook her head relief flooded him. 'Noel brought this on himself a long time ago and the duty-love I had held for him as a young girl has been these many years dead.' She threaded her fingers through his and brought up his hand to look at the injury, but he pulled away and turned his wrist against the heavy wool in his plaid.

'It will keep till we gain at least a few hours' riding between us and Stainmore. Who hit you?' His other hand momentarily dropped the reins as he surveyed the damage.

'Noel, when I told him that I would not marry Nigel Mummington. He was worse than he ever used to be at Heathwater.'

'I think he is mad. Was mad,' he corrected and turned away to speak with Quinlan.

He sounded so furious and distant that Madeleine was quiet, watching as he signalled to his men to ride north.

It was only when they slowed after a couple of hours that he allowed her speech.

'I take it Isabella Simpson was never your bride, then?' She could not meet his eyes as she waited for an answer.

'Nay. The idea of marriage was all I could think of to save you. Edward was demanding a fealty I could not give and a planned betrothal at least brought us some time.'

'And the child?'

'There was'na one. Isabella agreed to the pretence in return for a large sum of money. I was happy with the exchange.'

She did turn at that, her hand reaching out along the raspy roughness of his jaw. 'You look thinner.'

'I had the fever.'

'From the dungeons in the Tower of London?'

'You knew I was there?' Astonishment was reflected in pale eyes.

'Noel told me yesterday. He said he had gone to see you there. He said that you hoped for children and that my barrenness—'

He did not let her finish. 'You think it is children I am thinking of when I look at you, Madeleine? You think I would defy the might of England for the promise of an heir? When I already have one in Gillion?'

He looked around and saw his men waiting. Waving them on, he took up a position at the rear of the troop to give himself some privacy.

'When Edward said that he would kill you, I knew that it would take a lot to make you believe I no longer felt bound to you. Bound to the handfast. And if you did not believe, I knew that you would die.'

A smile of relief pulled reluctantly at Madeleine's lips, though she was still not quite ready to absolve him completely.

'You took your time in getting to me then, Alexander Ullyot. If Mummington had been a man who was not madly in love, I doubt even magic could have saved me from him.'

'Jesus.' His hand tightened over her own. 'I thought he liked men.'

'He what?'

'He liked men, so I thought you safe.'

'His mistress was the woman you saw just now at the head of the stairs.'

Alex blanched noticeably. 'But she was with child?' As the anger crossed into his eyes Madeleine began to laugh properly.

'He did not touch you?' The question was hard, giving Madeleine the impression that, should she have answered in the affirmative, he would turn his horse back here and now to kill Mummington. She placed her fingers over his, the blood from his hand dried now with the passing of time.

'He did not wish to. The woman you saw at the top of the stairs bears his child and I was as much a threat to her as anyone. She helped me by getting the potions I needed for my magic.'

Alexander pulled her closer. 'You're saying that the sorcery you did back there is explainable?'

'By knowledge. Old de Cargne knowledge. With the right training anyone might do it.'

'Not anyone, Madeleine. Only you, but when the tales of this witchcraft sweep the kingdoms of both England and Scotland I promise that I will keep you safe. And I promise, Lady Ullyot, that I will love you for ever.'

Tears came into her eyes at his confession as the death of Noel and the past weeks of uncertainty undid her. How had she deserved a man like this? One who took her sorcery as a gift and the difficulty of her circumstances as a challenge?

'I love you, too,' she whispered and brought her hand to his cheek as he leant down to kiss her. Not a careful kiss, either, but one full of lust and promise.

'And Jemmie?' she asked breathlessly a few moments later, reddening at the bawdy shouts of encouragement from the group of soldiers just in front of them.

'I promise that it will be safe for your sister to be a girl again and that no one ever need know of her lineage.'

She felt the warmth of his body against her back and

leaned in, smiling when he tucked her closer beneath his arm and pinned her there. She was going home. Home to Scotland. Home to Jemmie. Home with Alexander.

Tears blurred her vision as he spurred the big horse on and they headed north out of England.

Epilogue

Ashblane
Spring, 1361

Alexander paced up and down the Great Hall and listened all the time for the slightest noise from the chamber above the stairs. The chamber where Madeleine now laboured to bear their child.

He clenched his teeth and leaned against the window, parting the leather coverings and looking out. Nearly ten o'clock in the morning, he surmised as he read the light and the shadows. She had been labouring now for four hours and for the last two nobody had gone into her room or left it. Was that a good sign or a bad one? He could no longer rely on any conjecture. All he wanted was his wife. Whole. Well. In his arms. Laughing.

Quinlan watched him, a glass of whisky in one hand and

a long pipe in the other. Goult, Marcus and Stephen Grant stood near the doorway.

'It won't be long now, lad.' Goult's reassurance was kindly meant, though Alex doubted the old man had much experience in such matters.

'Ye are an expert on childbirth, then?' he returned irritably and turned away, angry that he should stoop to such pettiness. But everything seemed dangerous. It wouldn't be long now before what? Before Madeleine bled under the silence of haemorrhage, and died as Alice had, claimed in stillness before the bairn was even one day old?

He made himself stop. Madeleine was strong and fit and healthy and she wanted this child with a deep and desperate need. Two and a half years in its forming. He could not lose hope now.

The outside door opened and Gillion came in with a bunch of spring snowdrops. The candid innocence of youth in his eyes was a blessing beyond words.

'I picked these by Patrick's grave, for Mama grew them from bulbs and will be pleased for them.' His speech was no longer faltering and at eight years of age he had a comforting robustness that had not been there before. Madeleine's doing.

In truth, he had been blessed a hundredfold that day when he had captured her at the edge of the battlefield outside Heathwater. And now another battle and one in which he could take no part. Helplessness washed over him. And dread. He wanted this life with Madeleine.

Wanted the joy, and laughter and wonder. Wanted her warm in his bed every single night.

The cry of a child halted all thoughts and he was running up the stairs and into the chamber. Madeleine sat with a babe at her breast and Katherine and Jemima fussing over the bedclothes. In the light from the window Alex noticed downy amber at its crown and smiled. A redhead like her mother.

'You have a daughter, Alexander,' Madeleine said softly and held her hand out to him. He took her fingers and sat down beside her, for not even after his greatest battles had he felt this shaken before.

A warrior felled by love.

'And you are well?' He coughed as the huskiness in his voice undid him and was pleased when Jemmie and Katherine slipped into the other room.

'Better perhaps than you are,' she replied, laughter threaded with concern. 'I am all right, Alexander,' she added softly. 'I promised you at least fifty years and I mean to stand by it.'

'Starting now?'

He leaned over in reply, careful not to disturb the child as he ran his finger up across the line of his wife's cheek. Softly. When he had made her heart beat fast and her breath come shallow he leant back against the header on their bed.

'Ah, my Madeleine.' He smiled. 'The treasure you held was neither the money nor the lands. Nay, for sure it was this…' Pushing back her shift he placed his left hand across her heart. 'And this.' His right fingers ran over her forehead. 'Heart and mind, Madeleine. Intelligence, valour and beauty. What riches could be compared to these?'

'That of love, Alexander,' she answered.

'Our love,' he whispered back, and covered her mouth with his own.

1923,
the village of Kingshampton, Berkshire...

Sophie and Lydia Westlake have always been
close, thinking of themselves more like sisters than
cousins. Sophie has always been the prettier and
more light-hearted one, leaving the shy and
retiring Lydia to grow up happily in her shadow.
But everything changes the moment dashing
young architect Christian Mellor arrives at the
village summer fête...

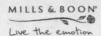

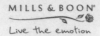

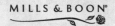

FREE

2 BOOKS AND A SURPRISE GIFT!

We would like to take this opportunity to thank you for reading this Mills & Boon® book by offering you the chance to take TWO more specially selected titles from the Historical Romance™ series absolutely FREE! We're also making this offer to introduce you to the benefits of the Mills & Boon® Reader Service™—

- ★ **FREE home delivery**
- ★ **FREE gifts and competitions**
- ★ **FREE monthly Newsletter**
- ★ **Books available before they're in the shops**
- ★ **Exclusive Reader Service offers**

Accepting these FREE books and gift places you under no obligation to buy; you may cancel at any time, even after receiving your free shipment. Simply complete your details below and return the entire page to the address below. You don't even need a stamp!

YES! Please send me 2 free Historical Romance books and a surprise gift. I understand that unless you hear from me, I will receive 4 superb new titles every month for just £3.69 each, postage and packing free. I am under no obligation to purchase any books and may cancel my subscription at any time. The free books and gift will be mine to keep in any case.

H6ZEE

Ms/Mrs/Miss/Mr..Initials ....

BLOCK CAPITALS PLEASE

Surname ....

Address ....

....

....Postcode ....

Send this whole page to:

The Reader Service, FREEPOST CN81, Croydon, CR9 3WZ